C334859697

Nicky Pellegrino

P.S. Come to Italy

ORION

First published in Great Britain in 2023 by Orion Fiction,
an imprint of The Orion Publishing Group Ltd,
Carmelite House, 50 Victoria Embankment,
London EC4Y 0DZ

An Hachette UK company

1 3 5 7 9 10 8 6 4 2

A CIP catalogue record for this book
is available from the British Library.

ISBN (Trade Paperback) 978 1 3987 0104 5
ISBN (eBook) 978 1 3987 0106 9

Typeset by Deltatype Ltd, Birkenhead, Merseyside

Printed in Great Britain by Clays Ltd, Elcograf S.p.A.

MIX
Paper from
responsible sources
FSC® C104740

www.orionbooks.co.uk

Nicky Pellegrino was born in Liverpool but spent childhood holidays staying with her family in Italy. It is her memories of those summers that flavour her stories: the passions, the feuds, but most of all the food. Nicky now lives in Auckland, New Zealand with her husband, her greyhound Harry and her horse Uno.

Find out more at www.nickypellegrino.com

Also by Nicky Pellegrino

Delicious
Summer at the Villa Rosa
(*originally published as* The Gypsy Tearoom)
The Italian Wedding
Recipe for Life
The Villa Girls
When in Rome
The Food of Love Cookery School
One Summer in Venice
Under Italian Skies
A Year at Hotel Gondola
A Dream of Italy
Tiny Pieces of Us
To Italy, With Love

For my mother-in-law, Margaret Bidwill

I

Now

Belle didn't know what she had expected, but it wasn't this. A grand *palazzo* with dark green shutters, time-worn stone walls and a doorway flanked by ornate columns, it was so imposing that for a moment she hesitated. Had coming here been a mistake? Was she going to regret being so impulsive?

And then she saw them standing in the vestibule, the whole family waiting to greet her. There was Enrico, his face so familiar. Behind him the others, his two sons and their wives sizing her up, and an older woman, Enrico's mother, holding onto his arm. Belle didn't think any one of them looked particularly pleased to meet her.

'Hello,' she said, dropping her battered suitcase on the marble floor, unsure whether she was meant to shake hands or kiss them.

'Welcome, welcome.' At least Enrico was smiling. He stepped towards Belle, touching his cheeks to hers, and briefly she was aware that his skin was smooth and his cologne woodsy and sophisticated. 'Such a long journey, all those thousands of kilometres, you must be very tired.'

'I am a little jet-lagged,' she agreed, although the truth was, she felt shattered. Hours and hours ago Belle had left behind a grey Auckland day. Since then, she had watched a lot of forgettable movies on a small seat-back screen and eaten too much horrible plane food, because there was nothing else to do. Now her ankles were swollen, her hair lank and stomach bloated.

'New Zealand is so far away,' remarked one of the wives, politely. She was dark-haired, plump-cheeked and very pretty, wearing a hand-embroidered smocked dress that showed off her bronzed legs.

The other young woman was dark-haired and lovely too, but her face was more angular and the skin beneath her eyes puckered with tiredness. One hand rested on the mound of her belly, and Belle tried to remember when Enrico had said his first grandchild was due.

'We were planning to eat lunch in the garden,' he told her, now.

Belle ought to have spent a couple of nights in Rome and then she might have arrived rested and refreshed. She was aware that Enrico's sons were staring at her stony-faced and his mother's frown wasn't shifting. Clearly, she hadn't made the best first impression.

'Lunch would be lovely,' she said, dismissing any thoughts of a long shower and a lie-down.

Enrico made the introductions, although Belle had already seen photographs so recognised the moody-looking elder son as Gianni with his pale and pregnant wife Katarina beside him. The other son Pietro had curlier hair and a couple of African woven friendship bracelets tied round one slender wrist. He was recently married to the beautiful Perla. And then there was Enrico's mother, the old Signora. Belle still wasn't sure what she was meant to call her, even once the introductions were over, and they were leading her down a long corridor, past a vaulted dining area and a room full of antique chairs and marble statuary.

Then they were on the terrace, which led down to a small formal garden, and down again to a rectangle of swimming pool, a loggia with more ornate columns, and a low limestone wall with a view of the red-earthed olive groves spreading out towards the sea.

'How long have you lived in this house?' Belle asked Enrico, taking a seat at a table shaded by the loggia.

'I was born here,' he told her. 'It has been in my family for a long time, passed down from eldest son to eldest son, as is traditional.'

'I didn't realise it was so ... magnificent.'

Whenever they had chatted, on those lengthy Zoom calls, Enrico had been in his home office. It hadn't seemed particularly fancy, just a small room, almost an alcove. Now Belle realised he must have another, much larger office wherever his business was based. It had never occurred to her that Enrico might be this wealthy.

Looking at him, seated at the head of his table, pouring out glasses of Prosecco, Belle realised what she knew about this man was that he made her laugh and felt like a friend, but still she didn't know him very well at all.

He was taller than she had expected, leaner too. Before today Belle had only ever seen him on a computer screen, mostly a head and shoulders view. Now she noticed other things. The way he moved, even his stance, signalled self-assurance. And as he passed her a glass of Prosecco, she observed that his fingers were long and tanned, the nails neatly manicured.

'We must make a toast,' he declared, once everyone had a drink. 'To Belle; we are so glad you have come to Italy and hope your stay here will be a very happy one.'

They all raised their glasses, but Perla was the only one that spoke. 'To Belle,' she echoed sweetly. 'Welcome.'

'Thank you, I'm very pleased to be here,' replied Belle, still feeling dazed, although whether by the place or the jet lag, she wasn't certain.

Everyone was staring, waiting for her to say something more. The old Signora whose eyes were set so deep in the fleshy folds of her face they looked like currants in a bun, the handsome sons, and the younger women, one smiling and the other even paler now if possible.

'This is very beautiful.' Belle touched a hand to the ivory linen cloth that was covering the table. 'One of your designs?'

'Yes, yes.' Enrico smiled at her. 'And the dress Perla is wearing, and my shirt, and Mamma's wrap – all artisan linen products from Casa di Ginaro. I sent you something of ours, didn't I?'

'Napkins,' Belle reminded him. They had arrived beautifully wrapped, eight white linen napkins with a subtle sheen of hand-embroidery and she had put them away in a drawer and not bothered taking them out again. Belle's table was covered in mismatched vintage china and jam jars full of foraged flowers. She liked to gather people around it for noisy, messy dinners – pulling apart roast chicken with fingers, spilling red wine, scattering crumbs. The napkins were a gift from Enrico so of course she kept them, but they weren't the kind of thing that Belle could imagine ever using.

She ought to have paid more attention to those napkins, to what they were telling her. They said that Enrico was a man who did things properly, not a person who casually tore off squares from a kitchen roll for his friends to dab their sticky mouths and hands with, not like Belle at all.

'Beautiful linen napkins,' she added. 'Embroidered with a crest.'

'Our family's crest.' The old Signora spoke, her currant-bun eyes fixed on Belle. 'It is historic.'

'You have your own crest.' Belle was impressed, as it seemed like she was meant to be.

'Many families do,' said Enrico, with a shrug. 'It is not so unusual.' Lunch was brought out by a woman wearing an apron. The portions were small but it all looked delicious. A swirl of spaghetti coated in a buttery tomato sauce and a puddle of jammy onions. Citrussy shaved fennel served with sweet-fleshed langoustines. Soft, dimpled bread rolls dusted with flour. Belle's mouth watered but she ate carefully. It was difficult to avoid splattering sauce all over the perfect linen cloth and almost certainly not OK to wipe a crust of bread around her plate to soak up every last delicious drop like she always did at home.

'My son says you are in the art world,' the old Signora remarked.

'I have a little gallery,' Belle told her.

'In the city?'

'No, it's in the seaside settlement where I live. Just an annexe of the house really, and I sell paintings, pottery, crafts, that sort of thing.'

'You do well? It is successful?'

'There are good times and bad, like any business.' Belle wasn't going to pretend otherwise. 'And it is very small.'

'This family is fortunate that we are very well established,' the Signora said. 'Casa di Ginaro was founded by my great-grandmother. She began in a small way, with the smocked nightgowns that she stitched and hand embroidered herself. Slowly, we have grown.'

Belle had checked out the Casa di Ginaro website, of course, and raised her eyebrows at the prices of the products it sold. Who paid that kind of money for linen clothes and homeware? Still for some reason she had continued to assume that Enrico was just like her, not rich or poor but somewhere in between. In the photographs she had come across there was no chunky gold Rolex on his wrist, no glitter or bling, nothing showy at all. What you noticed about Enrico, in pictures as well as life, was the sparkle in his eyes as he smiled and the traces of boyishness on his face.

She had found a few shots of him at fashion shows surrounded by his family and several images of them posing for magazines. In one Enrico was stretched out on a lounger beside his pool but there was nothing she came across that showed the *palazzo*'s grand façade. She felt vaguely affronted now that he had turned out to be wealthy, like he had been cheating or lying all along, holding out on her.

This trip was supposed to be the escape she needed, the answer to all her problems. Come to Italy, Enrico had said, and impetuously Belle had agreed. He lived in Ostuni, a dazzling white hilltop town rising up from a plateau of olive trees. In photographs it had wowed her and the descriptions she read did the rest. A labyrinth of alleyways, staircases and arches, houses built on houses, hundreds of years of history.

Now she was here, in this *palazzo* with this family and a man who seemed almost a stranger. Belle had come to Italy and she was going to have to make the most of it.

2

Then

When Belle got married to Ari, she always knew there was a chance she would be widowed one day. Not that she thought about it as they posed for wedding photographs in the wind-blown grass on the dunes above the ocean. She was wearing a summery dress and flowers in her fair hair and it was freezing cold because the weather had turned; still she was brimming with joy.

Not everyone was as happy. From the beginning her mother had made it clear that she disapproved of the age difference and throughout the ceremony, every time Belle glanced towards her or her stepfather, she thought that their faces looked pinched. Eventually Belle stopped glancing at them. She was in her mid-forties and Ari twenty years older. Dressed in a short-sleeved white shirt, the greenstone he always wore gleaming at his neck, her groom seemed a man in his prime.

Ari didn't look his age and never acted it. He went surfing when the waves were wild and galloped his horse down the black sand beach, leaping it over any driftwood in his path. You would have known he was older than her, but not that twenty years divided them. You saw his broad shoulders and strong hands, heard the deep rumble of his voice, you felt his energy; he never seemed frail. Belle had waited a long time for a man like Ari.

The first time she met him was at an exhibition of his paintings. A friend had invited her along; Ari had been her teacher at an adult art class, and the gallery showing his work was putting on a bigger party than normal because this was his final one, the end of a long career.

'My art has been everything to me but I believe there is more to life and it's time to experience that now,' he had said in his short speech. 'I don't want to be hidden away on my own in a studio anymore. I want to be out in the world, with people, doing some living.'

Pressed against the back wall, clutching a glass of warm Chardonnay, Belle had gazed at him over the heads of all those people, and thought he was amazing.

The second time she saw him was at a barbecue. Ari had been out surfing and was salty-skinned, his wet hair slicked back from his wide, brown face. Belle didn't talk to him that time either.

Their third meeting was on purpose. Belle couldn't stop thinking about Ari. She told her friend that she regretted not buying one of his artworks and, since the exhibition was over, the friend shared his contact details and suggested she go out to his studio near the beach at Muriwai. 'He's got loads of his old work out there; if there's something you like he'll sell it to you. He probably needs the money.'

Ari didn't remember her from the exhibition or the barbecue. But he said she should come out one Sunday afternoon and have a look through the paintings that were left in his studio.

'This Sunday?' Belle asked.

'If you like.'

'What time works for you?' she wondered.

'Any time,' Ari told her in his low, bass voice. 'If I'm not here then the key will be under the mat so let yourself in and put on some coffee. I won't be far away.'

His house was set in bush, down a short driveway that

dipped down from the coast road, a small wooden cottage with a covered veranda and a studio at one side. Belle knocked on the door and called out his name but there was no reply so she found the key beneath the mat and let herself in.

There was art everywhere, paintings propped next to piles of books, shelves of glassware and pottery bowls, a collection of woven flax bags on one wall, a half-finished mural covering the other. Belle stood there, taking it all in, more interested in Ari than ever.

He had been out riding and was dressed in dusty jeans, a tan-coloured dog at his heels. '*Kia ora*,' he said, striding in. 'You haven't put the coffee on.'

'I was just looking around ... being nosey really,' she admitted.

Ari shrugged. 'It's all here to be looked at.'

In this small space, so close to him, Belle felt giddy as a teenager; she hoped it wasn't obvious.

'Have you really stopped painting?' she asked, as he moved around his kitchen, making coffee and opening a packet of ginger biscuits.

'I really have,' said Ari.

'And you don't miss it?'

'Not really, it just feels strange because I never imagined stopping but then one day I didn't want to anymore, like something in me had changed. I looked at my paints, and my brushes and a blank canvas and it wasn't there, whatever made those paintings; I had lost it.'

'It sounds devastating,' said Belle. All her life she had been a creative person in search of something she was really good at. She couldn't draw or paint, her pottery was wobbly, her photographs weren't special, even the mosaics she made weren't amazing. To have actual talent and then lose it; she couldn't imagine.

'There's a lot more time to ride my horse now,' Ari told

9

her. 'To surf, see friends, listen to music, or do nothing at all. It's not so bad.'

Coffee in one hand, ginger biscuit in the other, he took her through to his studio. It was stacked full of paintings – a few earlier ones he had done of native birds, the portraits he was famous for and some newer stormy beach scenes.

'I'm not sure how I'll choose just one from all these,' said Belle.

'There's no rush,' he told her. 'Have a look round then go away and think about it. If there's something you like then you should come back again and visit it. Buying a painting, it's like a relationship; if you make the right choice, you'll be together for a long time.'

Belle loved his work, especially the seascapes that were abstract and saturated in colour. The one she was most drawn to was a smaller canvas, unframed and balanced on an easel. She stood there for a while, staring at it, knowing it was the right choice, but needing a reason to come back.

'No problem,' said Ari. 'Just let yourself in, if I'm not here. You know where the key is.'

So, Belle came back the following Sunday, and the Sunday after that, and then one final Sunday bringing a picnic they ate together beside a stream in the forest that stretched between his house and the ocean. By then she was absolutely sure it wasn't one of Ari's paintings that she wanted a relationship with. And seeing the smile spread across his face every time he set eyes on her gave Belle a reason to hope that he felt much the same way.

Right from the beginning there was an easiness between them. The more they got to know each other, the easier it felt. Sitting in the long grass, listening to the rush of water below and birdsong above, Belle questioned Ari about his life. She wanted to learn everything about him, to catch up on the years he had lived through before they met, and to do it as quickly as possible.

'You're not married?' she asked, because that was what she most wanted to know.

'Used to be,' he told her, leaning back on the picnic rug, hands behind his head and bare feet in the grass. 'She went to Australia to see her family and didn't come back.'

Belle didn't see how anyone could leave a man like him. When she said so, Ari only shrugged.

'Maybe I wasn't always so great to her. Artists can be difficult to live with. If our work isn't going well then nothing is. She put up with years of that. Probably she should have left me much sooner.'

'You're not an artist anymore,' Belle observed. 'So does that mean you're not as difficult to live with?'

'I hope so. You'd need to stick around to find out.'

'Would you like me to stick around?' she asked, staring away from him, towards a strand of silver birch, daring to ask the question.

Ari waited for a few moments before replying, then said in his soft, low voice, 'Hell yes.'

Belle leaned down and kissed him for the first time, softly and briefly. As she pulled away he smiled. 'Sunday girl,' he said. 'If I was still making paintings then your face would inspire me.'

Then his arms were around her and his lips were on hers. And to Belle it seemed that he had been waiting for her, just like she had been hoping for him.

She didn't drive back to the city that night, never really lived there again, and before long she had given up the apartment she was renting and moved in with Ari. He was bigger and bolder than any other man who had passed through her life, somehow more solid too. Getting to know him filled her mind and her days.

'Look at you,' she said, flicking through an old photo album she had found on a high shelf in the spare room, and coming across a faded shot of him with his cousins at the beach. He was stripped to the waist, the greenstone he still wore hanging round his neck, holding up a fish he had caught and grinning broadly.

'I thought I was Christmas,' he said, shaking his head at it. 'I was so full of myself back then.'

Belle smoothed the curled edges of the photo with her finger. Ari had aged, but he was still recognisably this man, a softer and mellower version.

'We met at the right time then,' she said. 'When we were ready for each other.'

'Yep, I reckon. We found each other just at the right moment.'

Just like her mother, a lot of people couldn't get past the age difference, as if it was the one thing that mattered. But so what if their musical tastes were poles apart and they grew up watching different movies? There was nobody else Belle would rather spend time with, and Ari felt the same.

They changed each other's lives. Belle had never known a man as kind as Ari, who rescued fledgling birds and released spiders he found in the house. To live with that kindness day after day made her feel more settled. And she filled the spaces in his life left vacant when art had left him.

It was Ari who encouraged her to open the gallery in the annexe. Belle had been working as a props buyer in the film industry but things were pretty quiet and there hadn't been a job in a while. If one did come along it would mean long hours and maybe working away from home. Belle didn't want to do anything that would take her too far away from Ari. This seemed the right time for a change; besides, she liked the idea of having her own gallery.

She began by selling off the remainder of Ari's paintings, and as the space emptied, she filled it up again, first with work from his old pupils and friends, later with pieces by local craftspeople. A woman who had built a mansion on the cliff-top commissioned Belle to source a series of artworks, and it seemed like she had left the film industry behind for good, just as she had her life in the city.

Sometimes Ari talked about painting. He would trace the planes of her face with his fingers, or run his hands along the length of her body and his voice would sound wistful. 'If only you'd come along a bit sooner,' he told her. 'I'd have painted you over and over.'

'Is it really too late?' asked Belle, who would have liked nothing more.

But Ari had cleaned all his brushes and put them away, given his empty canvases to the art school, whitewashed over the mural he never managed to complete and hung other people's artworks on the plain wall.

'It's gone, whatever it was that I had,' he said, regretfully. 'Ah well, it was good while it lasted.'

Later Belle wondered whether this had been one of the earliest signs of something going wrong, but no one had realised it at the time. His friends seemed to accept the change in him as part of growing older; everyone retired, didn't they? And mostly Ari didn't make a fuss about it. He enjoyed what he could still do. He enjoyed living.

Often when he surfed Belle would sit on the beach and watch, although she was never tempted to run into the waves herself. As for his horse, Ari showed her how to slip on the halter, and manoeuvre him through the gate and out of the paddock without the rest of the herd crowding her. Even though Belle hadn't grown up around animals, she did learn to love his tan-coloured dog, Waru, and stopped minding that he slept at the bottom of their bed. Still the big white horse Tama she never felt confident handling.

Ari rode all year round. He surfed in Maukatia Bay even in the winter. He seemed unstoppable. But there must have been signs even then and everyone missed them, even Belle.

To be fair he always did seem to have a sketchy memory.

She would find pencilled lists on the backs of old envelopes, things he had to do, people he should call, supplies to pick up the next time he was in town. He forgot birthdays and anniversaries, but remembered the important things. He remembered how Belle liked her coffee and the fragrance she wore and the flowers she preferred. He never forgot he loved her.

At times his mind did seem to wander, even go astray. He left pans on the hob to boil dry and forgot to fill the car with diesel. He made arrangements to go places and see people then didn't turn up. If they couldn't get hold of him, often they called Belle, and she made excuses. He was a typical creative type, she said, and his mind was always half on something else.

Belle ignored the small signs because she wanted to; she looked the other way on purpose. Until those signs started to get bigger and she couldn't pretend any longer.

3

Just Small Stuff

Belle had found a life she was happy in. She loved being here by the coast, walking on the beach every morning or along the path behind the dunes on wilder, windy days. She loved her gallery, and being surrounded by bush and birdsong. She belonged here, far more than she ever had in the dull suburb where she grew up, or the dilapidated villas on leafy streets where she shared a flat in her twenties, or the city apartment she lived in before now. This was her place and Ari was her person.

'Why me?' he asked her once. 'Why did you never settle down with some other fella?'

Belle knew the answer to the second question. Before meeting him she had never realised that she wanted to settle down. None of the unsuitable men she dated, even the couple of guys she'd tried living with, had made her feel settled enough. But why Ari? That was harder for her to put into words. All Belle knew was that he made her feel calmer. Even when the news was filled with grim stories, even when her mother rang and had nothing good to say, when winter chilled and the sky was grey, when her knees hurt and her head ached, being with Ari made it seem like everything would be OK.

'Why me?' she would sometimes ask in return and then he always laughed.

'You showed up and never left, that's how I remember it.'

He wasn't the kind of man who was constantly saying *I love you*. But Belle knew that he did and she loved him, fiercely and protectively. Every day she tried to do something that made him happy even if it was just baking his favourite buttery shortbread biscuits, or surprising him with a cup of tea or sitting on the deck with him watching the sun set and listening to stories she had heard about a hundred times before. That was love to Belle; those small and unimportant moments she and Ari had together.

'I'm getting old,' he told her, as they lay against each other in bed early one morning listening to the rain on the tin roof.

Belle had never heard him say anything like that before. 'We're both getting old,' she replied, trying to shrug off the words.

'Yes, but I'm starting to feel it, and I never did before.'

'In what way?' she asked, afraid of what he might say.

'Just … I don't know … me and Waru, we're showing our age now.'

The dog was lying on the end of their bed as usual and Belle felt his tail thumping against her legs as he heard the sound of his name. 'Waru might be looking a bit decrepit, but you're not,' she promised. 'You never seem old to me.'

Two days later she stopped at the farm-stand up the hill to buy peas freshly picked from the field, when she bumped into Greg. Blue-eyed, broad-shouldered and strikingly good-looking, he owned the property where Ari kept his horse, and the two of them were great mates.

'Hey Belle, how are you?' he asked.

'I'm fine but I need to tell you that I'm buying the last of these peas. Ari is making a risotto. You should come over to eat with us this evening. He'd love to have a night on the deck drinking wine with you.'

'That would be great.' Greg watched as she put her cash in the honesty box, and then he asked, 'Is Ari OK?'

'Yes, why? Does he not seem it?'

'There have been a couple of things, that's all,' said Greg, uncomfortably.

Ari had been hanging out at the stables more than ever these days. Since Greg's boyfriend had walked out, he had been quietly supportive. He helped with the chores, feeding out hay and bringing in horses for the farrier or vet. Ari was so practical he could turn his hand to fencing or shear a sheep if necessary, and he seemed to enjoy working outdoors, he always came back with a smile on his face.

'What things?' asked Belle, feeling a flutter of fear.

'Just small stuff,' said Greg, with a shrug. 'Like he left the barn door open and it rained so some of the hay bales got wet. He's forgotten to turn out a couple of horses. He said he'd pick up wormer but then didn't. Nothing major, but lots of little things.'

'He's always been a bit forgetful,' said Belle, relieved it wasn't anything more serious.

'Not really, not like this,' said Greg, who had known Ari a long time and was probably his closest friend now that he didn't have as much to do with the art world.

'Come over this evening,' Belle repeated, not wanting to hear any more. 'Pea and asparagus risotto, bring wine, about six o'clock, OK?'

'See you then,' said Greg, but his smile looked forced and as Belle got into the old Land Rover that Ari only ever drove on local roads these days, she could still feel the fear fluttering.

That night Ari was on form, pulling out dusty old bottles of wine from his cellar and a cedar box full of cigars. It was a mild spring night and they wrapped up in rugs and ate outside. Belle felt her fears ease as she listened to him plotting with Greg. They were coming up with some ridiculous plan to buy a young warm-blood horse and train it up so Greg could take revenge on his cheating ex-boyfriend in the dressage arena.

'You'd be playing a long game, obviously,' Ari was saying. 'But imagine how pissed off he'd be.'

'That horse of his was expensive,' Greg said, dubiously. 'I can't afford anything as flash.'

'You're the one with the talent mate, and talent wins over money, every time,' Ari assured him. 'We'll get the word out that you're looking and we'll find you something. You're going to go out there in your fancy jacket and your tight white jodhpurs and beat that little shit and it will feel amazing.'

'He broke my heart, you know,' said Greg, sadly.

'Yeah, I know,' said Ari, pouring more wine. 'You'll meet someone else though; it's never too late – look at me and Belle. You'll find the right guy and the right horse, I know it.'

By the time Greg left it was almost midnight. Belle walked him up the dark driveway with a torch. He probably shouldn't have been driving but the roads would be quiet now and he promised to take it slow.

'Ari seems all right, doesn't he?' she asked as he got in the car. 'His usual self?'

'Yeah, he does,' Greg agreed. 'It's probably normal to get a bit forgetful at his age. Sorry if I worried you.'

Even so, the next day while Ari was out surfing and Belle was alone in the gallery, she spent some time googling in the hope it would reassure her. *Symptoms of dementia*, she typed. There was a long list and most things definitely didn't apply to Ari. He hadn't developed balance and co-ordination issues. He wasn't apathetic. He didn't seem suspicious or defensive. He forgot a few things; that was all. Now and then he repeated himself, told her a story he'd already told the day before. Or he stopped mid-sentence because a word or name was eluding him. But that happened to everybody. Belle forgot words and names all the time. It wasn't a reason to be concerned.

Even so she signed up to a Facebook group, for partners of people with dementia. Open Minds, it was called. She was curious, that was all. She wondered what kinds of things they would post there.

Ari was mostly good for a while after that. He and Greg were caught up in the search for a dressage horse. They seemed to spend a lot of time online and speaking to each other in a language that Belle didn't fully understand. They talked about Donnerubins and some stallion called Secret they might buy frozen semen from. They travelled all over the country looking at horses. Ari was hugely engaged in the whole project. He hadn't liked Greg's ex-boyfriend much. 'The guy was a shit,' he kept telling Belle.

Some days she didn't let her worry spoil the life she loved. Ari repeated himself but she liked hearing his stories. He forgot names of people that weren't important. He left a chicken roasting too long in the oven, so she took over the cooking. There was a new expression that crossed his face, a blankness she didn't recognise, but it was there one moment and gone the next.

Then Ari stopped driving his old Land Rover, even down the road. Belle had to drop him off at the stables whenever he wanted to see his horse, and Greg would bring him home. She trusted Greg to look after him, and Ari seemed to need more looking after. As the months passed, there was no more ignoring that.

He was especially confused straight after waking, when sometimes he mixed up dreams with reality. Belle would hold him and talk about familiar things – the horse, Waru, a favourite painting on the wall – until real life came back into focus again.

Once Ari woke in a total panic, convinced he had borrowed Greg's horse truck without asking and then crashed it.

'I can't believe I did something so stupid,' he told her. 'I don't think I'm even insured to drive it. This could cost us thousands.'

Belle told him not to worry, that everything would be fine and Greg would sort it. Ari hadn't been anywhere in days so she was certain this must have been a particularly vivid dream. Still, later on, when he was busy in the garden, she called Greg and told him what had happened.

He reassured her that the horse truck was completely fine. Then he told her it was time to do something. 'Take Ari to a doctor, get him checked out.'

'I don't want him to realise what's happening.' The longer she could shield him from the truth, the better. 'Not yet.'

'He knows,' Greg told her. 'I'm sure of it.'

'What makes you think that?' Belle was watching Ari now, digging compost into the vegetable beds, the muscles in his arms and shoulders working. 'Has he said something?'

'Not exactly ... but Ari knows something is up, he just doesn't want to worry you.'

'It's getting worse,' she told Greg, bleakly. 'He's changing.'

'Yeah, I think he knows that too.'

The devastation hit Belle with such force that she couldn't breathe properly.

'There must be medications he can take to slow this thing,' Greg said. 'Or other therapies that will help. You need to talk to an expert. Get Ari scanned and see what's going on in that head of his.'

'I should have done it sooner.' Belle felt guilty. 'I've been trying to pretend this isn't happening.'

'Yeah, I reckon that's what Ari's been doing too.'

Belle didn't know how to bring the subject up. When Ari came inside for his lunch, she watched him scrubbing the dirt from his hands, and thought they should enjoy one last untroubled meal together. As he ate boiled eggs and buttery sourdough toast, he seemed cheerful. There was no mention of the dream that had so distressed him and afterwards he sat in the gallery with Belle, chatting over cups of tea, until a customer appeared, and he went back to his garden. For a while later she watched him digging the vegetable beds, stripped to the waist in this sunshine, the tattoo of a silver fern snaking over his still-muscular arm, whistling as he worked. Belle didn't have the heart to ruin a good day.

That night, after Ari had gone to bed, she did more research online. She learned there were medicines but they all had side effects, made people feel dizzy or nauseous, and none of them offered a cure. She read about art therapy and brain exercises and cognitive rehabilitation and wished there was someone she could talk to.

She almost called her mother. They had been closer once when her dad was alive, before her mum married again, but they weren't close anymore, hadn't been for years now. Belle still remembered realising this new man, this stepfather, meant more to her mother than she did, and that mum was choosing him. From now on she would take his side in arguments, believe him and doubt her daughter, agree with his opinions and change the way she looked because he didn't like her clothes or the colour of her hair. Her stepfather Rod wasn't a terrible person, Belle didn't dislike him exactly, but she hated the way her mum was around him.

If she called her mother now, Belle knew what she would hear. Rod says you should never have married him. Rod says the age difference was bound to cause problems. Rod says he expected this.

So Belle didn't bother. Nor did she try any of the friends who were at a different life stage, dealing with unruly teenagers rather than elderly husbands, busy with their careers and plans for the future. She struggled on alone until eventually she made her way back to the Open Minds Facebook page.

Some of the posts there were heart-rending, others darkly funny; lots asked for practical advice and the whole vibe seemed non-judgemental and supportive. Belle never posted on social media, except to promote the gallery. Now she found herself typing:

> I'm facing the fact that my husband has dementia. I've been slow to accept this and we still haven't talked about what it means for us. Once the words have been said they can't be unsaid. They'll make it real and we won't be able to act like everything is OK anymore. But how do I even bring it up? What do I say to him? Many of you must have been in exactly this position and I'm wondering if you've got any advice.

She went to bed and didn't check for responses until later the next morning. There were several and Belle read them, pausing to serve customers coming in and out of the gallery. Some people hadn't bothered to respond to her question at all, instead sharing their own experiences with partners who were angry or silent or abusive. She read those posts with a sinking heart, hoping none of this was what lay in store for her. Others suggested it was likely that Ari already recognised what was going wrong. A few said it was vital to get an early diagnosis and several that it had made little difference. Brow furrowed, Belle read through them all again, trying to find something useful.

> You'll know when the time is right to talk about this. It will be obvious.

> Dementia can move very slowly in older people, there are still happy times ahead for you both.

> We never use that word. We just talk about being forgetful. It's less threatening.

There was one message that she thought about again in the weeks and months that followed. It came from a man called Enrico who said his wife was suffering from early onset dementia.

> A doctor should break this news to your husband. All you
> need to do is love him, not make a medical diagnosis. And
> then do whatever you can to keep on loving him.

Belle couldn't imagine ever not loving Ari. For the first time, as she composed a short reply, she felt a little bit comforted.

> Thanks for your advice, Enrico. I'll find a way to get him to a
> doctor. I hope your wife is doing OK.

She didn't think Ari even had a regular doctor. He never seemed to trust them. Whatever ailed him, the solution was to drink a tea made from kawakawa leaves plucked from a tree in the garden. That plus two glasses of red wine a day was Ari's idea of medicine.

When she tried suggesting he visit a GP to have his blood pressure checked, his cholesterol measured, that kind of thing, he only laughed.

'Doctors find things wrong with you because they don't get paid otherwise,' he told her.

'I don't think that's entirely true,' said Belle.

'It's not entirely wrong either,' Ari insisted. 'It's a business like any other, isn't it? Anyway, I'm healthier than most doctors. I don't need anyone sticking needles in me.'

By then Ari was in his mid-seventies and, as far as Belle could tell, he had the strength and stamina of someone twenty years younger. There was only one reason for him to need a doctor's help. And still neither of them could say it out loud.

It was early summer and when he wasn't busy in the garden

Ari was taking the horses for a gallop down on the beach with Greg or heading out surfing with a couple of friends. The gallery was picking up, with passers-by stopping for a browse, and Belle spent a lot of her time there with Waru sleeping on the cool tiled floor, keeping her company.

The old dog couldn't run with the horses anymore and on hot days the black sand scalded his paws, so his gentle snoring became her soundtrack. When his breathing changed, growing more laboured, she noticed. When he struggled to get up it was Belle who had to lift him. And when his appetite faded, she was the one who decided it was time to take him to the vet for the final time. Ari agreed that it had to be done, but he couldn't bear to.

After they lost Waru, even Belle struggled to adjust. Often, she found herself stepping over the stretch of floor where he used to lie. She missed his hoarse bark warning her when customers arrived. The place felt emptier without him and she didn't like the emptiness.

But it was as though the loss had hit a switch in Ari. He couldn't seem to accept the dog had gone. Late at night, he would stand on the doorstep, calling Waru's name into the darkness. Some mornings Belle found him sitting in an armchair, his cheeks wet with tears, and no idea why he was crying. She had always known him as the most even-tempered man; now his moods came and went like wild weather.

'I think you should see a doctor,' Belle decided, expecting him to tell her not to be ridiculous, that there was nothing wrong with him, just like always. Instead, Ari stared at her for a moment and then spoke, sounding like a stranger.

'I reckon you should pack up your stuff and get out,' he said, gruffly. 'That would be the best thing.'

She was taken aback. 'What are you talking about?'

'You're still a young woman, so get out now while you've got the chance, no one would blame you.'

'Ari, I'm not …'

'Seriously, Belle, just leave. I don't want to be a burden on you.'

'You're not a burden,' she insisted.

'I will be though, eventually. It's early days yet.'

'I'd never leave,' she told him. 'I love you too much.'

'That's a problem then, isn't it,' said Ari.

After that he took the car keys from her desk and roared off in the Land Rover. It had been so long since Ari had driven anywhere that she was sick with anxiety until Greg texted to say he was at the stables. Later that afternoon, when he came home, his mood had settled, but still Belle went carefully, trying not to upset him.

In the weeks that followed, there was a shift in their relationship. Ari was prickly and everything Belle did seemed wrong. He had always been resolutely independent; now he wouldn't let her help him with anything at all.

'Stop fussing,' he would say. 'I can't bloody stand it.'

Often his temper flared for no reason and then he might retreat into silence. Belle felt like he was a changed man, not completely her Ari anymore. And she felt lonely. For the past ten years he had been the person she confided all her problems in. She wasn't sure where to turn. At night, lying sleepless beside him, she tried not to panic.

Belle had no plans. It was only possible to live day to day. She couldn't look too far ahead, because she was frightened of what she might see there.

During one of the more difficult weeks, when Ari seemed locked behind a wall of resentment and she couldn't get through to him no matter how she tried, she remembered that post on the Open Minds Facebook page, the man who had told her to keep on loving her husband. And for the first time she realised how difficult that might become.

Belle was in such despair that for the rest of the week she didn't bother opening the gallery. Instead, she went for long walks, breathing the resiny smell of pine trees, listening to the ocean crashing onto the beach, and trying not to worry too much about what Ari might be up to back at home.

One night she posted on the Open Minds page again. She felt awkward doing it, almost disloyal, but she had to talk to someone.

> My husband isn't the man I married. I still love him but
> I'm scared because it's getting so much harder. Someone
> on this forum tried to warn me this would happen. I didn't
> understand at the time, but now I do. What I need is some
> advice, but I'm not sure anyone can help me.

There was a flood of responses this time. People were so supportive that Belle grew tearful reading them. And it did make her feel less lonely to know others were out there and in the same position.

> Take it day by day.

> Don't expect too much from yourself.

> Never feel guilty about the way you're feeling.

> Remember you're important too. Make sure you get out, see
> friends, have a life.

A day later Belle checked in again and there were more responses, including one from Enrico in Italy, who said it might have been him who had replied to her original post, saying those things about love, and it was hard, really it was, but he did have some advice and would accept a direct message from her if she'd like to send one.

> Hi Enrico, thanks for your offer of advice. I don't really have

26

anyone here I can talk to who will understand what it's like.
I'm struggling a bit.

Ciao Belle, I asked you to send a direct message because
before I offer any suggestions, I need to know more about
your circumstances. Can you tell me what is going on?

The reply that Belle wrote took her a whole day to get right.
She kept coming back to it and tweaking it, adding bits
then deleting. In the end she told Enrico more than she had
told anyone else. She described Ari's mood swings, how he
seemed to be withdrawing, refused all help, wouldn't see a
doctor and at times seemed to hate her. When she re-read
the message for the final time, she paused and added one
last line.

It feels like all I've done is complain to you about Ari, but he's
a wonderful man, the best and he deserves all the love I can
give him.

It took another couple of days for Enrico's reply to come.
He was very kind and worried for her. They messaged to
and fro for a while.

You seem quite isolated, and that is going to become more
and more of a problem Belle. Would you consider moving
closer to friends and family?

No, Ari would never move from here, he loves this place too
much.

Then you need support. People will be willing to help. Often,
they are just waiting to be asked.

But Ari won't accept help, not even from me.

Maybe you can make it seem like he is the one doing the helping?

Belle asked him about his wife then and Enrico told her that he was struggling with the question of whether to put her into a care home, as she was deteriorating very fast.

Without help I couldn't have kept Luciana at home as long as I have. But now I am afraid she is going to hurt herself. And I have to think about my sons and my mother; they live here too. Still, it is a difficult decision.

Belle needed a friend and it seemed like Enrico needed one as well. While the days and weeks passed, they continued to exchange messages. He told her about the southern Italian hill-town where he lived. Belle googled pictures of it and was charmed by the huddle of whitewashed houses rising up from the groves of olive trees. She wrote back to him describing her stretch of dramatic coastline with its steep black dunes and restless ocean. They talked about TV shows they were watching and books they had read. Belle described her gallery and he mentioned his family's fashion business.

Whenever she found a message from Enrico, her mood lifted. The friendship that he offered was so uncomplicated. He didn't expect anything, never seemed judgemental, and was on the other side of the world, going through many of the same things she was.

The first time they chatted properly was after Enrico had come to terms with putting his wife in a care home. By then their messages were growing longer and longer. There was so much to say and too much tapping on a screen necessary to manage it. Enrico suggested chatting on WhatsApp instead, Belle said what about Zoom, and suddenly they were together, him with a coffee in his hand, her with a Chardonnay because it was night-time in New Zealand, staring at each other via a computer.

Belle thought Enrico looked very Italian. His silver-flecked hair was neatly trimmed, his pale linen shirt had been pressed and his face was clean-shaven. She wondered what he must think of her, with her unbrushed hair caught up in the scarf she wore to keep it out of her eyes. She rarely bothered with make-up and her clothes came straight from the washing line or the back of whichever chair she had thrown them over the night before.

'Are you in your gallery?' Enrico asked, and she tilted the screen so he could see the paintings on the wall and sculptures made out of driftwood and riverstones.

In return he showed her the view from his window, the narrow streets of clustered whitewashed houses set against a wintry blue sky.

'I've never been to Puglia,' Belle told him, wistfully.

'You should come one day,' said Enrico.

'I'd love to,' Belle replied, although she couldn't imagine when. She barely even went into the city now, and that was only forty minutes' drive away, because she didn't want to leave Ari for too long.

After that they talked for a while about his wife. Enrico still felt as if he had let her down, although in the end it had been clear there was no choice other than to move her into full-time care.

'The home is not far away so I see her most days. Often, she doesn't recognise me, but that is almost easier than the times when she does know me as her husband and begs to come home.'

'How are your sons coping?' Belle asked.

'My eldest boy, Gianni, he is sure there must be some solution. He keeps searching online to learn about surgery and experimental drugs, then wanting to know why we can't try these things for Luciana.'

'It must be hard for him to accept the way she has changed.'

'He hasn't accepted it. Instead, Gianni puts all his energy into trying to find a cure even though the doctors have said it is impossible.'

'And what about your younger son, Pietro?'

'He was always the wilder one,' Enrico told her. 'In the past this worried his mother but now he has met a lovely young woman and is settling down. Luciana would be very happy. I have told her, of course, but I am not sure whether she understands. She will miss so many things; Pietro's wedding, her grandchildren, so much that she was looking forward to.'

'It isn't fair,' said Belle.

'Not fair at all, but this is the reality. Somehow we must find a way to go on without her.' Enrico gave a very Italian shrug, head tilted and turning the palms of his hands upwards. 'The most difficult thing is that she isn't here with us, and yet she *is* still here. How are we supposed to behave? Should Pietro go ahead and organise his wedding? I say yes, but Gianni thinks it would be wrong to hold a family celebration and not have her among the guests. And so, we argue.'

'Your wife isn't well enough to go, not even for a little while?' Belle wondered.

'No.' Enrico paused, put down his coffee cup and rubbed his eyes. 'Pietro wants his mother there but she is too unpredictable. She might be in a rage or weeping, or say almost anything at all. It would be awkward for our guests and in my opinion undignified for her. And so, we argue.'

'It sounds complicated.'

'Families always are.'

In comparison Belle's own situation seemed straightforward. There was just her and Ari to worry about.

'I haven't got that sort of family,' she told him. 'We don't get very involved in one another's lives.'

'Do they know anything about what is going on?' asked Enrico.

'Not really,' Belle admitted. 'We're not close. My parents never really approved of Ari, they thought he was too old for me.'

'Then it must be hard for you too, but in a different way.'

In person Enrico seemed very like his messages, candid and kind, and she thought that Ari would probably like him if they ever met. Still, Belle didn't mention this new friendship to her husband. She kept messaging with Enrico, had another Zoom call, started to think of him as someone she really knew, but never talked about it.

Mostly each day seemed like the one before, and the life Belle had loved started to feel like a trap. She was a carer now, not just a wife, and she had to care for Ari slyly and subtly, in a way he barely noticed, otherwise she paid for it with his anger and frustration.

'I managed OK for a lot of years without you telling me what to do,' he would bark. 'I meant what I said. You should clear out and leave me alone.'

Sometimes Belle did imagine packing a suitcase, getting in the car and driving away. But then she would look at the wedding photograph on her desk, at the younger version of herself in Ari's arms, and know that woman would never have given up on him.

'I wish you'd stop saying that. I'm not going anywhere,' she kept telling Ari.

'You're a fool then,' he would huff and retreat into silence until his mood brightened for some reason and then he might bring her a coffee, or a bunch of dahlias picked from the garden, or simply come and put his arms around her and stand still for a while, so that Belle could take in the scent of him; salty from the sea, earthy from the land.

Holding onto what she had left of Ari for as long as

31

possible, enjoying every good day, keeping his mood light, it was all that Belle really cared about.

'Why don't you get another dog,' she suggested, thinking a puppy might make him happy.

'Nah, I don't think so. Waru was my last dog.'

'What if I got one then?'

'Don't tie yourself down,' said Ari, gruffly.

She remembered Enrico's advice, that the best way to help Ari was by making him believe he was helping her. At first, she couldn't fathom how to do that. But then it came to her one afternoon, when Ari arrived home from the stables, glowing with a good mood.

'Would you teach me to ride?' Belle asked.

'Seriously?' He was surprised. 'I thought you were still half-scared of horses.'

'I'm not scared really,' Belle lied. 'Maybe if you gave me a few lessons then we could borrow one of Greg's horses and go out for a hack together some time.'

'I'll teach you the way my father taught me,' said Ari, sounding pleased. 'You'll pick it up in no time. And Tama will look after you.'

Tama didn't look anywhere near as big from the ground as he felt when you were on his back. Belle tried to relax in the saddle as Ari adjusted the stirrups to the correct length and showed her how to hold the reins.

'Don't pull on his mouth,' he instructed. 'As he walks let your hands move forward with him. Relax your legs, your shoulders and your arms. Let everything feel fluid and soft.'

'What if he bolts?' she asked nervously, as the horse paced a circle around Ari, kicking up dust from the arena. 'What if he throws me?'

'He's not going to bolt or throw you. Just close your eyes for a minute and feel the movement. You trust me, don't you?'

Belle did trust Ari. Around the horses he seemed as capable as ever. And he liked teaching, that was obvious as he showed her how to squeeze her legs gently against Tama's sides so he broke into a trot, and how to rise up and down in the saddle, keeping her hands still and low.

Afterwards, Belle felt heady with relief. She hadn't fallen or hurt herself, which had been her biggest worry. Also, it seemed to have worked. As they split a cold beer, waiting for the horse to finish its feed, things between her and Ari were miraculously normal.

'I enjoyed that,' she told him, and it wasn't entirely untrue.

'Shall I give you another lesson tomorrow?'

'If I'm not too sore.'

'We'll make a rider of you,' Ari promised.

Belle changed the gallery opening times, so they could go to the stables early each morning. She always felt slightly fearful when she climbed onto the mounting block, put her foot into the stirrup and swung a leg over the horse's back. But she loved having Ari teach her. He might not be able to recall what he had eaten for breakfast or name the shows they watched on television the night before, but when he was around horses, Ari remembered everything that was important. For a while at least, Belle felt like she had her husband back.

The next time she sent a message to Enrico, she thanked him because his advice had made all the difference. She included a photo of herself on the horse, a bit sweaty and red-faced because it was a hot day and she'd had her first canter. His reply when it came was a brief one.

That is good Belle. I am happy to have helped. Be sure to make the most of these good times you have together.

4

Quiet And Empty

The beach was shimmering where black sand met salt spray, and the horse was straining against the reins that Belle held tightly. She wasn't sure if she was ready for this. Ari reckoned she had enough balance and control, and said it wouldn't be too different to riding over the farm tracks. But now she was here, with a long strip of sand stretching out in front of her, Belle was afraid to relax her grip, convinced the horse would be off and flying if she gave him the chance.

Greg had driven them down in his truck very early that morning and would be back later to collect them. So, it was just Ari bareback on a borrowed horse, and her on the usually trusty Tama who seemed a different beast here, with his ears forward and his stride much longer.

Ari's horse was jig-jogging towards the tideline now, in a way that concerned Belle, although he didn't seem particularly bothered. 'I never thought we'd ride together like this,' he called back to her.

'Me neither,' she responded, trying to sound more upbeat than she felt.

Ari was grinning now. 'It's very cool.'

The smile didn't leave his face even when his mount began cantering sideways and tossing his head. Ari had learned to ride without a saddle when he was a boy and was still at ease this way. From behind, Belle thought that he looked like a young man, his body barely moving as the horse rocked and reefed, so poised he seemed moulded to its back.

'I can't hold him much longer.' Ari was laughing now. 'I have to let him go. Will you be OK?'

'Yes, but not too fast,' Belle shouted.

As the lead horse lunged forwards, inevitably Tama followed. For a few moments all Belle was aware of was hoofbeats drumming on the sand and her own fear. She clung on to the mane, reins looped against Tama's neck and the canter growing faster and faster.

Then her head cleared and she remembered the instructions Ari had repeated patiently day after day. Sit up, breathe out, relax your legs, tighten and release one rein, but don't keep pulling on his mouth because he is stronger than you and he will win that battle. She tried it and the horse responded as he had promised it would, shortening its stride.

Tama calmed and so eventually did the chestnut horse that Ari was riding. For several minutes they were cantering slowly side by side, bordered by towering dunes and crashing waves, with miles of empty beach before them and, although still scared, Belle's adrenaline was surging.

As the horses began to tire, they slowed, and at last were settled enough to lope along at a walk, splashing through the shallow waves.

'Thank you,' said Ari, his eyes on the horizon. 'I know you only did this to make me happy.'

'I see why you love it now,' Belle told him.

He turned and looked at her. 'This is the happiest I've felt in a long time. Nothing could beat it,' he said softly. 'Nothing at all.'

Belle's spirits soared. She had helped Ari by letting him help her; the plan had worked.

'Perhaps you could teach me how to surf next?' she suggested.

Ari laughed. 'Steady on.'

'We could go boogie boarding together at least.'

'Let's just enjoy this, right now,' he told her.

When they turned towards home, the horses freshened again and broke into another canter. By the time they made it back to Greg, waiting in his truck beneath the pine trees, Belle's legs felt like jelly.

'You had a good time?' asked Greg.

'The best,' Belle replied, still buzzing with adrenaline as she ran the stirrup irons up the leathers the way that Ari had shown her, certain this had been an experience she would never forget, scary but worth feeling scared for.

'Thanks for the ride, mate,' said Ari, nodding towards the chestnut horse.

'Any time,' Greg told him.

Aferwards, although Belle was tired, Ari seemed energised. At home she lazed the rest of the morning away in a beanbag, while he kept busy fixing a broken window latch, tidying tools in his shed and then coming to fetch her, and taking her to bed where they made love for the first time in ages.

'This morning was perfect,' he whispered, as she lay curled against him, drifting off to sleep. 'I love you.'

She must have fallen into a deep sleep because when Belle woke again Ari wasn't in bed beside her. She found a scrawled note from him left on the kitchen table, stuck to one of his old art folders.

High tide … gone for a surf xxx

Belle hoped he hadn't gone alone. She thought about driving down to check on him but, after such a lovely time together, it would risk ruining his mood if he thought that she was fussing. So instead, she did a few chores in the gallery and then leafed through her recipe books, looking for something to cook for dinner using what she had in the pantry.

She kept listening out for Ari whistling as he walked down the driveway with his surfboard under his arm, having hitched a ride back up the hill. But as the afternoon shadows lengthened, and there was no sign of him, Belle started to worry. She told herself he would be sitting on the beach, drinking a cold beer with an old friend, talking about the waves they had caught and the boards they had ridden, losing track of time. But it grew later and she worried more. There was no distracting herself with recipes now. Belle could only think about Ari, and how this was unlike him.

She drove down to the smaller bay first as that was where he usually surfed. A few people were still in the water but Ari was distinctive, and as she looked towards the break at the southern end of the bay, she was sure that none of the surfers she could see were him. On the shore, Belle spotted somebody she did recognise, a younger guy who came by from time to time for a drink on the deck.

'Have you seen Ari?' she asked.

'Yeah, he was here earlier, I think,' the young surfer replied vaguely.

'You don't know where he is now?'

'No idea, sorry.' Squinting into the bright sun, he scanned the water quickly. 'He never stays out for long these days. Gets tired.'

'He hasn't come home,' Belle told him. 'I'm worried. He's been gone for hours.'

'OK.' This time the surfer took a more searching look and then zipped his wetsuit and picked up his board. 'I'll go and have a paddle around, check if I can see him out there, shall I?'

Belle paced the sand as she waited, the worry getting bigger until it filled her mind and there was no space for any other sort of thinking. She kept staring out to sea, although the hope of seeing him there was lessening.

The young surfer emerged from the sea at last, pushing

his long, wet hair from his face. 'No sign of him, as far as I can see,' he told Belle. 'You could check the main beach. He might have headed there for a change.'

'When you saw him earlier, did he say anything?' she asked.

'Nah, he didn't stop to speak. But hey, I'm sure he's fine. Ari knows what he's doing.'

Belle didn't feel reassured. She drove to the bigger beach to take a look, but she knew Ari was wary now of the riptides and strong currents, so wasn't surprised when she couldn't find him.

The sun was lower in the sky and the light more golden. Heading home, Belle clung to the hope that she would discover Ari there, wondering where she had got to.

But the house was quiet and empty, and his note still lay where she had left it, sitting on the old art folder. She turned it over, seeing the back was blank, then opened the folder. Inside she found a simple pen and ink portrait of her own face. Every line of it captured her exactly. Belle stared at the drawing that she hadn't known existed. When had Ari made this? Why had he left it for her now?

It was Greg she phoned first, trying not to sound as panicked as she felt.

'Could he have got confused and lost, do you think?' he asked. 'I mean I know it's a straightforward walk up the hill, but still he might have taken a wrong turn.'

'I suppose,' she agreed, doubtfully.

'You stay there, I'll have a scout around.'

Belle made a cup of tea but didn't drink it. She wasn't sure what to do with herself. When she heard the car coming down the drive, she rushed outside, hoping to see Ari sitting in the passenger seat. Her heart sank at the sight of Greg alone, his blue eyes dull, his expression grim.

'I reckon we call the police,' he told her. 'That's the best thing now. They'll alert the coastguard.'

'What if he's just at a mate's house?' Belle was clinging to the possibility.

'He's a man with dementia and he's missing. I think we should play it safe. Even an experienced surfer can hit their head or get caught in a rip.'

'You're right, I'll call them now.' Belle's voice shook.

Afterwards, the strongest memory Belle had of that time was how she kept wishing she could wind back the clock, be at the beach again with Ari on horseback cantering alongside her, exhilarated and happy. The images of that final morning played in her mind day and night, like a movie on a loop, until the memory took on an almost unreal quality. How could she have been so happy one moment and then so sad the next?

It was difficult to look at the portrait he had left her. To Belle it seemed worryingly like Ari's version of a goodbye note.

People seemed to think the kindest thing was to be re-assuring, so she stopped answering most of their calls. She didn't want to be reassured; it was pointless. Any hope of finding Ari safe had vanished very quickly. Belle was already grieving as she heard the first search helicopter overhead and in the days that followed grief tightened its grip on her. When she saw the newspaper stories about a missing pensioner with dementia, it seemed surreal that this was Ari they were writing about.

Her mother kept ringing until Belle picked up the phone.

'Why didn't you answer, we've been worried about you,' she complained, and then. 'What was he doing going surfing on his own at his age? Rod and I don't understand it.'

'He often surfs out there alone,' Belle replied, tiredly. 'He's always been fine.'

'The *Herald* is saying he has dementia. That's not true is it?'

'He's been having a few problems with his memory,' managed Belle.

There was a quick hiss of breath and then the phone went silent. Belle knew her mother must have covered the handset and was relaying those words to her stepfather.

After a few moments her voice came again. 'This doesn't look good does it; not good at all. You shouldn't be there by yourself. Rod will come and get you, bring you back here.'

'Mum, no,' Belle couldn't imagine herself in the little townhouse that her mother kept neat as a pin, in her child-hood bedroom, staring at the painted wallpaper. 'I need to be here.'

'But what if—'

Belle stopped her quickly with a lie. 'The police have said they want me to stay where I am.'

'Really?' Her mother didn't sound convinced. 'I can't see why you should need to, but I suppose if that's what they said. Is there anything you want? Can we bring you some groceries? A casserole?'

'Thanks but no.'

'We'll keep hoping for the best then. And you'll stay in touch? Call me if there's any news?'

'Of course,' promised Belle, just wanting to get her off the phone. 'As soon as I hear something.'

It was Greg who told her the surf-lifesaving club were out looking for Ari along with scores of people from the tight-knit local community. They were searching the beach, the dunes and the forest while the police helicopter covered the water.

'Maybe he's lost in the bush somewhere,' said Greg, cling-ing to the idea. 'Maybe he wandered off and got disoriented.'

'Yes, maybe,' agreed Belle, wishing she believed it.

They found his surfboard first, washed up on the beach a few kilometres further north. Belle felt numb by then. Not angry, not sad, just nothing at all. She closed the gallery, lowered the blinds and spent a lot of time lying in bed but not sleeping.

The day they found Ari's body, all she wanted was to run away. From the sympathy, from the people she needed to talk to, from the things she was meant to do; Belle couldn't face any of it.

'We don't know for sure that it's him yet,' said Greg, determinedly hoping.

But there was the tattoo of a silver fern on his arm, marks and scars on his body, there were dental records, and soon there was no doubt at all.

Just before it was confirmed officially Belle found Ari's carved greenstone pendant in a bowl on top of the fridge. She had been looking for her reading glasses at the time, sifting through the odds and ends that had been chucked in there, when she saw its gleam and closed her hand around its familiar shape. Ari never took that greenstone off. He wore it like a good luck charm. Belle couldn't understand why it hadn't been round his neck that afternoon when he went out for a surf. It didn't make any sense at all.

She tried wearing the pendant for a few hours after that. The jade warmed against her skin and she liked the feel of its weight but when she glimpsed herself in the mirror, it gave Belle a jolt to see it there. Taking it off again, she tucked it in a pocket, keeping it close but out of sight.

Traces of Ari were everywhere in the house. His blue Swanndri jacket on a hook behind the front door, his books on the shelf, his art on the walls – only he was missing. Belle kept closing her eyes and touching the piece of smooth jade in her pocket. She didn't want to be here, but neither could she face being anywhere else.

Whenever he had needed a break from his life, Ari went to the beach or the farm. Belle thought about it for a while and then, since she didn't think she would want to be near the sea ever again in her life, she drove inland to the horses.

Ari's gelding Tama was standing in the paddock, his head over the gate, dozing in the sunshine. She put on his halter and stood with her face pressed into his neck.

'He's gone,' she whispered. 'Ari's gone.'

The horse stayed still, letting Belle lean into him. She closed her eyes, slowed her breathing and thought of Ari, the hours he had spent with this animal, how much he had loved it.

'How could he leave us?' she asked, envying the horse for not understanding that its world had changed. Looping the lead rope over Tama's neck, she sank onto the ground, hands over her face, blotting out the brightness of the day. The horse didn't move very far away. She could hear him cropping grass and the occasional swish of his tail.

Eventually Greg came and found her there, touching her shoulder gently.

'Hey,' he said.

'You heard the news?' Opening her eyes, she saw his face, ashen and drawn.

Greg nodded, grimly. 'I know it's what you expected, but still I'm struggling to believe it.'

'Me too'

'I'm so sorry Belle ... I'm devastated.'

'Me too,' she repeated.

'Come for a ride?' he suggested, taking hold of Tama's lead rope.

'I don't think so.'

'Just over the farm for half an hour, and we can talk.'

'I don't want to talk.'

Greg opened the gate and led the horse out anyway, so Belle followed him to the yard where she stood and watched as he brushed the dust from Tama's coat, picked baked-in mud from his hooves and tacked him up.

'We'll go for a quiet hack, OK?' he said, passing her a hard-hat.

'OK,' agreed Belle who didn't have the strength to argue.

Greg held the horse while she mounted up, just like Ari would have, and riding behind him through the vineyard and up the steep track to the top of the farm, Belle found herself wishing he was the one who had gone, not her husband. Then she pushed the thought from her head because none of this was his fault.

At the top of the race track was an old chestnut orchard where a couple of retired geldings grazed. They halted there for a moment and Greg asked, 'So what do you think?'

'About what?' asked Belle, confused.

'Him, the new boy over there,' Greg pointed out a youngster, a glossy black horse with a silver tail and a white blaze down its face. 'He arrived on a truck a couple of days ago, sent up by a cousin of Ari's from the East Cape.'

'That's the dressage horse you were looking for,' Belle realised. 'I didn't know you'd found one.'

'Neither did I.'

'You weren't expecting him?'

Greg shook his head. 'He appeared out of the blue. You should see the thing move, it's incredible.'

Belle stared at the young horse, head down and peacefully grazing, and couldn't escape the thought that this was another goodbye present.

'Ari was a good surfer, careful,' she said, as they turned and began riding back down the hill, ducking beneath the overhanging branches of the rata trees. 'He wasn't a person who had accidents.'

'Yeah, I know.'

'So what if this wasn't an accident?' It was the thought that kept going through her head. 'What if he did it on purpose?'

'Belle, you shouldn't—' Greg began, but she interrupted.

'I'm to blame,' she told him. 'Ari hated to be a burden, he kept telling me that but I wouldn't listen.'

43

'This isn't your fault,' Greg insisted. 'It's the one thing I'm sure of.'

'I should have forced him to see a doctor, like you said.'

'He was determined not to though.'

'I just wanted to keep him happy,' Belle said, her voice breaking.

'Ari was happy. I've watched him teaching you these past weeks and that was obvious.'

'Why, then? Why has he left me like this?' Belle remembered him that morning on the beach, strong and certain as he cantered the chestnut horse through the shallow waves. 'I thought we had much more time together.'

They rode down through a strand of bush, a wood pigeon flying low overhead and as Belle's eyes followed it, she glanced at Greg and saw the tears streaking his cheeks.

'I loved him too, you know,' he told her.

'And he loved you,' she said, softly.

The hardest thing was other people. Belle had no patience with their best wishes at this difficult time, their offers of help if there was anything she needed. What she needed was Ari, and since she couldn't have him then she didn't want anyone.

Still there was no getting away from people; at least in the first few weeks. Ari had a traditional Māori funeral, a *tangi*, and Belle knew that she was meant to find comfort in the rituals, but it felt drawn out and exhausting. All those acquaintances from the different corners of his life, his art world friends, the local surfers. The waves of pity she felt coming off them; they were so glad not to be her. And then there were flocks of his cousins, groups of her own friends, her parents tight-lipped and uncomfortable through the speeches, songs and chants. Too many people, pressing in, hugging her tentatively like grief was catching, or holding on too tightly and long, repeating the same details about her husband – a talented artist, a gutsy rider, a loyal friend, a man who would be missed.

The whole thing went on for three days and once Ari's casket had been buried and the minister had walked through their home to cleanse and bless it, all Belle wanted was to be by herself.

At first it seemed impossible. Friends left more messages, mailed cards or even popped round. Her parents appeared on the doorstep with flowers and food. Ari's cousins called to check if she needed anything. Belle rebuffed kindness after kindness and eventually people got busy with their own lives. She was glad to be forgotten. She had no energy for other people, she had no words. What she needed was to move slowly and live quietly. To be alone inside her grief.

Only Greg refused to go away. If she didn't answer the door, he kept knocking, knowing she was inside. He brought food and made sure she ate it. He cleaned the kitchen, put on laundry and made endless cups of tea. Belle assumed that at some stage Ari must have asked him to look after her.

It turned out that her husband had taken care of everything. Just as he had tidied his tool-shed on that final day, in the months prior Ari must have organised his life. All the documents Belle needed were gathered together. His will was recently updated and, aside from a few bequests to family and friends, everything he owned was left to her. In a drawer she found the list he had made, with everything ticked off on it, so he wouldn't forget.

It enraged Belle that he had been quietly plotting to abandon her. She felt angry when she wasn't sad, aside from brief periods of feeling nothing at all, numbed by sleeping pills or wine, when it was a relief to let life slip out of focus.

Greg insisted on being with her. They spent night after night binge-watching trashy TV shows together. He headed into town to pick up groceries and brought her takeaway coffee from the beach café. Often, he was the only person that Belle spoke to. She felt like a fading version of herself now, less solid somehow, as though when Ari had gone, a part of her had been erased as well. If it hadn't been for Greg, she might have disappeared altogether.

Her interest in the outside world was minimal, and Belle wasn't looking at newspapers or switching on the radio, so it took a while for her to realise that everyone else was being forced to retreat, just like she had.

'Lockdown?' she asked Greg, when he phoned to check in. 'What does that mean exactly?'

'We stay in our homes, only go out for essentials, wear a mask, try not to catch this virus,' he said, grimly.

'You seem really worried.' Belle was surprised.

'Haven't you seen what's happening overseas?' Greg sounded impatient. 'China? Italy? Yes, I'm worried.'

That night Belle watched the TV news rather than old episodes of *Sex and the City*. She turned on the radio and logged onto international websites. As she caught up with what was happening, her concern grew. It was difficult to believe that the whole world was being affected. She watched videos of locked-down people singing on balconies in Italy, using pots and pans for percussion, and thought about getting in touch with Enrico, but then for some reason didn't.

'Should we even be seeing each other?' she asked Greg, when he came round with a few bags of extra groceries, just in case. 'Aren't we meant to distance?'

'If we live alone then we're allowed to join up with one other person,' he told her.

'Am I your person then?' asked Belle.

'Seems like it,' said Greg.

Lockdown didn't make much difference to her life, but it felt as though the way she had been behaving was allowed now. Hiding away in your home and refusing to see any-one; that was the responsible thing to do, it was what the government had ordered, and so Belle carried on doing it.

They slipped by, those golden late-summer days when out on the coast everything seemed quieter. Belle wasn't sure how she filled the time. Her gallery stayed shut; she couldn't have opened it even if she wanted. The car battery went flat. The phone hardly rang.

Whenever she spoke to her mother, the conversations always left Belle feeling drained. Every word she said seemed loaded with disapproval.

'You're so isolated out there. I don't like to think of you all alone in that house at a time like this,' she kept repeating.

'What's wrong with my house?' Belle wanted to know.

'All those trees around you, it must be a fire risk, especially with everything tinder dry this time of year. Who would help if something happened?'

'There's really no need to worry.'

'Someone has to,' her mother's voice was high-pitched and querulous. 'Rod and I wish you had somebody there with you.'

Now she was widowed like her mother had been, now she was grieving, Belle had thought they might find a new understanding, but it wasn't the same at all apparently. Belle's father had died young, while Ari was an older man who had dementia. Her mother didn't go as far as saying that perhaps it was a blessing, but Belle assumed it was how she was thinking.

'Rod and I would just like to see you settled somehere more suitable,' she would almost always finish.

'I'm settled here, Mum,' was always Belle's reply. Then she would touch the greenstone in her pocket, and tuning out her mother's voice, would fill her mind with thoughts of Ari.

Belle was lonely but it felt right to feel that way. Loneliness was almost a friend. The farm was the only place she ever left home for these days. She would check on Tama, give him a feed and brush the dust from his coat. If Greg was

47

around then usually he would put the kettle on and make a cafetière of coffee that they would drink leaning against a stable door or sitting on a mounting block, chatting about whatever came into their heads.

'Can you still go out hacking?' she asked Greg, one day as she stroked the long glossy neck of his young horse.

'So long as I don't leave the property, I can do what I like,' Greg told her. 'Do you want to come for a hack?'

Belle shook her head. That wasn't what she had meant at all.

'I watched three seasons of *Sex and the City* reruns with you,' Greg pointed out.

'You enjoyed that,' she countered.

'Not really.'

Belle almost smiled. 'I get that you're doing this for Ari, but you don't have to keep an eye on me,' she told him.

'I need a friend too, I lost one remember,' said Greg, and then he threw a saddle blanket over Tama's back before going to fetch his tack.

Belle started riding again, cantering up the hay paddock on Tama one day, trotting the rows of the vineyard behind Greg the next. It felt as if she was waking up from a long sleep that hadn't really refreshed her.

One day they risked breaking the rules to ride over a neighbouring property. Coming over the brow of a hill, they paused to look at the view that stretched towards the harbourside city with its towering buildings. Auckland felt like a foreign place to Belle now, a town she had visited, but long ago. She had no desire to go back to the life she'd had there before Ari.

By then she was trying to face the choices his death was forcing her to make. Ari had left her his art collection and much of the small sum he had saved, and the house of course.

'Sell the place,' suggested Greg, as they were riding through a strand of kauri trees. 'Start again, somewhere new.'

'Where though?' wondered Belle, who couldn't bear the thought of selling.

'There's no rush, you can take your time thinking about it.'

Whenever Belle tried to consider her future, she went completely blank. It was like trying to imagine the entire universe; too big, too mind-blowing. She assumed that she would manage to get her head around it at some point, but for now she stopped trying to make plans and focused on living day-to-day.

On the first anniversary of Ari's death, she went to visit Greg at a place where he was house-sitting, a modern home high on the cliffs above the beach. It was the first time she had looked out at the sea since she lost her husband to it and raising a glass of champagne with her eyes on that wide expanse of blue, she wondered what he was thinking when he rode the final wave. Had he really imagined that he was setting her free?

Her life was off-kilter and it stayed that way. The gallery was still closed and neglect had left a layer of dust over it but the idea of cleaning was exhausting. It was almost a relief when Auckland went into another lockdown and she could keep driving to the farm every morning and spending the afternoon pottering around in Ari's garden.

When it was stormy the wilder weather suited her. Belle preferred it if the wind was lashing the trees and howling through the chimney, when the rain was so heavy it drummed on the metal roof, and she could huddle beneath an old plaid wool rug that she liked to imagine still smelled of Ari.

One night she was listening to cracks of thunder overhead and looking for the flashes of lightning that followed, when her phone pinged with a message from Enrico. Belle hadn't been in touch with him since she lost Ari. For some reason it seemed more disloyal now, this long-distance friendship with the Italian man, and besides she couldn't bring herself to tell him what had happened.

Now she glanced at this new message. What could Enrico have to say, after such a long time? She almost didn't open it but, curious, changed her mind.

Dear Belle, I wanted to let you know that my wife Luciana died. We are all heartbroken and things are very difficult here. I hope it is easier in New Zealand and that you and Ari are OK. I like to think of you, still enjoying your good times.

Instantly Belle felt terrible. She had become so caught up in her own troubles that she had forgotten other people had them too. Watching the storm, she tried to decide how to respond. There could be no sending deepest sympathy or offering best wishes. All those well-meaning clichés trotted out at times like this; it made Belle tense just remembering them.

Finding the words to use wasn't easy. She wanted Enrico to know that she understood his grief, because she felt it every day beneath her own skin too, prickling and stinging. But at the same time, she couldn't make this all about herself. She was meant to be comforting him.

Pouring a glass of wine, Belle waited for the storm to pass, then sent a message back.

Are you free to Zoom?

Not long afterwards, a reply came from Enzo.

Now, yes why not, I have a little time before work. One moment, I will send you a link.

And there they were again, staring at each other, Enrico with his morning coffee, Belle with her evening wine. Framed by the screen, their faces looked almost unchanged, which seemed incredible given how much both of them had been through. His hair was longer, hers was a knottier mess of curls, but judging only by appearances, they were the same people.

'It is very good to see you again after such a long time.' Enrico smiled. 'How have you been?'

'Yes, it's been far too long,' Belle said, avoiding his question. 'I'm so sorry about your wife. How are you doing?'

'Not great to be honest.' Enrico ran a hand through his silvery hair, pushing it out of his face. 'Luciana was unwell, of course, her life wasn't a good one and we expected this ... even so it is very hard.'

'Of course it is,' said Belle.

'Luciana stopped eating,' he explained. 'They said her body was shutting down, that we should let her go.'

'Oh Enrico ...'

'I wish she had been at home with us. I realise now that would have made things less difficult for my family.'

'How are your sons doing?' Belle asked.

'Dealing with it in their different ways. Gianni loses himself in work and Pietro drinks with his friends. I worry about them both. And seeing their grief every day ... it kills me.'

His eyes were flat and dull, his smile was missing. Belle wished she knew what to say. But perhaps there were no words of comfort in times like this. That was why people repeated all those meaningless phrases, because they had to say something.

'Tell me how you are doing in these crazy times?' Enrico asked. 'Are you and Ari still riding your horses and having good times?'

'I ride almost every day.' Belle couldn't bring herself to tell him the truth.

'It sounds idyllic.' He was wistful. 'I have thought about you often and wondered how you were getting on. But even though you were on my mind, I never contacted you, I'm sorry.'

'There's no need to apologise; I could have got in touch as well but ...' Belle paused. If she was going to explain about Ari, this was the time.

'You were busy too,' Enrico finished.

'Yes, I don't know where the time has gone,' she told him, relieved the moment had passed. 'It's like a blur, this past year, it seems unreal.'

'Unreal and yet at the same time too real,' said Enrico. 'But please let's talk about something else, anything but this pandemic which I am so sick of talking about. Tell me about riding horses. It is not something I have ever tried. What do you love about it?'

Belle tried to describe being astride an animal that was so much stronger and faster than you, the trust it needed, the feeling of exhilaration and the moments of peace it brought.

'You aren't frightened of being thrown?' asked Enrico.

'No, Tama looks after me. I feel very safe when I'm on him now.'

'You are very daring.'

Belle shook her head and smiled. 'I'm not really.'

'You go fast on this horse? It gallops with you on its back?'

'Sometimes, yes,' she admitted.

'Then you are daring.' Enrico glanced at his watch. His day was about to begin and there were things he needed to do. 'You haven't told me about Ari yet, how are things going with him.'

'Never mind,' replied Belle, quickly. 'Next time.'

Once they ended the call, she poured herself another glass of wine. She wasn't sure why she hadn't been able to speak about Ari. Maybe because Enrico's own news was so sad. Or perhaps, for a few moments, she wanted to be the old Belle, the one who hadn't lost her husband, the more carefree version of herself. Now it was going to be awkward. If they spoke again, how would she explain herself?

Sipping her wine, she wrote it all down in a long email.

Told Enrico what had happened. Explained her reluctance to believe it was an accident, but the impossibility of thinking he might have done it on purpose. Described the funeral that seemed to go on forever and the first anniversary, watching the sunset with Greg on a clifftop. And finished by apologising for not telling him when they had spoken.

Sometimes it feels as though I lost Ari twice.

She sent the email before she could change her mind then went to bed. Even now Belle still stayed to her own side of the old queen-size that sagged in the middle, as though Ari was going to come and climb in beside her. And every night she would wake, stretching a hand into the empty space. She never slept well.

The next morning there was a reply waiting from Enrico. He said how sorry he was and that she and Ari should have had more time. And he told her yes, it felt the same to him, like he had lost someone twice.

We will talk again very soon. In the meantime, go and be daring, ride your horse and find those moments of peace ... don't fall off!

Belle liked the idea of being daring. It was a new way of seeing herself. And it was true that now she could saddle up Tama and ride around the property without Greg to babysit her. For the first time in ages, she felt a tiny bit proud, almost like she had achieved something.

Still, Belle would never ride on the beach again, even though Greg had suggested it once or twice. She wanted to hold onto a clear image of cantering down that long stretch of black sand alongside Ari, and not have other memories layered over it. She stuck to hacking round the farm and riding to the top of the hill, to check on the young gelding that had been one of his parting gifts. Greg had noticed he was getting cheeky with the older horses, who kicked up their heels and bared their teeth to drive him away, and reckoned it was time to start his education.

'You can give me a hand if you like,' he told Belle.

'I don't know anything about breaking in young horses,' she pointed out.

'We don't *break* them anymore, we *start* them. And the first step is giving young Ari some new experiences.'

'You've called the horse after him?' Belle was taken aback.

Greg grinned. 'Well, he's headstrong and handsome.'

The next day they brought the young horse into the yards. He wasn't happy at being separated from his herd, calling out to them plaintively and jig-jogging on the end of his lead rope as they walked down the steep track. But once in a stall, with hay and a bucket of feed, and Tama beside him for company, he settled quickly enough.

Belle's job was to introduce him to things he might not have encountered before. She walked past his stall with a squeaky wheelbarrow, drove a quad bike through the yards, played with Greg's dogs, put up an umbrella, made a noise, waved things around.

The horse – which Belle flatly refused to call Ari – seemed pretty unfazed. Before long, he had graduated to being taken for walks and very quickly Belle discovered that he was skittish and much quicker than Tama, far more likely to pull her towards a patch of grass or tread on her toes. When something worried him, he made a huffing noise.

'When will you try to get on him?' she wondered.

'There's no hurry,' said Greg. 'He's got some growing to do yet. And this work we're doing now is the foundation for that. It'll make everything easier later on.'

'You have a plan for him, then.'

'Exactly.'

Even a half-wild young gelding had its future mapped

out; meanwhile, Belle continued to flail. While she enjoyed helping with the horses, this was Greg's life not hers, and she couldn't keep following him around forever. Her gallery was still there waiting, dim and dusty, and some evenings she sat at her desk, looking at the empty spaces on shelves and walls, knowing she ought to fill them. But the next morning it always seemed easier to climb in the old Land Rover and drive to the farm, where Tama was waiting in a paddock, and Greg had a list of chores to keep her busy all day and by the end of it exhausted.

Greg never asked her about the gallery or showed any interest in what her longer-term plans might be. He seemed to assume that she would just keep turning up every day.

Sometimes, as she was leading the young gelding down the race track past the house, then looping back to the stables, Belle would start to feel panicky. Time was escaping from her and she needed to hang onto it.

A friend had offered to help reopen the gallery or close it up for good, depending on what Belle wanted. The trouble was she didn't know. Some days one thing seemed best, the next the other.

'I'm not normally so indecisive,' she told Enrico, early one morning when they were catching up over Zoom. He was settled in his study with an *aperitivo*, she was in her kitchen with a cafetière of coffee. 'The problem is what I want is the one thing I can't have and that's Ari.'

'You are still grieving,' Enrico reminded her. 'Changing your life when you are feeling this sad seems a bad idea to me. But then my situation is different. I had to keep going, there was no other choice. Although I had lost Luciana, everything else seemed much the same, and I found the old routines comforting.'

'Would you have changed anything if you could?' wondered Belle, as she moved around the kitchen, peeling a

55

banana and putting it in a bowl with a dollop of Greek yoghurt and a sprinkle of flaked almonds.

Enrico paused to think. 'I haven't even considered it. At times I feel restless, I suppose, but doesn't everyone ... don't you?'

'I feel like if I open the gallery then my life will be back the way it used to be, except not as good.'

'I can understand that,' said Enrico, finishing his drink. 'But if it doesn't work out then you can close it again, surely? You have no staff to worry about, no premises that you are leasing?'

'That's true,' agreed Belle, taking a bite of her breakfast.

'I am not sure it would be wise to try something different right now; not unless you have to.'

Belle swallowed a chunk of banana and said wryly. 'I don't even know what that different thing would be.'

Enrico seemed distracted, suddenly. He glanced away from the screen and spoke in Italian to someone she couldn't see.

'I am sorry,' he told her, turning back. 'It is time for dinner and my family is waiting so I must go. Let me know what you decide to do.'

'If I ever manage to make a decision.'

'You will, when you are ready.'

They said goodbye, before clicking off Zoom. As Belle finished her breakfast, she thought about him eating dinner with his family. She knew that both his sons still lived with him, along with his mother, and at least one daughter-in-law, so his home must be a busy place, full of people and noise.

Belle's house was ridiculously quiet. No tapping of Waru's long claws on the wooden floors anymore, no sounds of Ari softly snoring in the bedroom, not even the ticking of a clock. Putting her single bowl and spoon in the dishwasher, leaving the half-drunk cafetière of cold coffee, she went outside and listened to the birdsong.

What were you supposed to do when you were lonely but couldn't deal with other people? Like everything in Belle's life right now, there seemed no easy answer. But she knew for sure that she needed to find a way to be happier; it had to be possible. She couldn't go on like this for very much longer.

5

Somewhere New

Restarting the gallery wasn't as difficult as Belle had envisaged. Dusting surfaces, mopping floors and polishing windows was a slog but then came the reward of hunting out artworks to restock it. Local pottery and Corten steel sculptures, woven flax bags and silver jewellery; objects it was a pleasure to be surrounded by. Belle missed Ari's advice as she arranged it all. He had an instinct for knowing what looked best where. But by the time it was finished, she felt reasonably satisfied with the job she had done without him.

She was planning to open three days a week, partly because a lot of business was happening online these days, but more importantly Belle wasn't ready for anything more.

'Why don't you do coffee too?' one friend suggested. 'A few little cakes even?'

'Have an artist-in-residence,' contributed another. 'Put on art and pottery classes.'

None of those were bad ideas; still Belle wasn't interested. She was edging back into life, not running towards it at full tilt, and that was fine, she decided. This way she still had time to spend at the farm, helping Greg muck out stables or bring in horses. When she slept badly, she could lie in a little later. If she felt low, she didn't have to pretend to be cheerful. And if she needed company, she could have her breakfast with Enrico while he enjoyed his *aperitivo*, or drink an evening glass of wine while he had his coffee.

Several times he had contacted her in the middle of his night-time when he couldn't sleep. Usually, she called him early in the morning after waking to another day without Ari. They spent so much time together they had started reading the same novels, first a twisty murder mystery he suggested. Both had differing opinions on the likely villain's identity. Between each conversation they progressed through its pages until it became evident that Belle had been misled by a series of red herrings.

They shared movies and TV shows, and listened to the same podcasts. They sent each other funny cartoons and video clips. When Enrico hurt his back, Belle thought Pilates might help, so they took a Zoom class together.

Whenever she thought about their friendship, Belle didn't completely understand what made it work, but moment by moment, she enjoyed it. She looked forward to spending time with him. Her spirits lifted whenever she saw that he had sent a message.

'So, it's like a long-distance romance?' Greg asked, when she happened to mention Enrico's name one day then had to explain how she knew him.

'Of course it isn't,' Belle replied, horrified at the idea. She was mucking out a stable, forking manure into a wheelbarrow while Greg waterproofed a canvas horse rug. 'We're friends, that's all; we get each other.'

'How often are you in touch?'

'Most days we'll message or catch up on Zoom.' Belle flung another pile of manure into the barrow.

'Seriously?' Greg raised his eyebrows.

'We've lost our partners, been through the same things,' said Belle, defensively. 'He's my friend, like you are.'

Grabbing the handles of the loaded wheelbarrow, she pushed it to the manure heap. She was annoyed with herself for introducing Enrico's name into the conversation. She and

Greg had been talking about where they would most like to travel once they could and without thinking, Belle started telling him about her friend who lived in a hilltop town overlooking olive groves in southern Italy and how wonderful he made it sound. Then she felt the need to explain how she knew this friend. And now Greg seemed determined to misunderstand the whole situation.

'There wouldn't be anything wrong you know, if you did have a new relationship,' he told her.

'But I'm not having a new relationship,' Belle said, exasperated. 'You're reading too much into this.'

'I'm intrigued, that's all. It sounds like you've been spending a lot of time online with this guy.'

Belle shrugged. 'Maybe I have.'

'You are being careful, right?'

'I'm not about to transfer all my savings into his bank account if that's what you're worried about. Enrico runs a fashion business, he's not a scammer.'

'So, it's a long-distance friendship?'

'Yes, and a really nice one.'

'That's good, then,' said Greg, but she noticed him arching his eyebrows again, before he went back to painting chemicals onto canvas.

Belle thought about it as she finished mucking out the stables. She was pretty sure she wasn't misreading the signs like she had the clues in the murder-mystery. They had a lot in common, she and Enrico. They had been through the toughest of times, and now she was lonely in her empty house while he felt the same in his full one.

Enrico was easy company. He didn't have any expectations, never spoke in platitudes, always made her laugh, but he definitely wasn't any more than a friend. Besides Belle loved Ari and couldn't imagine ever not loving him.

Grief coloured her life. She continued to feel sad from the moment she woke in the morning to closing her eyes at night, but there were times now when that sadness felt a shade or two lighter. She could look at the portrait that Ari had sketched of her without a spike of anger. And glimpse the sea without anxiety. Belle didn't feel better exactly, but it was possible that she didn't feel quite so bad.

She started doing everything possible to lighten things further. Reading self-help books and taking an online meditation course, eating well and exercising, spending time in nature, even starting to connect with a few friends again.

It wasn't easy working in the gallery. Having customers come in to buy a little something for a person that they loved, wrapping birthday presents and anniversary gifts, being caught in small pockets of other people's happiness; it was a sharp reminder of what she had lost.

Still there were reminders almost everywhere. Some were comforting like the old Swanndri jacket of Ari's that she put on when it was cold, and the Swiss Army knife she kept in her bag, and his greenstone pendant that was always in her pocket.

Other reminders were sad. The clothes she needed to throw away but somehow couldn't because she had memories of him wearing this torn old bush shirt and that faded denim; the belongings that had been pushed to the backs of drawers and half-forgotten like the hip flask he used when he went out on long rides or a programme from a theatre show they had enjoyed together.

Even if she was readier to move on with her life, mostly Belle still felt stuck in it.

'Perhaps I do need to start again somewhere new,' she said to Enrico one morning. They were playing chess over Zoom and, although the hand-carved marble set belonged to him, Belle was the one winning.

Enrico frowned down at the pieces on the board. 'Would a change of place make a big difference?' he wanted to know.

'I'm not sure,' Belle admitted. 'Imagine going to all the

61

bother of moving then discovering that it made no difference at all.'

'What if you went away for a while?' he suggested, looking up from the chess board. 'Took a trip somewhere you always wanted to go. That might be all the change you need.'

'Travel is so difficult right now,' pointed out Belle.

'True, but you could plan for when it isn't.'

Belle started thinking about dream destinations. For the next week she and Enrico messaged back and forth with details of luxury safari lodges in the Masai Mara, houseboats in Kerala and glamping in the Galapagos Islands. They talked about these trips like she was actually considering them. When was the best season to visit? What would the food be like? How long would she stay for?

'There are too many choices. How does anyone decide on anything?' Belle wondered, eating cheese on toast for dinner while Enrico breakfasted on a crisp, sugar-dusted pastry. 'There are still whole parts of the world we haven't looked at. Scandinavia, Asia, the Middle East.'

'Meanwhile I have been taking my summer holiday each year in our villa by the sea then going skiing in winter,' said Enrico, ruefully. 'It is starting to feel like I have never lived.'

'Galapagos is waiting,' Belle told him. 'You can sleep in the wilderness and enjoy all the romance and charm of camping without sacrificing comfort.'

'That does sound tempting,' agreed Enrico. 'Definitely more tempting than the horse trek in Mongolia.'

Belle wasn't even sure where her suitcases had got to. Possibly Ari had stored them in the loft after she moved in. He felt happiest here, so they had never pulled them down again.

'Luciana always wanted to travel,' Enrico told her. 'But we were waiting until our son took over the business, thinking we would have more time and freedom then.'

'Where did she want to go?'

Enrico thought about it for a moment. 'A place with history and culture,' he decided. 'She was a stylish woman and very clever. This is why it took us so long to notice the change. Luciana managed to hide her confusion at first.'

'Like Ari,' Belle said, nodding. 'He had ways to play down forgetting someone's name or an arrangement we'd made. And he remembered things from the past so well.'

'Luciana could name a piece of music from an opera she loved but wouldn't be able to tell you what she had for lunch.'

'Ari was the same with paintings and artists; he had so much knowledge stored way but his short-term memory was shocking.'

They faced each other screen-to-screen, Enrico's expression sober and Belle swamped by sorrow.

'One day we will only think of them the way they really were,' Enrico said. 'Your artistic husband, my elegant wife.'

'I hope so.'

'In the meantime, we have a dilemma to solve. Where in the world to go for your adventure?'

'Probably nowhere,' Belle said, wistfully. 'Not right now.'

'But you are daring,' argued Enrico.

'Not daring enough.'

Belle wasted a lot of time researching exotic journeys when the reality was that she would never visit giant tortoises in the Galapagos or ride over the Mongolian steppe. She stayed in the life that she had made with Ari, even though it felt strange and sad, because she couldn't imagine any other life was possible. She kept reminding herself that she had plenty to be grateful for – enough money, a lovely place to live, people who cared about her. The self-help books instructed her to focus on what she did have, rather than what was missing, so that was what Belle tried to do.

*

The package arrived by courier one morning. When she saw the postmark and the Italian stamps, Belle knew it must have come from Enrico. Impatiently cutting it open, she found the napkins, eight of them, made from the finest linen and embroidered with a crest. Belle held one to her face; it even smelled expensive. Then she opened a card, printed with the same design, and read Enrico's careful calligraphy.

Dear Belle, I wanted to send you a gift, something from our collection, as a thank you. It was difficult to know what you might like, but everyone needs napkins don't they? Probably you are asking yourself what exactly I am thanking you for? Just your company, which has been more important than I can say. Just our unexpected friendship. You have brightened days that would otherwise have seemed very dark. I hope I have managed to do the same for you.

Napkins seem like a promise of enjoyment to come, of having friends round your dinner table, talking, laughing and eating. I know you have been in and out of lockdowns in New Zealand, but hopefully this will be possible now. I also hope we will be able to sit together at a table some day and share the same meal in the same time zone; wouldn't that be nice? For now, I give you this small gift and my great thanks.
With very best wishes – Enrico

P.S. Come to Italy Belle, come for sunshine, and pasta, and red wine and long walks, come for as long as you like.

That final line looked to have been scrawled more hastily, an afterthought before putting the card in the package, and she wondered if Enrico had really meant it? Belle had never been to Italy. She had come close, visiting Spain, France and Greece when she was young and travelling around Europe. She had intended to get to Italy but then run out of time and money.

Holding the napkins in one hand and the card in the other, she was filled with a feeling she couldn't immediately identify, but then realised was excitement. This might be the escape she needed? An opportunity to travel somewhere entirely new but still a place where she had a friend if she needed one.

Belle read Enrico's words again. Sunshine and pasta, red wine and long walks. It sounded perfect and not entirely impossible.

Winter was coming and the gallery was always quieter in the colder months so it wouldn't be a huge deal to close it again. Greg would look after Tama. Her parents had each other and never really needed Belle at all. No one needed her now; she was free to go if she wanted.

The more she thought about it, the more attractive the idea seemed. Belle frittered away an afternoon looking at flight options and reading more about Enrico's hilltop town, Ostuni, the white city, full of history and charm.

The next time they Zoomed, she had the napkins ready.

'Look what arrived,' she said, holding them up so Enrico could see them. 'A surprise gift.'

'Finally, you have received them. I couriered that parcel weeks ago.'

'Deliveries are taking such a long time.'

'I thought perhaps they had arrived and you didn't like them but were too polite to say.'

Belle smiled. Starched linen napkins weren't really her thing, but she wasn't going to tell him that. 'It was such a treat to get them, so thoughtful of you, thank you.'

'You are very welcome.'

'Enrico,' she said, more hesitantly. 'Your invitation?'

'I'm sorry, what?' He sounded puzzled and Belle thought that either he can't have heard her properly or he had forgotten his quickly scrawled offer.

'*P.S. Come to Italy*, you wrote,' Belle reminded him. 'In the card you sent with the napkins.'

A smile flashed across his face. 'Yes, I did. Are you considering it?'

'I have been giving it some thought.'

'That is great news. I would love you to be our guest here. We have a very spacious house and you could use it as your base or stay the whole time, whatever you preferred.'

'I thought it would be a chance to have a complete break, get some perspective.'

'Yes, yes,' he agreed. 'When do you think that you might like to come?'

Belle imagined Italy: hearing foreign languages, trying new foods, seeing different places. She imagined herself there but as a slightly different person, happier, tanned, glowing even.

'As soon as possible,' she told Enrico.

But when she discussed the idea with other people, they were mostly negative. Her stepfather thought it was a terrible idea and her mother agreed. Why would she leave the country right now? And who was this man and how did she know him? That was a predictable response and normally Belle wouldn't have taken much notice. She had never lived her life to please her parents. Then several friends weighed in, advising her to sit tight and stay safe. This wasn't the time to travel, seemed to be the consensus.

Only Greg didn't think Italy was the stupidest idea Belle ever had in life. He listened while she listed everyone's reservations, then shrugged them off.

'I don't know what you're worried about; the worst thing has already happened hasn't it?' he said, as they sat drinking a cocktail he had mixed out of random bottles pulled from Ari's drinks cabinet.

'True,' she agreed. 'It has.'

'We're all going to have to engage with the world eventually and find a way to live with this thing.'

'Also true,' said Belle.

'If you want to go to Italy, then you should go.'

'You'd look after Tama?'

'Yep.'

'And you promise that you won't try getting on that young horse unless somebody else is around.'

'I'll make sure there is at least one person to pick up my shattered body from the ground,' agreed Greg.

'Don't joke, it isn't funny.'

Belle felt a spike of anxiety at the thought of leaving him. They had supported each other through the loss of Ari, their friendship was tighter now, and it struck her that Greg might be the one person who did need her.

'You don't mind me going?' asked Belle. 'I'm not leaving you in the lurch.'

He smiled. 'I'll manage without you for a bit.'

'Shall I think about booking a flight then?'

'Why waste time thinking? Let's book it right away.'

'Now?' Belle was hovering between drunk and sober, and perhaps that was why being impulsive seemed like such a good idea.

'Yes now,' said Greg. 'Go and find your laptop and your credit card. You're going to Italy.'

When she woke the next morning with an aching head and a dry mouth, Belle had a suspicion that she might have done something rash. Then her mind cleared and it came back to her.

'Oh shit.'

She checked her laptop and there it was, flights from Auckland to Rome, in only three weeks' time.

'Shit, shit, shit,' muttered Belle, searching for the terms and conditions to see if she could cancel. Then she paused to think about it. Why not go? What was there to stop her?

She spent the whole day swinging between dread and anticipation. One moment Belle was desperate to leave, the next as keen on staying. She wondered what Ari would have said she should do. But there was no message from beyond, no voice in her head, no eerie signs, not even a rainbow. Belle was on her own.

Before drifting off to sleep that night she was convinced she would cancel, but then she woke at daybreak with a different feeling altogether. Muriwai was her home. It was where Belle had spent the happiest days of her life and she hoped to be happy here again. But she needed a break from it, to be somewhere where she didn't keep hoping to see Ari striding through the door in dusty jodhpurs or with his hair full of saltwater and sand.

Italy was her chance to escape. That was what Belle told herself before sending a message to Enrico.

I'm coming to Italy! I'm coming for sunshine, and pasta, and red wine and long walks.

Belle said goodbye to Ari on the beach. She and Greg went down one evening to watch the sunset. Listening to the waves crashing on the shore, they talked about how much they missed him, swapping memories, laughing and crying, as the moon lit the black sand and the darkness beyond it deepened.

'Italy,' said Greg. 'What are your plans when you get there?'

'I'm not sure yet. I may do some travelling around but Enrico seems keen for me to spend a few weeks in Ostuni first.'

'Oh, yes?' Greg's face was pale in the moonlight but Belle could see he was smiling.

'Not a romance,' she said, sternly. 'Just friends, remember.'

'That might change.'

'I don't think so.'

'All I'm saying is that you shouldn't close yourself off to the idea.'

'It's the furthest thing from my mind,' she told him, a little impatiently. 'Friendship is enough, I don't need love anymore, Ari was it for me.'

'You think that now ...'

'I'm not going to change,' Belle promised.

6

Now

Rising up from a plateau carpeted with olive trees, the dazzling white mountaintop town of Ostuni begged to be explored. After so long in her own little bubble, everything felt new and interesting to Belle. Even Rome airport, with Italian voices all around, and the dark-roasted smell of espresso drifting through, was foreign and interesting. On the long road trip down to Puglia, when she wasn't dozing, there had been tantalising glimpses of ancient stone buildings and villages clinging to steep hillsides. As they drew further south, leaving the mountains behind, the roads were fringed with oleander.

Enrico had sent his car and driver to collect her. This was the first clue that he inhabited a very different world, the sleek Alfa Romeo and the dark-haired, dark-clothed man behind its wheel, who was very discreet on the subject of the family he worked for. Belle felt more nervous now, about the prospect of meeting them.

Then there was the *palazzo*, far grander than any house surrounding it, with views that stretched across the plains towards the sea. And the three generations gathered round the lunch table in the garden, all somehow glossier than her, neatly pressed and looking cooler in the heat.

Glancing from face to face, Belle was forming first impressions. The old Signora seemed like the kind of woman who always wore lipstick, even in her own home. The older son

Gianni looked solemn while the younger one, Pietro was quicker to smile. Their wives Katarina and Perla were both beautiful in different ways. And then there was Enrico. All those hours spent chatting over Zoom hadn't prepared her for this quietly well-mannered man, successful in business, the head of his family. Suddenly her friend felt almost a stranger.

'How long are you planning to spend in Italy?' serious-faced Gianni asked, as dessert was placed in front of them.

'I thought I'd stay for the summer,' she replied, 'although I haven't made any firm plans.'

'Belle is a free spirit,' Enrico told his son, and Belle was surprised by the image of her he had formed during their Zoom calls, and left wondering whether in real life she could match up to it.

She tasted the delicate fried pastry shell filled with roasted almonds, spices and honey, and served with a spoonful of rich vanilla-laced gelato; and couldn't suppress a tiny sigh of pleasure.

Sitting beside her, Perla smiled. 'I love sweet things too,' she said. 'These are called *cartellate*. In Puglia we eat them at Christmas time, but also on special occasions like today, welcoming a new friend.'

Perla seemed as warm as she was lovely, and already Belle felt charmed by her.

'This gelato is so creamy,' she said, appreciatively.

'It is a secret recipe,' Enrico told her. 'Passed down through my family for generations.'

Since Ari's death, most meals for Belle were something on toast, eaten while she was watching television or reading. She took another bite of the pastry. Its crispness and creaminess, its richness and spiciness, now almost overwhelming.

'We have a very fine cook,' said the old Signora. 'She has been with us for many years and we eat well.'

So, there was a cook in the kitchen, and a woman who

waited on the table, plus a driver and presumably a gardener to care for these landscaped grounds; Belle wondered how many members of staff the household employed and what Enrico would make of her little home, often cobwebbed and dusty, usually with dirty dishes in the sink, always a little messy. She thought back over those Zoom calls, searching for clues that might have given his status away. But Enrico had always been low-key. He never flaunted his wealth, made no mention of what he had at all. His business might have been successful or it might have been struggling; it wasn't what they talked about. Belle understood that he worked hard, and noticed that often he was tired particularly late at night, and in the mornings he could seem distracted. She had been aware he was close to his family. But she had never guessed at all of this. All she had seen was a rectangle of his world, framed by her laptop screen, that gave no idea of its scale.

Now she looked around the table at the family she would be getting to know better in the coming weeks. They wore their wealth carelessly, like it was something they took for granted.

Pietro had finished eating and was leaning into Perla, playing with a strand of her long hair. His fine linen shirt was unbuttoned, revealing an expanse of smooth tanned chest, and turned up loosely at the sleeves; his trousers were crumpled and rolled up at the ankle.

Gianni was more neatly pressed and on his finger he wore a wedding band with a discreet glitter of diamonds, but other than that no jewellery at all. He was staring at his wife and frowning, as she pushed the food around her plate, tense and pale, hardly touching a bite.

He said something to her in Italian and Katarina shook her head then dropped her spoon and went rushing from the table.

'She is having a difficult pregnancy,' Perla confided. 'Poor Katarina, she is very often sick.'

'Oh dear, how awful.' Belle sympathised.

'It is not awful at all,' countered Gianni. 'She is expecting Papa's first grandson, an heir for the family. We are very happy.'

'Katarina doesn't seem happy right now,' Perla pointed out.

'My wife and I are planning a large family,' added Gianni, as if he hadn't heard. 'At least four children, that is our goal.'

Belle hoped they also planned to add a nanny to their staff. She felt for Katarina, having to sit through this long lunch when she was nauseous and wondered if the thought of all those future pregnancies might be weighing heavily on her.

'Is it true you have no children?' the old Signora questioned Belle, her currant-bun eyes piercing.

'My husband and I met later in life,' she replied. 'So, we didn't have the chance.'

That was true enough, but it wasn't the whole truth. Belle had thought about the possibility of having children when she was in her mid-thirties and people kept warning her she was running out of time. There had been pressure from her mother in particular, and Belle pushed back against that. Plenty of people were childless and happy, she told her. Having a family wasn't obligatory. Still occasionally, when she held a friend's newborn baby Belle was swamped by a wave of wanting this for herself. It was just hormones, she would reason later. Her life wasn't suited to being a parent. Not with the hours she worked and the travel it involved. Not with the way men came and went from it.

If she had met Ari earlier then things might have been different. Surely they would have had a child together and often she imagined what that child would have been like. Ari's darker skin, his athleticism, her fair hair, his artistic talent. But Belle had to wait another ten years before they met and what she thought of as her real life began. By then it was too late. As it became clear there weren't going to be

73

any miracles, she had let go of the idea of being a mother, let it slip away. She and Ari had each other and that seemed enough.

'How sad that you lost him.' Perla covered Belle's hand with her own and squeezed gently. 'Enrico told us how it happened. Such a tragedy.'

'Yes,' said Belle, not wanting to talk about it.

As the dessert plates were cleared and coffee served alongside a platter of fresh fruit, she was grateful that this long lunch seemed to be nearly over. She needed a shower and then to flop onto cool sheets for a few quiet moments of not being on her best behaviour.

'You are tired from your journey,' observed Enrico. 'Do you need to rest?'

'Yes, I'd love to,' she said, with relief, longing to lie down.

Gianni frowned. 'You mustn't rest yet. What you need is to adjust your body clock to Italian time as quickly as possible. That is the correct thing to do.'

'You're probably right,' conceded Belle, reluctantly. 'It would be better not to sleep now.'

'You ought to take a walk instead,' advised Gianni. 'Keep moving, that is the best idea if you want to stay awake.'

Belle knew it made sense. Exercise would be a wiser option than a nap right now. Even though she longed to close her eyes, she would go for a long, slow stroll and try to find some of the intriguingly narrow lanes she had noticed while being driven through the whitewashed town.

'OK, a walk then,' she agreed.

'I have a commitment this afternoon so won't be able to join you,' said Enrico, regretfully. 'Unfortunately, I was unable to reschedule it.'

'We can come,' Perla put in. 'Me and Pietro; we will show you round. Then there is no chance of you getting lost.'

Belle might not have minded being lost for a while; still it would be rude to refuse their company.

'We will take you through the old town and up to the cathedral.' Perla sounded enthusiastic. 'It is the walk that everyone must do when they visit Ostuni.'

'They will be excellent guides,' Enrico promised. 'And tomorrow I have a free day so I was thinking that we might go out on my yacht.'

There was a yacht, naturally there was. And a holiday house too, she remembered, maybe even more than one.

'The coastline is spectacular,' he was telling her. 'We will take a picnic, spend the day on the water, visit my favourite place, how does that sound?'

Belle was less than enthusiastic. Sailing had never been her thing and she had avoided being near the sea since losing Ari to it. But Enrico didn't know that as she hadn't told him – or in fact anyone at all really – how she felt. This was something special he had planned. Her good manners won out.

'That sounds lovely,' she said, trying to sound like she meant it.

Up in her room, Belle made the most of a few moments alone. She stood at the window looking over the jumble of whitewashed houses, the mass of olive trees in the valley below and the shining band of blue beyond, and tried to gather her thoughts.

The town was beautiful as she had known it would be, Enrico as friendly and kind. At some point Belle would find an excuse to head away and go travelling on her own. In the meantime, she was going to make the most of this.

Her room was grand, dominated by a large bed with a lacquered wooden headboard and made up with fine white linen and plump pillows. The walls were covered with satiny paper embossed with the family's crest and from the ceiling hung a vintage Murano glass chandelier. Nothing here was creased or dusty. Everything looked antique and gleamed.

There was a smell that Belle couldn't identify but eventually decided must be some sort of minty furniture polish.

Her ensuite was less magnificent. A small plastic shower cubicle had been crammed in beside the original fittings and the ancient toilet made a loud groaning noise when she flushed it, as if exhausted by its many years of service. At least Belle felt fresher, once she had showered and towelled herself dry.

Although she rarely bothered with make-up, now it felt as if she ought to make the effort. Belle smoothed on tinted moisturiser, flicked a little bronzer onto her cheeks, treated her lashes to a coat of mascara and glossed her lips. Then she sent a quick message to Greg.

> Arrived safely. This place is not exactly what I expected but all is fine. Hope horses are OK. Talk soon. xxxx B

There had been rainstorms before she left and the winds were chilling. As winter set in Greg would be busy trudging through mud and feeding out hay, and Belle felt guilty that she wasn't there to help. What had she been thinking, running away from her life? How had she thought it was going to help anything?

She changed her outfit twice. Everything looked worn-out or unsophisticated when she glanced at her reflection in the gilded Rococo mirror. Her faded denim and vintage silks, her suede Birkenstocks, the scarf she liked to wear in her hair, none of it worked here.

In the end Belle settled for a turquoise tiered maxi dress with billowy sleeves and a pair of white trainers that were comfortable to walk in. She tied back her hair with her coral-coloured scarf, stacked silver bangles on her wrist, and decided she was ready.

Perla was waiting in the vestibule, hair in a sleek ponytail, but there was no sign of Pietro yet.

'He is always late, even on our wedding day.' Her tone was resigned. 'But he is so charming that nobody minds.'

They waited for at least fifteen minutes and Belle distracted herself by looking at a collection of framed family wedding photographs arranged on top of a carved walnut sideboard.

There was Perla with Pietro gazing into each other's eyes and beside them a portrait of a far younger version of the old Signora standing stiffly beside the handsome man she had married, then Katarina and Gianni as a photogenic bride and groom, and finally Enrico with Luciana on the day they exchanged their vows. Enrico's hair was much darker and his face a little fuller. The woman beside him was wearing her hair in an elaborate up-do and her wedding gown shimmered with crystals. The impression was of someone very glamorous.

'Luciana was elegant,' said Perla, following her gaze. 'Even in the nursing home, she was well-dressed with manicured nails and nice hair. It upset her not to look her best.'

Belle stared at the young bride, smiling on the happiest day of her life.

'Always she would demand to see her reflection in the mirror,' continued Perla, 'and if she wasn't happy with how she looked then she would scream.'

'She couldn't speak by then?'

'Hardly at all,' recalled Perla. 'And the screaming was terrible. We used to take some make-up when we visited so we could make her look pretty again, and then she would look at herself and be happy for a while.'

'Poor Luciana, what a terrible thing.'

'She wasn't well enough to come to our wedding. That made Pietro very sad. And now she is gone and she will miss out on her new grandchildren.'

With a secretive smile, Perla smoothed down the front of her smocked linen dress to show off the slightest roundness of her belly, then put a finger to her lips. 'Shhh, no one knows yet.'

'Congratulations,' Belle whispered. 'That's lovely news.'

'Yes,' she said, with a smile. 'And I am not sick like poor Katarina; I feel fine.'

'When will you tell everyone?' asked Belle, wondering why Perla had chosen to confide in her, a stranger, and at the same time feeling a little flattered.

'We are waiting for the right moment,' she said, vaguely.

Pietro appeared at last, his linen shirt untucked, friendship bracelets knotted round his wrist, glossy dark hair curling to his shoulders.

'What is everyone waiting for? *Andiamo, andiamo,*' he called, clapping his hands.

'*Disgraziato,*' responded Perla, fondly. 'Always he is like this. It drives me completely crazy.'

The pair walked briskly arm in arm, crossing a wide piazza and then plunging into a labyrinth of cobbled lanes flanked by crooked buildings, Belle already beginning to lag behind. Here in the old town a waiter was setting up tables outside an *osteria*, a well-dressed woman was standing in the doorway of a smart boutique smoking a cigarette; there were white houses with window ledges spilling over with geraniums and people drifting through the streets.

The whole place was dreamlike and Belle had a strange jet-lagged sense of disbelief. Was she really here, in this romantic old city? She wished Ari was there too and they could walk its streets together. He would like this place. It might even make him want to reach for his sketchbook again. What would he think and say about everything? Belle kept wondering.

The lane looped upwards past shops selling bright ceramics, wine and olive oil, towards a couple of churches with colour-ful majolica-tiled domes at the town's highest point. Stopping every few steps to gaze at something that had caught her eye, she reached the cathedral a short while after the others, and found them standing in a doorway, arms wrapped round each other, both gazing at their phones.

'OK?' asked Perla, looking up. 'Not too tired?'

'No, I'm fine,' Belle told her. 'There's so much to see here. It's lovely.'

Perla gave a dismissive shrug. 'Ostuni is very small and not so exciting.'

Belle would have liked to take a look inside the cathedral but neither of them seemed particularly keen so she decided to come back another time. Instead, she followed as they wended their way back through the old town, reaching a towering plinth crowned with the statue of a saint then turning down a short flight of steps that swept into an annexe of the main piazza.

There they stopped at a bar where Perla claimed a table with a view of the statue above them. 'We are meeting some friends here,' she announcd. 'I think you will like them. Don't worry, everyone has some English.'

Belle had been concerned that language would be a barrier but so far everyone she had encountered spoke English surprisingly well.

'Some of the older ones won't understand you,' Pietro warned her now. 'A few mostly speak Salentino, the local dialect. But the younger people are better educated.'

'I ought to make an effort to learn some Italian while I'm here,' said Belle. 'Perhaps there is a language school I could go to.'

'You are here to have fun though, surely, not study?' asked Perla.

What was she here for? Belle still wasn't entirely certain. 'Learning could be fun, don't you think?' she asked.

'Maybe,' Perla agreed, her expression dubious.

As their friends began to appear and gathered round the table, Belle saw that like Pietro and Perla all of them were attractive and wore expensive clothes casually. They ordered icy ruby-red cocktails and lots of snack food: discs of double-baked bread seasoned with salty tomatoes and drizzled with grassy olive oil, little puffs of pastry filled with melting moz-zarella and creamy béchamel, a dish of crispy fava beans dusted with Parmesan and a platter of fried artichokes.

'Perla says that you met Enrico online.' The young woman seated next to her was wearing a skimpy handkerchief top and tight cropped pants, and had introduced herself as Mia. 'Is that true?'

'It is,' confirmed Belle. 'Both of us had partners with dementia. We met in a Facebook group and became good friends.'

'That is very sad, but also nice that you have made this friendship,' said Mia. 'And now you are living at Palazzo Ginaro?'

'Just for a while over the summer.'

Mia smiled, tossing back her long black hair with perfectly manicured fingers, heavy gold hoops gleaming in her ears. 'It is magnificent, yes? My parents are friends of the family, so I have spent lots of time there with Pietro and Gianni. We grew up together. I have known them all my life.'

'You must be very close then,' said Belle, thinking how glamorous this young woman was and how confident she seemed. She remembered herself at that age as being awk-ward and dreamy, rather than self-possessed. A girl who lived in jeans and a puffer jacket, and if she was attractive, didn't know it.

'Close, yes.' Mia gave another toss of her head and her glossy curls flowed over her shoulders.

'Did Perla grow up with you too?' Belle wondered.

'No, she is from Rome; that is where they met. All of us were every surprised when Pietro said they were to be married.'

Belle glanced at the newlyweds. Pietro had an arm resting over Perla's shoulders, and every few minutes one of them would kiss the other. They seemed very much at the centre of the group and when they spoke, the others listened.

'Poor Pietro, his life is very difficult,' said Mia.

'It is?' Belle looked at the young man leaning back in his chair, encircled by friends and laughing like he hadn't a worry.

'He is the second son,' said Mia, as if that explained everything, and seeing Belle's blank look, continued. 'Gianni will inherit the *palazzo* and the business. His life is assured while Pietro must make his own way.'

'That seems extraordinary in this day and age,' said Belle, wondering what sort of world she had walked into.

'It is the system here, eldest son to eldest son, still the same tradition.'

'So, Pietro will be left with nothing at all?' Belle found that difficult to believe.

'Maybe some money, I don't know the exact arrangement. But Gianni will get the important things, and that is hard for Pietro.' Mia lowered her voice. 'When Enrico retires, then it will be interesting I think. There may be trouble then.'

Belle was taken aback. 'Enrico is only in his fifties, he might not retire for decades.'

Mia gave a quick, one-shouldered shrug, before turning and speaking in Italian to a friend, while Belle thought over what she had heard. She hadn't known any of this about Enrico and she wondered how much more there was she didn't know. This was a foreign country, after all, and people were bound to have different customs. Belle had rushed to be the guest of someone who was really a stranger.

As she half-listened to chatter that she couldn't understand, she sipped the last of her drink. Downing cocktails in the late afternoon wasn't her usual style, but Belle's body had no idea what time it was at this point, and the alcohol had given her a lift, so she decided to have another.

A second spritz didn't make her feel twice as good. Instead, she started yawning. She found herself thinking how nice it would be to find somewhere peaceful and lie down. The piazza was busy and for Belle, who had grown unused to crowds, there seemed to be too many people sitting close and talking loudly.

'I'm going to head off,' she said to no one in particular. 'I feel completely exhausted.'

'You do look tired.' Only Mia appeared to have heard. She stared into Belle's face and frowned. 'Actually you look terrible. Do you need a ride?'

'Would you mind? I think the jet lag has caught up with me and this probably hasn't helped.' Belle held up her glass.

'No problem. My car is close by, in the main piazza.'

Perla gave Belle a wave as she left. Pietro only smiled then looked away. So much for them being excellent guides. Still, they were young and it made sense that they were more interested in hanging out with their friends than a middle-aged stranger. Belle wasn't going to hold it against them.

Mia drove a dented silver Smart car, which she had left at a rakish angle next to a no-parking sign. Belle was grateful that she didn't have to walk. Keeping her eyes open was a struggle, despite the young woman's constant stream of chatter as she drove the short distance.

'Here we are, Palazzo Ginaro,' said Mia, pulling up outside.

'Thanks so much.'

'Your home for the summer.' Mia gazed up at the elegant building as if it was a prize that Belle had won, adding almost enviously. 'Aren't you fortunate to have met Enrico.'

Even through the fogginess of her jet lag, Belle realised people were going to assume that she had latched on to Enrico for his wealthy lifestyle and this fancy house. Like Mia, everyone must admire it. But standing on the doorstep and ringing the bell, because she hadn't thought to ask for a key, she was sure that she would never feel properly at home here.

Belle had a yearning for her own little house, for Ari and

everything familiar, such a strong yearning that she wanted to turn and run. Instead, she smiled at the maid who opened the door and said a polite, '*Buona sera.*'

7

Southern Italian Royalty

Falling asleep at dinnertime meant that Belle came to in the middle of the night, wide awake and ravenous. She couldn't go poking round in someone else's kitchen searching out snacks and the only food in her bag was a chocolate biscuit that she had saved from the flight.

Sitting at her window, she opened the shutters and munched on it while looking down over the darkened town and up at the star-studded sky. Then she checked her phone and was pleased to find a message that Greg had sent earlier.

The place is not what you expected? Don't be cryptic. Tell me everything!

By now most likely he would be busy schooling someone's dressage horse or coaching kids on their ponies. On the off-chance she might find him free, Belle tried to FaceTime and was surprised when he answered.

It was good to see his familiar face on her screen, his startlingly blue eyes, strong jawline and the slightly crooked nose, broken after a horse had bucked him off.

'Why aren't you sleeping?' he asked.

'Jet lag,' she told him. 'I've never been more awake in my life.'

'What's the place like then? Show me.'

Belle held up her phone and gave him a quick tour, hearing a low whistle of appreciation as she panned across the room.

'That mirror is insane. And is the bed as big as it looks?'

'Massive,' she confirmed. 'The whole place is completely over the top. Palatial. You have no idea.'

'Who are these people?' asked Greg.

'Quite possibly southern Italian royalty.' Belle kept her voice low in case anyone else was awake and listening through an open window.

'Are they nice? Do you like them?' he wanted to know.

'Hmm, not completely sure yet.'

'Enrico?'

'I thought I knew him, but I don't at all. It's weird.'

'He's not sinister though?' Greg sounded worried.

'Oh no,' Belle was quick to reassure him. 'Completely charming, just not exactly who I thought he was.'

'You've been there less than twenty-four hours though, right?'

'That's true.'

'And you're jet-lagged and not feeling yourself?'

'I got a bit pissed this afternoon,' Belle admitted. 'Went out for cocktails with one of the sons and his wife.'

'I want to drink cocktails in the afternoon,' sighed Greg, plaintively. 'Why aren't I there?'

'If only you were,' she said. 'Enrico's got a yacht. And staff. Also, I think his mother disapproves of me.'

'Give it some time,' Greg advised. 'You're bound to feel out of place at first.'

'Yeah, I know.'

'Poor Belle, stuck in a *palazzo* with nothing to do except daytime drinking,' he teased.

'Think of me whenever you are ankle deep in mud and lugging bales of hay, this winter.'

'I will,' he promised. 'You'll be in my thoughts and prayers, don't worry.'

Eventually Belle managed to get back to sleep and had vivid dreams that she couldn't remember properly when she woke the next morning. She lay in bed for a while, staring up at the fine cracks in the plaster ceiling. This was her first proper day in Puglia, if you didn't count the plane-weary afternoon of her arrival and Belle decided not to.

It had steadied her, that talk with Greg in the depths of the night. Looking round at the grandeur of her room, she recognised that he was right; things could have been a lot worse.

It wasn't quite what she had expected but she should let go of any expectations and treat it like the chance for adventure it was. Ari had wanted her to be free and Belle owed it to him to make the most of that freedom.

Springing out of bed, she went to take a shower.

The house was nearly silent by the time she was ready to venture downstairs, the only sound the loud ticking of a clock. Reaching the marble vestibule, Belle caught a faint whiff of coffee and, following its scent, managed to find the kitchen.

Katarina was there, at one end of a long table, staring at a packet of dry toast crackers, a cat sitting beneath her chair.

'Good morning,' Belle greeted her. 'How are you today?'

'Not so good,' said Katarina. 'My husband says I must eat but I feel too nauseous even for these *fette biscottate*.'

'Oh dear.' Belle felt awkward about her own keen appetite. 'Isn't ginger supposed to help.'

'Nothing helps,' said Katarina, who was very slender aside from her rounded belly, and whose dark hair hung long and straight almost to her waist. 'Sometimes I can eat, but I have to wait for the right moment.'

The kitchen was large, its walls covered in blue and white porcelain tiles, a bank of shining copper pans hanging from the ceiling, and the long table at its centre. Aside from a modern cooking range and stainless-steel fridge, everything looked old and well-used.

'Would you mind if I made some coffee?' asked Belle.

'Let me.' Katarina got to her feet and shooed away the cat. 'You must eat, also. We have bread, *marmellata*, fruit, yoghurt and some *pasticciotto*. What can I offer you?'

'I'm fine to help myself,' Belle told her. 'If you could just show me where it's all kept.'

Everything was hidden away in small cupboards, bread in one, coffee in another, sugar somewhere else. Belle discovered where the Moka pots were kept and was offered a paper-wrapped tray of little pastries.

'The cook comes to prepare lunch and dinner. At breakfast we are free to eat whatever we want,' explained Katarina.

'Where is everyone this morning?' asked Belle, busy piling ground coffee into the basket of a small Moka pot.

'Enrico and Gianni went to work early as usual. Nonna left for an appointment to have her hair set. And Pietro and Perla came home late last night so I expect they are still sleeping.'

Belle took one of the pastries, some fruit and a small pot of yoghurt. 'Are you sure there's nothing I can get you?'

Katarina shook her head. She was standing by an open window, where she could breathe fresh air. 'You are the guest; we are supposed to be looking after you.'

'Yes, but you're feeling sick so that cancels out me being a guest.'

Belle was rewarded with a fleeting smile then the young woman looked stern again. 'Perla and Pietro have no excuse for leaving you to find your own way back to the *palazzo* last night. That was unforgiveable.'

'It's OK, I got a ride from a friend of theirs, Mia.'

'Mia, of course, she would be there. She is a part of Pietro's club and wherever he goes she follows.'

Belle's sweet pastry tart was filled with a rich, creamy custard. She was so hungry that she had to consciously chew slowly and take sips of coffee between each mouthful.

'Did you say that Enrico has gone to work?' she asked, wondering if this meant that their sailing trip was cancelled, hoping so.

'Only for a short time, to do one or two things that probably he should have left to Gianni but ...' With a shrug, Katarina came and sat at the table, took a cracker from the packet and broke off a corner, asking curiously, 'Enrico told us that he met you on a Facebook page, a support group?'

'Yes, a while ago now.'

'Did he spend a lot of time in this group?'

'Actually, I have no idea, I never asked that question.' Belle peeled the top from the yoghurt and dipped in her spoon.

'It seems strange that he would do this, without telling any of us.' Katarina gazed at the shard of dry toast in her hand but didn't take a bite.

'It's a very supportive group full of people in the same position, it's helpful,' Belle explained.

'But Enrico has his sons, his family, so why talk to strangers?' Katarina crumbled the rest of the toast onto her plate. 'And if you were spending all this time together, why did he never mention you? Not even to any of us ... not until suddenly you were coming to Italy.'

Belle hadn't spoken much about Enrico either. What they had together happened in the early hours of the morning or late at night and it seemed separate from their everyday lives. Now she sensed how that might seem to other people.

'We're friends, that's all.' Belle put down the yoghurt. 'Everyone does realise that, I hope?'

'Friends, yes, this is what Enrico has said. But he has many friends, right here in Italy, so why does he want a new one from the other side of the world, this is what his sons are wondering.'

Belle realised she had been naïve, that she ought to have forseen that his family might imagine more than a friendship between her and Enrico; hadn't Greg assumed the same?

Katarina removed another toast from the packet, took a tentative bite, crunched on it and closed her eyes, forcing herself to swallow. 'I am only telling you what they are saying,' she murmured. 'Better that you know, I think.'

Belle hated the idea of them discussing her and making wrong assumptions. Surely, they didn't really believe Enrico would bring her to stay here in his home if they were having some sort of affair?

'We were going through the same things, that's what brought us together,' she said, defensively. 'Having a partner with dementia, being widowed, grieving, trying to cope ... we supported one another.'

Katarina stared down at her crumb-covered plate. 'I have upset you; I am sorry,' she said, in a small voice.

'I'm not upset,' said Belle, although actually she sort of was. 'I just want to make sure there is no confusion. Enrico invited me here because he knew I needed to get away, and because he's a kind person and a friend, it's as simple as that.'

'Friends, yes, I understand,' said Katarina, in a way that suggested she was placating Belle. Then taking another cracker, she picked up a knife and took a deep breath. '*Va bene*. This one I will try with a little *marmellata*.'

Belle was alone in the kitchen, washing up her few breakfast dishes, when Enrico arrived home.

'Leave those, you don't have to clean,' he said, finding her at the sink. 'The maid will take care of them.'

Smooth-shaven and in a pale linen suit, he seemed a more highly polished version of the man Belle had thought she knew and taller than he appeared on a screen. It was strange having to look up when she spoke to him.

'I'm not used to having staff,' said Belle, putting down the dishcloth then not quite knowing what to do with her hands.

She wondered if Enrico had any idea what his sons were thinking about her presence here and what he might say if he did. Not that she was going to be the one to tell him; that would be much too awkward. Over Zoom their friendship had developed into an easy one, but standing beside him now it seemed newer again.

'Did you sleep well?' Enrico wanted to know.

'Not brilliantly,' she admitted. 'I think it's going to take a few days for me to adjust.'

'I expect it must feel surreal being here.'

'It does.' Belle was glad he understood. 'And this house, it's ... quite something. You never told me you lived in a *palazzo*.'

'Didn't I?' Enrico looked round at the rows of gleaming copper pans, the long kitchen table and the wall covered in boldly patterned tiles, as if seeing it all for the first time. 'When you have lived somewhere your whole life, when you were born here, then you take it for granted. For me this seems normal but I suppose it isn't really?'

Belle laughed. 'Not normal at all.'

'I could show you round,' he offered. 'Unless Katarina already has?'

'Not yet,' said Belle, just as pleased for a chance to delay the sailing trip as she was to take a proper look at the place. 'I'd love to see it.'

'In that case we will go on a tour.'

Enrico led as she followed, and Belle discovered the scope of the *palazzo* was even greater than she had imagined. A salon with a frescoed ceiling and a cavernous fireplace ran almost the full depth of the building. It was over-filled with elaborate Rococo furniture, none of which looked particularly comfortable and the walls were decorated with dark oil paintings in gilded frames.

Walking her through the *palazzo*'s many rooms, Enrico spoke about the rhythms of its day, explaining that he and his sons were in the habit of leaving early every morning so they could be home in time to eat dinner at the hour that his mother preferred. Saturday was when they entertained friends and might dine a little later, which would certainly be the case this weekend as Pietro was celebrating his twenty-first birthday. And every Sunday they gathered for a long lunch in the garden or the orangery, depending on the weather.

'Mostly we lead a quiet life. I hope you won't find us too boring,' he said.

'My life is quiet too,' she told him. 'At least these days it is and I've got used to it.'

Enrico took her through a music room and on to an annexe teeming with sculptures, where she saw more frescoes and portraits. She couldn't imagine living with so many memories of previous generations. Would it be comforting, Belle wasn't certain.

She tilted her head to marvel at an elaborate ceiling fresco and glancing back, saw that Enrico was smiling at her expression.

'I imagine this isn't much like the place in Auckland where you grew up?'

'It couldn't be more different.' Belle smiled back at him. 'My family's house is modern and very minimalist. Smaller too, of course.'

'And are you a minimalist?' he wondered.

'No, I reacted against that. I quite like a bit of clutter.'

Belle didn't explain why her childhood home was so austere or that it hadn't always been that way. It was a story she had taken a long time to tell, even to Ari, and it began on the dark wintry evening when an oncoming van full of drunken teenagers crossed the centre line and crashed head-on into the car her father was driving home. For a week after they lost him Belle's mother had cried until her eyes were raw. Then she stopped crying and went into a frenzy of throwing out or giving away their belongings. Not only his clothes but her own, along with books and artworks, furniture and kitchen crockery, lots of Belle's things, keeping only the barest of essentials. Belle was six and they lived in that stark empty house for six years until Rod came along and his possessions soon followed.

'Some people would call me messy,' she admitted to Enrico now. 'My mother certainly does.'

'She hasn't seen my son Pietro's rooms,' he replied. 'Really, I am not joking. He and Perla are outrageous.'

After the tragedy that reshaped their lives, Belle's mother couldn't bear anything to be out of place. She tidied and cleaned constantly. If you put down a magazine you were reading then it would be whisked into a neat pile; if you sat on a bed then the cover was smoothed after you stood. Only perfection made her mother happy and nothing was ever perfect. Once she left home, it took Belle a while to train herself out of living that way.

'A little mess and clutter makes things seem homely,' she told Enrico.

They moved on through the staff quarters, and a cellar for hanging prosciutto, storing preserves and olive oil, and a snug for watching television. At the very back of the *palazzo* was a vaulted space with whitewashed stone walls and windows looking out onto the garden. There, amid the rattan furniture, were large urns planted with orange trees.

Almost everywhere they went Belle spotted cats: peering out from the leaves of a pot plant, prowling across the decorative marble floor, curled up on a baroque chair.

'Those cats are not supposed to be inside,' said Enrico dismissively when she wondered about them. 'Apparently they aren't aware of that, so here they are. They belong to my mother.'

How many cats exactly lived here? Belle would have

asked except now Enrico was leading her back towards the vestibule and listing what she might want to bring along on their sailing trip. A hat and a swimming costume, something to cover up against the sun.

'Everything else you will find on board,' he promised and Belle stopped thinking about cats as her mind was filled with that wide expanse of Adriatic Sea, out there waiting.

Fleetingly, as she packed a small bag with what she was planning to take, Belle considered faking a headache or telling Enrico she was too tired to go sailing. Even the sight of the sea made her stomach turn over. Those waves had taken Ari away then thrown him carelessly back onto the shore. She thought of them as her enemy.

But Enrico saw her as daring rather than fearful. So she packed her bikini and a sarong, some sunscreen and a hat.

When she came back downstairs, he was already there waiting, looking less formal in a long-sleeved T-shirt and loose shorts, his bare legs lightly tanned.

'Ready?' he asked.

'As ready as I'll ever be,' Belle replied.

They were driven to the marina at Villanova di Ostuni where his yacht was moored in the small harbour. It wasn't an especially large vessel, but even Belle could see it was something special. The hull was navy blue, the deck polished wood and the fittings shining brass.

'She is a classic, we had her restored,' Enrico explained. 'When we found her, she was almost a wreck but Luciana was determined to save her. It was our last project.'

'Did you sail together?'

Enrico nodded. 'We managed to get to a few regattas before things became too difficult. Since then, mostly I have sailed alone. Our sons don't share my passion.'

'I haven't done much sailing,' Belle warned him. 'I won't be a lot of help, I'm afraid.'

'That is fine, you are a guest, remember; mostly you can relax.' Enrico smiled at her.

Belle recognised that quick, boyish smile and the way he tilted his head as he talked. Focusing on his face, she found what was familiar from all those Zoom calls and it was reassuring.

He took her arm and helped her onto the yacht. On board, feeling the gentle shift of the deck, she faltered.

'Are you OK?' Enrico asked. He was still holding onto her, his touch lighter now, and his gaze met hers.

Belle told the truth. 'I haven't wanted to be near the sea since Ari died in it.'

His brow furrowed and he let his hand fall. 'I am so sorry, I didn't even think. You would prefer not to go?'

'I'm scared.' It was almost a relief for Belle to admit it. 'I've developed this ridiculous phobia.'

'Not ridiculous at all. Let me call back the driver, we can do something else.'

Belle stared out at the less settled waters beyond the harbour walls. She knew that Enrico was an experienced sailor and could see this was a calm, clear day. Probably it was safer out at sea than on the roads, given what she had seen so far of people's driving. And she hated being afraid of something so beautiful.

'We're here now,' she said. 'Could we just take a short sail?'

'The moment you wish it, we will come back to the harbour,' Enrico promised.

'OK,' she agreed, making up her mind. 'Let's do that then.'

They motored out of the marina, Enrico at the helm and Belle beside him on a bench covered with a striped canvas squab and cushions. Once clear of the harbour wall, he showed her how to hold the wheel and keep a steady course, while he hauled on ropes and hoisted sails. It felt good to have something to focus on as they headed into deeper water and the sea surrounded them.

Once the engine had cut, all she could hear was low waves gently slapping against the hull, the creak of old wood and the screech of seabirds overhead. At the wheel again, Enrico was quiet. He smiled when Belle caught his eye and checked if she was doing OK, but mostly he seemed lost in thought which left her space to think too.

This seemed a different kind of sea than the one that had stolen Ari. There were no white-topped breakers curling to a dark shore, but instead depths of indigo, rocky coves and cliffs topped by ruined towers. Belle glimpsed people sunning themselves on the rocks and stretches of sand studded by brightly coloured parasols. She felt a little of her tension ebb away. This wasn't so bad after all.

'Do your sons never come out here with you?' she asked, turning to Enrico.

He shrugged, regretfully. 'They have their own interests. My hope is that my love of the sea might skip a generation and my grandchildren will be sailors.'

'Then this yacht will be handed down through the generations, like the recipe for gelato?'

He laughed at that. 'Luciana always planned for it to be a family heirloom, but who knows.'

They anchored in a bay with a sweep of sand fringed by rocks. Enrico wanted to swim and Belle wasn't sure she would join him but went down to the cabin and changed into her bikini anyway.

She emerged onto the deck, a fringed pink sarong wrapped round her waist, in time to see Enrico diving gracefully from it. He hit the glassy surface of the sea, briefly disappearing and when he surfaced his wet hair was spiky and beads of water sparkled on his face. He looked up towards her questioningly.

'Do you think you might want to come in?'

Belle stood beside the ladder at the stern of the boat and reminded herself that she actually wasn't too bad a swimmer, the sea was calm and clear, and Enrico would be right there beside her.

Cautiously, she climbed down the ladder, feeling the chill of the water and holding on for a few breaths to get used to it, then launching off and starting to swim. Belle felt surprisingly buoyant, as though the sea was supporting her. Swimming alongside Enrico, gradually she found a rhythm.

At first they circled the yacht, staying close until Belle was confident enough to swim towards the rocky shoreline.

She wasn't fast and soon Enrico was a few strokes ahead of her. 'There is a sea cave here, a secret place where we always swim,' he called back.

'I don't see it,' said Belle, stopping to tread water and catch her breath.

He waited for her to catch up. 'We would have to dive under the water to find the entrance.'

'I don't think so,' she said, reflexively.

'Another time maybe. It is only a few seconds underwater and the grotto is magical.'

Belle tasted the saltiness of seawater as she stared up at the cliff face. She had come this far. Her instinct was to trust Enrico in the water, in the same way she had trusted Ari to take her cantering down a beach on horseback. She had been daring then, she remembered, and surely she could be again.

'Just a few seconds?' The thought of her mother flickered through Belle's head. She never wanted to be like her, living a clean safe life.

'Hold on to me and I will show you. We will be fine, I promise.'

She followed Enrico towards a crease in the rock wall. It took everything Belle had to place a hand in his, close her eyes and hold her breath. Together they plunged forwards and down, through a gap in the rocks and into a short tunnel. Panicking now, Belle kept her eyes clenched shut as Enrico continued to swim, pulling her strongly after him. When they rose to the surface, she gasped for a breath, opening her eyes to find herself in a large chamber beneath a ceiling of stalactites lit by shafts of sunlight.

'Amazing,' said Belle, once she could speak. 'Magical even.'

'There are sea caves all along the coast, but I like to think that my family discovered this one,' Enrico told her. 'We have been coming here since I was a child.'

They swam through the colder, darker water, then turned onto their backs and floated, staring up at the soaring arches of the grotto's ceiling.

'It's like being in a cathedral.' A thought occurred to Belle. 'Do you think there are bats?'

Enrico's deep laugh echoed from the limestone walls. 'Almost certainly there are bats,' he promised.

They left the cave the way they had arrived, Enrico holding her hand until they were out in daylight and swimming towards the yacht. Belle climbed up the ladder first and grabbed a fluffy white towel she had taken from a stack in the cabin.

'That was really great,' she said, winding the towel round her body, pleased to be back on board, but also full of what she had done and proud of herself. 'Just like you said it would be.'

'I want to show you all my favourite places,' said Enrico. 'I have been looking forward to it.'

He went below to fetch the picnic he had brought and laid it on a table beneath the shade cloth. Crusty bread and ripe cheese, thinly sliced cured meats, a salad of yellow tomatoes and sweet red onion, another of fennel and orange, and a bottle of chilled *Rosato*.

Belle's appetite seemed to have sharpened. Piling her plate, she settled back on the cushions.

'It is good to take an afternoon off and enjoy all of this.' Enrico topped up her glass with blush pink wine. 'I haven't been sailing for a while. Lately it has been difficult to find enough time.'

'You work very hard,' Belle observed.

'Too hard, Luciana always said.' Enrico looked back towards the shore. 'But I am responsible for our family's business.'

Belle had hardly done any work over the past couple of years. She wasn't quite sure how the time had flown past but suspected she had wasted it.

'Work isn't everything,' she said, lightly.

'Luciana told me that too. Unfortunately, I can't steal back the hours I spent at my desk, take the trips she always dreamed of, have more time with her, however much I might like to.'

'What about now?' Belle remembered that Mia had implied he might be retiring. 'Would you think about passing the business onto your sons?'

'I think about it all the time, but ...' Enrico glanced at Belle. 'My eldest son Gianni has big ideas. He wants to expand, open more shops, have a base in Milan, move into the UK, perhaps even America. I am not sure this is the right moment for any of that. More importantly, why must we keep getting bigger? Already we have so much.'

'He is young and ambitious,' said Belle, although she never had been, not even at Gianni's age. She had fallen into a job helping source props for a movie. A friend's mother had helped, probably because she felt sorry for Belle. She made a real effort to steer her in the direction of work that might suit her, recognising she was an arty, visual person and that achieving academically was never going to be her thing, however much Belle's mum might have liked that. Without her kindly interference who knows what she might have ended up doing. And working in film suited Belle. It paid enough to live on, took her to interesting places and she liked the camaraderie of a crew. Becoming more successful had never really occurred to her.

'Gianni wants to make his mark,' agreed Enrico.

'How old were you when you took over the business?' asked Belle.

'My father died when I was thirty but he had been unwell for some years, so by then I was already running things, for a long time with the guidance of Mamma.' Enrico told her. 'Now though, she has retired and hardly ever visits the office.'

'Did you always know this would be your job, right from when you were a boy?' That seemed extraordinary to Belle.

'I knew the business would be mine; that it was my destiny,' said Enrico. 'Just like it will be Gianni's one day.'

'Because it is passed down from eldest son to eldest son?'

'Which seems unfair, I know, but it means that everything is kept intact, rather than being broken up to be shared around. My younger sister worked with us for a while then started her own business making baby clothes. Pietro will find his way too. He has a wife now and she makes him happy, so his life is progressing I hope.'

As she ate the bittersweet salad of crisp fennel and juicy oranges, Belle recalled what Mia had said and thought she may have been right. There were problems ahead for the Ginaro family unless the youngest son had found a path in life before the father retired.

'My wife was convinced that Pietro is creative,' Enrico continued. 'She pushed him to write or paint or make music, but he never stuck with any of these things.'

'That's why you have the piano.' Belle had seen a shining baby grand in one of the reception rooms off the main vestibule.

'Also, a guitar, a violin, an oboe,' he said, wryly. 'The one thing that Pietro does seem to enjoy is playing the bongos but I think it is only because they make the loudest noise.'

Belle laughed. 'The bongos do sound like fun.'

'You haven't heard them yet. Trust me, you will change your mind.'

Once the remnants of their picnic had been cleared away,

they sailed on further until Enrico decided it was time to turn for home. Sun-kissed and salty-skinned, with his guidance and encouragement Belle took the wheel again and held the course steady while he hoisted sails to catch the wind and the yacht cut through the water.

'You are OK?' he asked, coming to stand beside her. 'It hasn't been too stressful being at sea with me?'

'I'm glad I came,' Belle told him, and she meant it. 'I feel like I needed this.'

'For me the sea is where I feel most free. Luciana was the same. Any problems always seemed smaller the further we got from the land. Even when she was ill, we came out together, until it got too risky. The very last time was sad, because I knew it but she didn't, and I couldn't explain to her. For a long time afterwards, I stayed away. I didn't even want to look at the yacht.'

This was their friendship, thought Belle, this shared understanding of what had happened and how it made them feel. It was what had drawn them together and kept them as friends despite the distance and their differences. They had lost someone.

'Sailing solo must have been hard,' she said.

'At first yes, but then in a way I would feel closer to Luciana out here ... closer to the person she used to be.'

'I'm closer to Ari when I'm riding his horse,' said Belle. 'But I think he would have liked me being here, doing this with you.'

'I hope so,' said Enrico. 'To be truthful, I am not certain how Luciana would feel about it. I don't think she ever imagined my life without her at its centre. Niether did I.'

Belle was curious to know more about this woman who sounded so formidable but Enrico went to trim a sail that was flapping, then slipped down into the cabin for a few moments, and by the time he took the helm again, the moment was lost.

His car was waiting for them at the marina. As they were being driven back Enrico remained preoccupied, checking messages on his phone while Belle gazed out at the groves of olive trees, and before long they were at the *palazzo*, its walls pinking in the evening sun.

'There is time to clean up and change for dinner,' said Enrico, glancing at his watch. 'Mamma likes to eat early.'

Belle had enjoyed their day together more than she had expected. Stepping through the heavy wooden door, she couldn't help wishing they had the place to themselves, at least for one evening. She wasn't used to being surrounded by people. And three generations in one house seemed too many, even in a *palazzo* as large as this one.

Who stayed at home with their parents anyway, once they were old enough to go flat sharing with friends? Belle had moved out the moment she was able to, so she could have parties and make messes, eat when she wanted and live how she liked. Her late teens and early twenties had been about wild nights and terrible hangovers, brilliant flatmates and bad ones, far too many takeaway curries. What she remembered most was a lot of laughter and freedom. Pietro and Gianni were missing out on that, just as presumably Enrico had, and she didn't envy them.

'We will eat in the dining room this evening,' Enrico told her. 'Afterwards if it is still warm, we will drink a *digestivo* in the garden.'

His life was regimented, realised Belle, as she was getting ready for dinner. For that short time on the yacht, he had seemed lighter and freer. But here he had responsibilities, people who expected things of him, here he was the head of a family as well as the CEO of a business.

Not wanting to be late, Belle spritzed her wrists with a little of her favourite citrussy fragrance, tidied her hair then stared into the wardrobe at the row of clothes she had unpacked into it. All she saw were the same old things

– her beloved loose linen trousers and billowy silks, a faded gingham wrap dress that possibly looked like a tablecloth, a blue striped sun frock with a low-cut back which arguably was too revealing.

Belle settled for a dress she had found in a designer recycle shop. It was boldly printed with green leaves and purple aubergines, and must once have been expensive but by the time she chanced on it the silk organza had seen better days and needed some mending. Much as Belle loved it, this was one of those outfits that she hardly ever seemed to find the right time to wear.

Walking into the dining room, she found the family waiting. Their heads turned to look in her direction and Enrico's mother stared at Belle's frock, like it was an old acquaintance that she was trying to place.

'Dolce and Gabbana,' she said, as Belle took a seat. 'From at least ten years ago. How nice you are still wearing it.'

'An old favourite,' Belle murmured, not prepared to admit the dress had come to her second-hand.

'I have some vintage pieces that I continue to wear.' The older woman's hair was a rigid helmet and her demeanour stern. Still, she seemed to have defrosted very slightly at the sight of the frock. 'They come from our own label of course. It is very unusual for me to wear anything else.'

'Your jacket is gorgeous,' said Belle. Long-line, primrose-coloured linen and hand-embroidered with red and ochre flowers, it really was very striking.

'This is from our new autumn collection. It isn't available to buy yet.'

'Nonna makes sure samples of her favourite designs are made up in her size,' explained Gianni. 'She always looks good in them.'

'Like a model,' added Pietro, grinning at the older woman.

Enrico's mother made a tutting sound, but looked flattered. 'I never throw anything away,' she told Belle. 'If I no longer wear a garment then it goes into my archive. I still have some original designs of my great-grandmother's, stitched by her own hand. We were hoping to create a display room. Luciana had plans for it but sadly ...'

'I'd be keen to take a look,' said Belle, who adored beautiful things whether they were clothes, jewellery or paintings, ceramics or sculptures, 'if that's possible.'

'You would be interested to see?' She seemed to thaw a fraction more.

'I'd love to,' said Belle. 'Also, don't you have a shop in Ostuni? I was thinking that tomorrow I might take a walk and find it.'

'If you go, then you should choose something to wear, as a gift from us,' said Enrico.

'You already sent me those lovely napkins.' Belle hadn't intended him to feel as though he had to give her stuff.

'I chose those napkins because I wasn't sure what would suit your style.'

'You should have asked me,' put in Perla. 'I know exactly the dress that Belle should have. I will go along tomorrow and show her.'

'Which dress?' asked Enrico's mother, currant-bun eyes boring into Belle.

'The white one with the embroidered blue grapes ... it is a little boho but still stylish,' said Perla.

'No, no, at her age she needs more colour,' insisted the old Signora. 'I say the red dress with the pale blue embroidery on the sleeves and neckline.'

'That one is too short,' argued Perla.

'Once she has more of a tan it will look fine,' the Signora insisted.

The noise around the dining table seemed to rise a few decibels. Their voices echoed in the cavernous room with its marble floor and high frescoed ceiling. Perla was waving her phone, showing them the dress that she thought best,

Pietro was adding his opinion. One moment they seemed to be fighting, the next they were laughing, and Belle felt bewildered, as they switched from English to Italian and back again, arguing about what might suit her without bothering to ask what she thought.

Once everyone had quietened down enough, Enrico turned to her. 'Why not have both. At least try them on and see which you prefer.'

'I'd love to, thank you,' said Belle, because she didn't want to prolong the argument, and it was always fun to try on new things.

'Shopping tomorrow.' Perla was beaming. 'It is my superpower, you will see.'

Gianni rolled his eyes. 'I thought that staring at your phone all day was your superpower, Perla?'

'*Ohhh*,' Pietro objected, glancing concernedly at his wife, but Perla smiled and shrugged.

'I am very good at that too,' she said, coolly.

And Belle, after such a long stretch of time on her own, envied Enrico and his days filled with colour and noise, but at the same time was not at all sure she could cope with it.

Dinner was three courses that stretched out slowly through the evening. First an array of antipasti: sweet red peppers stuffed with garlicky breadcrumbs, pleasantly tart pickled aubergine, tender slices of seared *polpo* on a creamy puree of fava beans. Then a slab of salted cod baked in the oven with potatoes and pecorino until it was crisp and golden on top. Finally fresh fruits soaked in a spiced red wine syrup. Each plate to Belle seemed like an adventure and she savoured every mouthful, noticing the flavours and textures.

Once the dessert plates had been removed, the old Signora declared it was time for her to rest. The others trooped outside, Enrico with a bottle of liqueur, and his sons carrying cut-crystal glasses.

By night, the garden was magical. Its rough-hewn walls were spotlit as were the columns of the loggia and the blue rectangle of swimming pool. The boughs of the ancient olive trees made ghostly twisted shapes, the air smelled sweet and floral, and the eyes of watchful cats glinted green.

They settled down on two long, low divans, arranged beneath a pergola covered in bougainvillea and Enrico poured a little of the liqueur for each of them.

'Did you enjoy your sailing today?' asked Perla, leaning into the curve of Pietro's arm.

'It was beautiful out on the water,' confirmed Belle.

'For our next adventure, should we sail north, towards Polignano al Mare?' Enrico suggested. 'That is just as spectacular.'

Gianni gave his father a quick sideways glance. 'Perhaps we will join you, the next time you go out, if you don't mind.'

'Yes, of course.' Enrico sounded surprised and pleased. 'It is a very long time since I have taken you sailing.'

'Too long,' agreed Gianni 'This summer, while Belle is here, we should make sure to enjoy some time together. We can help you to show her around Puglia.'

Pietro nodded. 'We must take her to Lecce. And maybe a day trip to Matera.'

'And she will want to see Alberobello, the caves of Castellana, and Locorotondo.' Gianni ticked off the local beauty spots on his fingers. 'We can take turns showing these places to her.'

'That's really kind,' responded Belle. 'But I'm still quite jet-lagged and very happy to spend the next few days just wandering around Ostuni.'

'Perla will show you Ostuni ... and Katarina too,' Gianni told her. 'My wife has many commitments with her charity work; but it would be good for her to take a few days off.'

Belle might have preferred to explore alone, to walk

through the labyrinth of staircased streets until they started to seem familiar, to find the café where she would regularly stop for coffee or lunch, to discover the best place for a gelato. She was longing to sit quietly inside the cathedral perched above the buildings that were clustered on the hilltop, walk beneath the archways of the blazingly white houses, soak up the history and find the best views.

'I really don't want to put you to any trouble,' she murmured.

'We cannot leave it all to Papa though,' said Gianni. 'He is busy too.'

'It is no trouble at all for us,' Pietro promised.

'Shopping tomorrow morning,' Perla reminded her. 'We will find you some beautiful things to wear.'

Sipping the dark, pleasantly medicinal liqueur, Belle told herself she would get to know this family; get used to them. It was time for her to be out in the world and with other people.

'We will take you to the *festa* at Martina Franca; the lights are always beautiful,' said Gianni.

'And to a beach party at the lido,' offered Pietro. 'They are laid-back, lots of fun, I think you will like it.'

'Someone should write a list, or we will forget what we have decided,' suggested Perla.

'I will do it.' Katarina pulled out her phone. 'First the family sailing trip up to Polignano al Mare and where after that?'

They started bickering about what Belle might like best, Katarina tapping on her screen as Gianni raised his voice to be heard above the others.

'It is going to be a good summer.' Enrico was beaming. 'Belle, I am very glad that you came to Italy.'

His sons and their wives smiled back at him, but no one except Perla said anything. She held up the crystal glass of liqueur she had been sipping from despite her pregnancy, and proposed a toast.

'To Belle,' she smiled. 'And to our summer together.'

8

A Better Belle

In her dreams Belle was home again, pottering round the gallery, so when she opened her eyes to see a vaulted ceiling above her bed, she had a moment of feeling disoriented. Then she heard a knocking sound, which must have been what had woken her up in the first place.

'Belle, I have brought you some coffee.' Perla's voice was muffled by the heavy door. She knocked again, insistently. 'We are going shopping today, remember. Can I come in?'

'Yes, sure,' Belle called back, propping herself up on the pillows and stretching her legs which always ached a bit first thing, until she got going.

Perla appeared with a tray, putting it down on the ottoman, before passing Belle a cup filled with milky coffee and a paper-wrapped pastry.

'I am excited about finding you something beautiful to wear,' she said.

'Actually, I feel a bit awkward about this,' Belle told her. 'I don't expect Enrico to be giving me free clothes.'

'Only a dress or two and he can afford it.' Perla helped herself to a pastry from the tray and sat at the foot of Belle's bed, curling her legs beneath her and scattering crumbs as she ate.

'Even so ...'

'He is happy to have you here. All of us can see a difference in him. I was asking Pietro how long it is since his father sat outside with us in the evening to enjoy a glass of Amaro. Neither of us could remember.'

'That's great but it doesn't mean he has to give me frocks.'

Perla stared at Belle's toes, poking out from beneath the sheet and frowned. 'You need a pedicure too. We could do that after we have been shopping. I know a good place.'

'I suppose we could.' Belle's feet were a little rough, but she tended to go barefoot all summer then lived in boots over winter, so there seemed no point in making them look fancy.

'Do you need new shoes too?' asked Perla, hopefully.

'No, definitely not.'

'OK, let me see what you have here already.' Perla climbed off the bed, skipping over to the wardrobe, where she started looking through Belle's things, and judging by the shaking of her head, was unimpressed with what she found there.

'This one I do like,' she said, pulling out the tiered maxi dress in a vivid shade of turquoise that Belle had worn on the day she arrived. 'Gilda is right, you suit colour.'

'Gilda?' Belle was confused for a moment. 'Oh, you mean Enrico's mother?'

'We never call her Gilda, not to her face,' Perla warned, rifling further into the cupboard. 'To me she is Nonna and to you Signora Ginaro, unless she suggests otherwise. It is about respect.'

'OK.' Belle was pleased to have been warned.

'Nonna Gilda has a good eye, but so do I, and I say you can wear paler shades too. For now, though, this one is OK.' She tossed the turquoise frock on the bed. 'And on your feet … hmm, but I think you do need shoes.'

At the sight of Belle's old Birkenstocks and worn trainers, Perla's eyes widened. Finally, she found a pair of beaded sandals that she deemed acceptable.

'In half an hour, I will meet you in the vestibule. Don't be like Pietro and keep me waiting,' Perla warned, taking the tray.

'Is Katarina coming too?' asked Belle.

'I didn't ask her.'

'Do you think we should?'

'No,' said Perla, closing the bedroom door behind her.

Belle was tempted to wear something else, purely to assert her independence, but she had a strong sense that it wasn't worth the hassle. Besides she liked Perla, who seemed lively and warm, and she needed a friend here. So she pulled the turquoise dress over her head, slipped her feet into the blingy sandals, then tied up her hair with a scarf. Checking the mirror, she viewed her reflection more critically. Her hair had grown longer and the greys were streaking through it. Her fingernails were bitten and her toenails ragged. If Ari had been here, he would have said she was beautiful, but he always told her that, no matter how she looked.

She was five minutes early and found Perla ready and waiting, dressed in a dusky pink linen shift dress that skimmed her body, with her glossy dark hair falling over her bare shoulders.

'I tried calling for the driver but he is busy,' she complained. 'So, we will have to walk.'

'Is it very far?' asked Belle.

'Not really but ...' Perla looked down at her stilettos and sighed. 'Enrico needs two cars now there are so many of us.'

Belle was curious about the way this family fitted together. 'Will you and Pietro stay living in the *palazzo*, or find a place of your own?' she asked as they set off.

'It is a matter of money,' explained Perla, marching across the road then down a narrow side street. 'My husband doesn't earn enough for us to be independent.'

'I thought he worked with Enrico and Gianni?'

'Yes, but he is very junior and they don't pay him enough.' Perla turned a corner into an even narrower street.

'What about you and Katarina?' asked Belle. 'What do you both do?'

'Katarina has her charity work; always she is organising fundraising auctions and gala dinners. And me? I am crazy busy,' Perla replied, without elaborating.

They emerged onto a winding street lined with small boutiques and shops selling bright ceramics, wine and olive oil. The Casa di Ginaro shop was among them, a simple building with pearl-white walls and shuttered doors.

'This boutique has been here almost since the very beginning,' Perla explained. 'They will never close it, although it is small and very ordinary compared to the other shops.'

Inside, two racks filled with clothes were set against opposing walls, and a curtained changing area and mirror were positioned at the back of the shop. Belle saw no sign of an assistant.

'*Salve,*' Perla called, striding in and pulling aside the changing room curtain to reveal Mia sitting on a low stool, scrolling on her phone.

She looked up, scowling. 'What a nightmare. This is the worst job in the world.'

'There must be much worse jobs.' Perla was unsympathetic.

'Easy for you to say, you don't have to do it.'

'If customers come in, they will think there is no one here,' Perla pointed out.

'Exactly,' said Mia, getting to her feet.

'Belle wants to try on some dresses,' Perla told her. 'But I will find them. No need for you to go to any trouble at all.'

'Ciao Belle, how are you doing?' asked Mia, tossing her head as she came out of the changing room.

Looking through the rack of bone-coloured linens, Belle noticed the prices on the labels and couldn't imagine there being many people in this small southern Italian town who were able to afford them.

'What about this one?' asked Mia, who was searching

the other rack and had picked out a bright apricot-coloured frock with white embroidery around the hem and neckline. She held it up against herself so that Belle could see how good it looked. 'It is my favourite.'

'That dress looks pretty on you, because you are dark,' said Perla. 'But Belle is fair-haired ... or maybe grey ...'

'She is both,' said Mia, helpfully.

'Either way this shade is totally wrong for her. I think she should try the white one with the grapes, but Nonna Gilda prefers the shorter red dress with the pale blue embroidery.'

'Take the one that Signora Ginaro has suggested,' Mia advised. 'It is best to agree with her.'

'We will try them both,' decreed Perla, continuing to flick through the rails.

Mia held up another dress, this one with frilled sleeves in a shade of vibrant watermelon.

'Too pink.' Perla dismissed it.

Quietly doing her own thing at the other rack, Belle had come across a flowing, bone-coloured maxi dress with full sleeves and a tasselled belt at the waist. It had dark blue embroidered panels on the skirt and over the shoulders. She held the dress against herself and peered in the mirror. It was more her style.

'This one,' she said, making up her mind without even putting it on.

'Yes, try it,' agreed Perla, taking the dress from Belle and passing it to Mia to hang in the changing room. 'And we will see what else might work.'

In the stuffy changing room, Belle found herself trying on dress after dress. Soon she was hot and very much over it. The boho dress she had preferred in the first place was the kind of thing she could imagine drifting around in at home. Loose and cool, stylish but not shouty, and it fitted her perfectly.

'Definitely this one,' she said, pulling back the curtain and holding it out.

'It is not sexy.' Mia screwed up her pretty face.

'I'm going to take it,' Belle decided and started delving in her handbag, sorting through the muddle of tissues, lip balm, hair ties, phone and face masks, trying to find her credit card.

'Your money is no good here,' Perla reminded her, when she pulled it out. 'This dress is a gift from Enrico. He wanted you to have.'

'*Va bene*,' said Mia, untroubled. 'And what about you Perla? Which one will you be taking today?'

'The dress you liked, the apricot. No need for me to try it on, I know my size here. We are going to have our pedicures now so will leave everything here and collect it on our way back.'

'Pedicures.' Now Mia was wistful.

'At the little nail bar, you know, the one I like. I hope there will be a polish to match my new dress.'

Belle wondered if Perla really had licence to help herself to any frock she liked. She feared they were both taking advantage of Enrico's generosity and, watching the two young women kissing goodbye, touching lightly cheek to cheek, decided to avoid any future shopping trips if possible.

The nail bar was a few doors further down. Clearly, they knew Perla here, as she was greeted with more kisses and offered a range of bright polishes to choose from.

'This,' she said, lighting on a vivid apricot. 'And Belle, do you prefer a turquoise to match your dress? Or this lilac?'

'Just something natural,' Belle replied.

'A French pedicure, perfect,' said Perla, settling at one of the basins and gesturing for Belle to take the one beside her.

It was good to sit down and put her feet in cool water. Belle leaned back in the padded chair, preparing to be pampered, as Perla scrolled on her phone.

'Mia has no eye at all,' she remarked, conversationally. 'She has that job only because she is a friend of the family. It won't last. She didn't stay very long in her previous job either. Of course, she is in love with Pietro and Gianni. She always believed she was going to marry one or other of them.'

Belle was watching as the pedicurist struggled to clip her toenails, which she had noticed were getting thicker these days; presumably it was yet another age thing like her creakier knees and salt-and-pepper hair. Perla didn't seem to need a response; she continued chatting and scrolling.

'Gianni met Katarina while he was at university in Milan,' Perla explained. 'And then Pietro got together with me in Rome, so both of them were taken. Poor Mia.'

Belle's feet were proving to be high maintenance. Her hard skin needed pumicing and the pedicurist seemed to spend a very long time probing and picking beneath her toenails with a sharp metal instrument.

'Maybe Mia will meet someone online, like you and Enrico did, that would be nice for her,' said Perla.

'Enrico and I are friends, that's all,' Belle said, quickly, wondering how many times she would have to explain this to everyone.

'Friends, yes,' replied Perla, looking up from her screen. 'But you met online, and that is what Mia must do. There is no one here in Ostuni for her.'

'Poor Mia,' Belle agreed, thinking that perhaps in a small town like this there weren't too many options, whether it was people to meet or jobs to apply for.

Perla watched approvingly as her nails were prettily glossed. 'After this we should have a nice lunch together. I will let them know we won't be home.'

'Will they be expecting us?' Belle didn't want to upset any plans, at least not this early in her stay.

'Probably.' Perla seemed unconcerned. 'But it is nicer to eat out. This way we get to choose. At home, the menu is planned, and none of us have any say.'

'Who plans it?' wondered Belle.

'Gilda, of course, she controls everything.'

Belle wondered if that were true. Wasn't Enrico meant to be the head of the family? His mother might be a strong character but surely she didn't run his whole life, even deciding what he had for dinner? If so that would be stifling.

'Let's go for lunch then,' she agreed.

Pedicures were time-consuming. You had to wait for the polish to dry which seemed to take forever, even though there were fans blowing cool air to speed up the process. And Belle was restless; there was a whole world outside the window waiting to be explored.

'No smudging,' Perla warned. 'Make sure it is set properly.'

'It must be by now.'

'A few minutes more,' she insisted.

Finally, Perla agreed that they could move. With the pedicurist's help, Belle managed to insert her feet into her blingy sandals without doing any damage. Her feet did look better, she had to concede, smoother and softer. She liked the natural shade of her nails, it was simple and practical, which was how Belle preferred to look. Gingerly, she followed Perla back to the boutique to collect their shopping.

'Where are you going next?' asked Mia, who had been transfixed by her phone when they arrived but was at least standing at the counter.

'We're having lunch somewhere,' said Belle.

'Lunch?' Mia's eyes widened. 'I will come too. It is nearly time for me to close up anyway. Bar Pausa?'

'Why not,' replied Perla.

Together they returned to the bar in the annexe of the main piazza where Perla chose a table shaded by a large cream parasol and the waiter brought over chilled water and menus. The process of ordering food and drinks was long-winded. Belle only wanted a seafood salad but Perla rattled off several things then changed her mind and called the waiter back, to re-make the order.

'Would anyone like a spritz?' Perla asked.

Belle recalled how woozy she had felt the last time. 'Not me.'

'Yes, I will have one,' said Mia.

'But you have to go back to work later,' Perla reminded her.

'If I can't do my job after drinking a spritz then I am no good at it,' declared Mia.

Perla didn't bother trying to hide her amusement. 'You are a terrible shop assistant, *cara*.'

'Maybe I am,' conceded Mia. 'Still one drink won't make me any worse, and besides I need cheering up.'

'Perhaps what you actually need is a different job,' suggested Belle, kindly. 'If you hate that one so much.'

'I am only doing it because I hope to transfer to another of the Casa di Ginaro shops. Rome, Milan, Florence, even Venice, anywhere but this place.' Mia cast a despairing look around the small piazza with its sun-bleached buildings and tears welled up in her eyes. 'All I am doing here is waiting for something to happen and nothing ever does.'

Belle reached into her bag for a packet of tissues. 'What would you like to happen?' she asked, passing her a couple.

'To meet someone online like you did Enrico,' Mia said, as if that was going to change everything. 'And fall in love.'

'They are just friends,' chimed in Perla, before Belle could say the words herself.

'For now, maybe.' Mia shrugged.

'For always,' Belle insisted.

'But Enrico would be easy to fall in love with,' Mia pointed out, turning towards her. 'Imagine the life you could have with him.'

'I lost my husband.' Belle had no patience with well-meaning people who thought she was too young to be alone for the rest of her life. She wasn't interested in moving on or starting afresh or second chances; and she was quite sure she never would be. 'I'm not looking for love.'

Perla gave her a searching look. 'You don't want to be loved again?'

Belle shook her head.

'But that is so sad.'

'Not really,' Belle told them. 'I've got friends, like Enrico, and that's all I want.'

'I suppose this explains your hair,' said Mia, thoughtfully.

'My hair?' Belle touched her wayward curls. She hadn't thought they looked that bad.

'All the grey,' Mia clarified.

Belle was hoping the greys would tone in with the blondes, until at some point, they took over. Anyway, wasn't it acceptable to go grey now? Even quite on-trend?

'It makes you look old,' explained Mia. 'I am never going to let that happen to mine.'

She had beautiful hair, very dark and thick and Belle had noticed how aware of it Mia seemed, flicking it dramatically to make a point while she was speaking and fidgeting by twisting it in ringlets round her finger.

'Me too, my hair will stay this exact colour until the day I die,' said Perla.

'It will look too harsh,' Mia warned. Tapping and swiping on the screen of her phone, she held it up to show a picture. 'Bronze streaks are more flattering, so this is what I will do when I am in my forties like Belle.'

'My fifties actually,' she corrected, and saw them looking more closely at her. 'I wonder where you will both be by then.'

'I will be here, living in Ostuni, with Pietro and our family.' Perla sounded certain. 'That is my future.'

Mia ran her hands through her long mane. 'I have no idea at all, but I know my hair will look good.'

At their age Belle hadn't given much thought to life in her fifties. It seemed a distant shore and she assumed by then she would be a different person. Belle felt no wiser than before, no more sorted or certain. Although there were signs of age she couldn't ignore. She ached, she flushed, she didn't sleep as well, and her reflection in the mirror was proof that things were changing.

'Do you think I'm making a mistake?' She touched her grey-streaked hairline, feeling insecure about it now. 'Should I go back to being blonde again?'

'Yes,' the two younger women, chorused.

'OK, then I'll pick up a box of dye, if we go past a pharmacy.'

'You can't do it yourself.' Perla sounded appalled. 'We need to find out where Mia's mother goes. Her hair always looks expensive.'

'I've always done it myself,' said Belle. 'I only stopped because we were in lockdown and it didn't seem to matter because I hardly saw anyone.'

'I know exactly where Mamma goes.' Mia turned back to her phone. 'I will see if I can get an appointment.'

Normally Belle would have resisted anyone trying to change her appearance. Her style was her own. But while she had been busy grieving and hiding from the world, her style had seemed to take a break. Belle had worn Ari's old clothes, let her hair grow wild, there had been dirt beneath her fingernails most of the time and she never cared at all. Now, glancing down at her smoother, polished feet, she thought that perhaps her hair could do with some attention. Here she was, trying to find her way towards a new life; why not have a fresh look too? Mia was already on the phone to the salon. She beamed as she announced that there had been a late cancellation and they could fit her in this afternoon. Immediately Perla was scrolling through pictures of hairstyles on her phone and saying that Belle should be honey blonde with highlights. It was impossible not to be at least a little charmed by their enthusiasm.

'You will look fantastic,' promised Mia.

'*Bellissima*,' Perla agreed. 'From top to toe.'

The salon was hidden in a warren of side streets, a shabby whitewashed limestone building that inside was modern and viciously air-conditioned. Since the stylist spoke no English, a detailed explanation of what she wanted was delivered by Mia, and the two stood either side of her, hands in Belle's hair, pulling it this way and that, apparently disagreeing.

'What are they saying?' she asked Perla, tugging free of their fingers.

'There is a discussion about the style. The hairdresser suggests a layered bob but Mia says no, absolutely not.'

'Honestly, I just want it tidied up a bit,' said Belle, who didn't know how there could be this much to say about one person's hair. 'And the colour sorted.'

'That is exactly what Mia is telling her,' promised Perla. 'Don't worry.'

It was a painstaking process, this covering of greys and painting on of highlights, with Mia supervising, while Perla retreated with her phone. Spending hours on improving her appearance had never been Belle's idea of a treat. She preferred to be outdoors, going for long walks or getting muddy in the garden. And she would always rather have an extra twenty minutes in bed than iron her clothes or style her hair.

She wondered how long it had taken Mia to perfect that careful flick of eyeliner along her lash-line, how much volumising mascara and lipliner she got through, and whether she bothered applying the whole look every single day then removing it again at bedtime.

'I will do your face,' offered Mia, noticing that Belle was studying her. 'It will be the finishing touch.'

Belle was quick to refuse. 'I don't wear much make-up.'

'A natural look,' Mia promised.

Belle muttered a phrase that her mother liked to use. 'I don't want to look like mutton dressed as a lamb.'

'What did you say?' Mia was confused.

'I don't want to try and look like something I'm not,' Belle explained.

'Of course not. You will look like yourself, only better,' Mia promised. 'And it is only make-up, I will remove it if you aren't happy.'

Belle stared at the three of them reflected in the mirror, at herself sitting with foils in her hair, looking tense and uncomfortable, while they fluttered around. These girls were having fun, she realised. Was that something she had forgotten how to do during Ari's illness and the long, empty months that followed? Had her personality dulled, along with her appearance?

'Please,' Mia begged, and since she really seemed to want to, Belle agreed.

'OK then.'

Both young women carried around full make-up bags, and sorting through them, pulling out tubes of gloss and pots of colour, Mia sang along to the music that was playing through the salon speakers, her earlier despair forgotten.

By the time they had finished, the afternoon was almost over. Long layers had been cut into Belle's hair to give it some shape and it fell below her shoulders in relaxed, beachy waves. The grey was gone, its hue was honeyed and her skin seemed to glow. As Mia had promised, she was a better version of herself.

'You look fantastic,' said Perla, approvingly.

'And sexy,' added Mia, dabbing a last touch of gloss on her lips. 'Tonight, you should wear your new dress, and then wait till Enrico sees you.'

'She and Enrico are just friends.' Perla rolled her eyes. 'Remember?'

'Oh yes, friends,' echoed Mia.

Belle didn't bother trying to argue. Being in love must seem like everything at their age and it would be beyond belief that she preferred to be single. Her recollection of her own twenties was almost always having someone on the scene; guys she met at work, in bars, through friends, guys that she was flirting with, dating or secretly attracted to. Searching for the right one had taken up a lot of her time and energy.

And still she had never found what she had much later on with Ari; so much love, it was all-consuming. Even if she could feel like that again, Belle wasn't sure she wanted to.

When you lost that kind of love, there was so little of yourself left. Perla and Mia didn't understand that yet. All they saw was grey hairs on her head and lines on her face. They thought fixing those fixed everything.

'You like it?' Mia wanted to know. 'You are happy.'

'Yes, I'm happy,' she agreed. But glancing towards the mirror one last time before stepping out of the salon and into afternoon sunshine, Belle thought that hair and make-up could only do so much.

Perla was in a rush to get home, to be sure there would be enough time to change before dinner. As they hurried towards the *palazzo*, the streets they passed through seemed to be coming to life. Shops were unshuttered, people were out and about, stopping to exchange a few words with an acquaintance or sipping a drink at tables outside bars. Perla called greetings to friends she encountered on the way, but didn't stop.

'Gilda likes us to eat dinner together,' she explained, stepping quickly in her stilettos. 'Except on Sundays when she prefers a long lunch. This is the family tradition.'

'So many traditions,' observed Belle.

'You will get used to it.'

Belle doubted that. She was beginning to see how Enrico had formed his impression that she was a free spirit. In her world there was no hard-and-fast schedule, no one to dictate that things must be done the way they always had.

Rounding a bend, she saw the *palazzo* ahead, its old stone walls glowing in the soft evening light. Even with his family around, Enrico must have been lonely here at times. Why else had he struck up a friendship with Belle, a woman on the other side of the world? He must have needed her company, just like she had needed his.

Inside the *palazzo*, she found that nothing had altered except the light. For years and years, it must have been this way, the same antique chairs and marble statuary, the same dark oil paintings in heavy gold frames, the same ticking clocks.

'Wear the new dress,' Perla reminded her, as they parted ways. 'Don't change anything else.'

'I wouldn't dare,' said Belle, and she was rewarded with a smile.

She did love the dress. Floating downstairs wearing it half an hour later, Belle felt less at odds with her grand surroundings.

Again, the family was already gathered, waiting for her at the table. This time Belle felt as if they were taking in every aspect of her changed appearance. Looking from one to the other, she witnessed a Mexican wave of expressions. Gianni was frowning slightly, both Pietro and Katarina seemed surprised, Perla looked smugly pleased and the old Signora was appraising her, as though trying to work out her real value.

'That dress was made for you,' Enrico said. 'It is perfect.'

'Thank you so much, it's the nicest gift.'

'Better than napkins,' said Perla, pointedly.

'And your hair is different too?' asked Enrico.

'I have given Belle a makeover.' Perla explained. 'Mia helped. Doesn't she look beautiful now?'

'Of course she does,' said Enrico, lightly. 'She always looks beautiful.'

Around the table, she sensed a widening of eyes and an

intake of breath; and Belle suspected that she wasn't the only one to be startled by the unexpected compliment.

'We also had lunch at Bar Pausa; it was fun, wasn't it?' chirped Perla.

'Yes it was,' Belle agreed. 'The most fun I've had in ages. And I have this lovely dress now, which is such a treat.'

'You deserve treats,' Enrico told her, warmly. 'We will make sure there are plenty more.'

Belle was aware of his sons tensing, of Katarina's frown and Perla's smile. Only his mother's face was unreadable.

We are friends, she wanted to announce to the whole room, *I am here because I lost love, not because I am looking for it*. But then the maid appeared to serve a first course of *orecchiette* pasta with peppery leafy greens, a salty crush of anchovy and a fiery bite of chilli. And Belle stayed silent.

Trying to focus on the food, she continued to be distracted by a sense that they were watching her. The old Signora's gaze seemed especially beady.

'Do you like it, Signora Ginaro?' Belle touched the billowy folds of the new dress, assuming that her choice hadn't met with approval.

'It is from our label, so of course I do,' the older woman replied. 'You suit the Casa di Ginaro style. It looks good on you.'

'Tomorrow we will go looking for shoes,' said Perla.

'No more shopping.' The Signora was stern.

'But Nonna, I promised ...'

'You will be too busy. Katarina needs help to organise a charity gala.'

Perla cast a glance at her husband, then stared down at her plate. '*Va bene.*'

'And tomorrow Belle will be coming with me to see the archive,' added Signora Ginaro, beckoning for the maid to refill the bread basket. 'So everyone has a plan for the day.'

The meal was delicious, with skewers of pork stuffed with

melted *caciocavallo* cheese to follow the pasta. Still, Belle wondered if they ever got tired of dining like this. What if actually all you felt like was something plain on toast. What if you didn't want to be told what to do and how to eat?

Belle was here for the summer and would do her best to fit in. Any longer and she sensed that she would get the urge to push back against the rules and routines. She certainly couldn't imagine living this way.

'You are interested in my archive, yes,' said Signora Ginaro, and it seemed more a statement than a question.

'Yes, definitely,' Belle confirmed. 'I'm looking forward to seeing it.'

Once again, they finished the evening sitting on the outdoor sofas, drinking a *digestivo*, although tonight it was cooler so Enrico lit the brazier. Belle wanted to ask him about the garden. How old were those olive trees with the thick twisted boughs? Was it the white wisteria or honeysuckle that smelled so fragrant? Who trimmed the perfect balls of topiary planted in the stone urns? And what about the cats that kept stalking through, did they really all belong to the old Signora? But his sons were holding his attention, telling stories and making him laugh. Seated between them, looking from one to the other, Enrico seemed relaxed and happy. Belle listened as the conversation drifted in and out of Italian and the light from the flames flickered on their faces. She was an outsider here. Once it was late enough, she excused herself and went upstairs to bed.

Belle was about to get to work with a cotton wool ball and make-up remover, when she heard the ping of a message arriving. Checking her phone, she found a video and, peering at it, her hand flew to her mouth.

'Oh,' she said, grabbing her reading glasses for a clearer look. 'He's done it.'

The clip showed Greg up on the young horse, walking

him quietly around the arena on a long rein. Belle watched a second time, feeling a pang of regret at missing the moment. Then she sent a message.

Was that the first time?

Yep.

Are you free for a FaceTime call now?

Yep.

And then there he was, blue eyes sparkling, wearing a black furry hat with ear flaps.

'Cold here this morning.' Greg held up his phone to show her the frosted grass and a herd of horses in winter rugs, their breath puffing into the frigid air.

'You're riding him already,' said Belle. 'What happened to not rushing things?'

'He reckoned it was time for us to crack on and have some fun.'

'Oh, he told you that did he?'

'He's very direct. What you see is what you get with this boy.'

'Like Ari then?'

'Pretty much,' agreed Greg.

'Please tell me you're not still calling him that?'

'I changed his name to Aroha.'

It was a Māori word for love and affection. 'That suits him,' said Belle.

'Yeah, he seems to like it.'

'So, what's next?' she asked, switching on a couple of lamps and settling back on the cushions mounded on her vast bed. 'Will you be doing dressage on him by the time I get back?'

'Winning at dressage hopefully.' Greg squinted at her face on his screen. 'What have you been up to? You look really great.'

'I've been taken in hand by a couple of twentysomethings who think I've let myself go.'

He laughed at that.

'You should see my feet, if you think my face looks better.'

'You're starting to have a good time then?'

'It's beautiful here, the sun is shining.'

'What about the Italian royal family?' asked Greg.

'I think they all assume that I'm here to make a play for Enrico,' Belle told him.

'No shit Sherlock.' Greg grinned. 'So, are you?'

'Of course not.' She was indignant.

'Just checking.'

'Tomorrow I'm going to spend the day with his mother.'

'And how much fun will that be?' wondered Greg.

'My expectations are fairly low, but you never know.'

Afterwards, once she had said goodbye to Greg, and finished removing her make-up, then taken all the cushions off her bed so she could sleep in it, Belle felt unsettled. She couldn't see herself ever being entirely at ease in this house filled with so many ornate things and other people. She was more at home in the place she had just glimpsed on her phone, in Greg's wide paddocks, whether they were baked hard in summer or wet with mud over winter, with his horses and a couple of farm dogs for company. Or in her gallery, with customers coming in and out and long stretches of empty time between them.

Belle knew how families worked, even if her own had been a lonelier childhood. Growing up she had escaped to the cosier homes of schoolfriends whenever she could. She had sat round other people's kitchen tables listening to their bickering and debates, watched TV in their cramped living rooms and seized the chance of a sleepover. She had moved in and out of other people's families and learned how things were done. Belle had particularly enjoyed hanging out with Ari's many cousins. They were noisy and funny; there was always some sort of feud going on and she never went to a gathering that didn't feature tears as well as laughter, but they were also warm and welcoming.

Still, nothing in her life had prepared Belle for a family quite like this one.

Lying in bed, staring up at the lofty ceiling, she thought about Ari. He had a knack of being at ease wherever he went and an ability to talk to anybody. At the same time, he was always entirely himself. Closing her eyes and drifting off to sleep, Belle was still thinking of him.

9

Clothes, Clothes, Clothes

The Casa di Ginaro archive was housed in a climate-controlled room, at the fashion label's headquarters. Enrico's driver took them there, even though the imposing building, with its pink stone slab façade, was only a short stretch away in a newer part of town with wider boulevards.

Belle had woken early that morning thinking about what she should wear and, in the end, chosen the new dress again. As always Enrico's mother was encased in her uniform of a tailored long jacket; this one a shade of bright chartreuse that matched the woven leather handbag she was carrying. Following her into the foyer of the Casa di Ginaro building, and across a stretch of shining marble, Belle saw the woman behind the reception desk sitting up straighter at the sight of them.

'Signora Ginaro,' she said. 'We weren't expecting you this morning.'

With a brisk nod in return, Enrico's mother paused at the foyer table, where a collection of magazines wasn't fanned out to her liking, then seemed to take exception to a flower arrangement, remonstrating with the receptionist in Italian, while the young woman nodded and repeated. '*Si, si, va bene.*'

Furnished with a key to the archive, they moved through a set of heavy wooden doors and into the hush of a large office where Belle was aware of a ripple of surprise as they passed by workers at their desks. Several offered a restrained greeting of '*buongiorno*' and the Signora nodded in acknowledgement.

At the far end of the room was an old-fashioned lift with a cage door. She halted there and pressed a button that set its mechanism rattling.

'This building was one of my husband's investments,' she explained, once they were in the lift and lurching downwards. 'During his time, there was a lot of expansion. He created the space for the archive and then my daughter-in-law Luciana worked with me to store all our most precious pieces there.'

The archive was in the basement, behind a heavy metal door that swung open to reveal a dark void fragranced with cedar and lavender. As the Signora switched on the lights, she stepped aside to allow Belle to enter.

'Come, come,' she urged.

Every item was shrouded or boxed, still Belle could tell this windowless room was a treasure trove, with racks and racks of clothes and shelves stacked high. It seemed a waste to hide everything away. Weren't clothes meant to be worn and loved, to take people places and become caught up with their memories? Belle had always thought so.

'Old textiles are very fragile,' explained the Signora, in a measured way that suggested she had repeated those same words often. 'Here in the archive, they are kept at a constant temperature with no light to spoil them. The garments are hung properly and protected by muslin, or folded in acid-free paper. We always wear gloves before we handle them. I don't put on any fragrance and I remove jewellery that might catch on a loose thread. These are precious things and the wrong treatment could destroy them forever.'

The first box she opened contained a smocked nightgown embroidered with small blue cornflowers. Removing it from the acid-free paper that cushioned its folds, she laid it out reverently with her white-gloved hands and gestured to Belle to take a closer look.

'How pretty,' Belle remarked, seeing that it was very simple but beautifully hand-made.

'This is one of the first pieces, created by my great-grandmother. She started this business to help put food on the table, then my grandmother built on that, my husband and I made our contribution and Enrico has held a steady course. Soon Gianni will do great things, and eventually his son will continue our legacy.'

The viewing process was slow. Every garment was un-wrapped carefully then stored away again, before the next could be revealed. A wonderful jacket with a Nehru collar that her father had worn on his wedding day; the Signora's own bridal dress still pristine, Enrico's tiny christening gown, a stylish frock with a nipped-in waist that Belle could imagine herself wearing.

'Each generation has lifted up the one that came after it,' the Signora explained with pride, removing the lid from yet another box. 'We are a part of this town and its past, but everything we do is for the future.'

Eventually Belle understood that she was meant to be impressed. This family's success and its achievements were being laid out for her along with a summer skirt the Signora had worn as a young woman and the modest pale linens she had favoured later as a mother. It seemed there was a mes-sage in all of this. Look at our family, see how well we have done, the Signora was saying. We are important, admire us along with all our beautiful creations.

And although she was impressed because all these gar-ments were very beautiful, Belle felt claustrophobic in the cold, clinical room. She wondered how much longer all this showing-off of expensive things would drag on for. Surely by now the Signora had made her point. Her status was in no doubt at all.

Then one of the bridal dresses caught Belle's interest. As it was unboxed, she realised she had seen it before in a framed family photograph at the *palazzo*. It shimmered with thousands of crystal beads; the waist was narrow and the train extravagant.

'That is the gown that Enrico's wife wore on their wedding day,' she guessed.

The Signora smoothed it out tenderly and to Belle's surprise her eyes welled with tears. 'How happy we all were that day, imagining the long life they would have together.'

It was the first time she had seen a trace of emotion in this carefully controlled woman and when Belle replied her voice was gentle. 'There are so many memories in this room. It must be difficult for you at times coming here.'

'Difficult, yes. I have hardly been back at all since my daughter-in-law became ill.' The Signora was already busy wrapping the gown again, her face turned away from Belle, any emotion hidden. 'She and I were always together here so I was among the first to see that things weren't right. Luciana was such a meticulous woman. I noticed when she became careless and started to misplace things. I worried about her. Of course, she tried to cover up her confusion.'

Belle was flooded with sympathy now. 'It was the same with my husband.'

'Yes, but Luciana wasn't elderly like him. This was entirely unexpected.'

Belle's sympathy ebbed away just as quickly as it had come. The idea that Ari's age made anything less heartbreaking offended her. Even if people thought so, they should know better than to say it.

'We had so many plans,' continued the Signora. 'Luciana was the person I trusted with my legacy. Now I must train someone to take her place.'

'Perla loves fashion. Perhaps she could help work on it,' Belle suggested, as she seemed the obvious choice.

'That child?' The Signora sounded unconvinced. 'She is interested in wearing clothes but not caring for them properly. All she does is stare at her phone and take selfies. Enrico thinks that being married will mean she and my grandson settle down but I see no sign of it.'

Belle thought it would be daunting for anyone to marry into the Ginaro family and be governed by this older woman, who seemed almost impossible to please. She didn't envy Perla.

'Yesterday when we went shopping she was very helpful.'

'Helpful? One dress, that is all you brought home.' The Signora threw up her white-gloved hands, exasperated.

'I only wanted one,' said Belle, reasonably.

'If you are going to be spending the summer with us then you will need many more. Our lifestyle is very important to the Casa di Ginaro brand. People don't only want to dress like we do, they want to eat, live and holiday like us. We are telling them a story of what their lives could be like. For now, you are involved in that story.'

Belle understood the value of marketing but this seemed entirely over the top. 'I'm just a guest.'

'As our guest you will go places and meet people, be seen as part of the family, so I have had some clothes sent over for you to try,' the Signora said, imperiously. 'If there are pieces you dislike, then of course there is no obligation to wear them. But I have a good eye and I am sure you will enjoy what I have chosen.'

There was an expectant look on the Signora's face, as if she was waiting to be thanked, but Belle's mouth couldn't seem to form the word. She was entirely speechless. It was difficult to know what was more distasteful, the idea that her own style wasn't good enough, or that she was meant to become a walking advert for the family's fashion house.

'The delivery should have arrived by the time we return to the *palazzo*,' the Signora continued. 'You have all afternoon to try the clothes on.'

As always, the person Belle longed to turn to was Ari. She imagined his deep belly laugh and how he might have played things down and calmed her 'Don't stress about it,' he would' have said. 'What's the problem? Just wear the free stuff.'

But the thought didn't make her feel much better. Making her hair blonder and glossing her lips was one thing. Spending the entire summer dressing like someone else was quite another.

'Thank you,' she managed somehow, and the Signora responded with a tight smile.

'In return perhaps while you are here in Italy, you could help me?' she surprised Belle again by asking.

'Help with what?' Belle couldn't imagine.

'With the display room that Luciana and I were going to create. You do run a gallery, after all, so you must understand how things should be exhibited.'

'I'm not as well-qualified as you might think.' Belle pictured her little gallery, housed in what amounted to a lean-to on the side of the house. She was quite certain the Signora wouldn't be impressed.

'We had some plans drawn up. I will show them to you. Then perhaps you could assist me, and we will start to make some progress.'

'Isn't this a project that Enrico would expect to be involved with?' asked Belle, doubtful that she was likely to be much use.

'My son is focused on the business. The design team, manufacturing, marketing, distribution, staff – he must concern himself with all of it. The archive has always been my project. A display room would be the final achievement but, with Luciana gone …' Again the Signora's emotions simmered closer to the surface. As she held a hand to her face, Belle saw that it was shaking slightly.

This woman's make-up was flawless and every last hair lacquered in place, but she was fading. It showed in the curve of her spine and the stoop of her shoulders, in the careful way she moved, and a dullness in those deep-set eyes. When Belle looked more closely at her, it was more obvious.

'If there's anything I can do to help,' she found herself saying.

'You will have some time while you are here,' the Signora responded, more briskly. 'And I am sure you are going to find the plans interesting. Later, we will look at them. Now though it is almost time for lunch and I need to take a rest.'

Belle helped her to stack boxes back on shelves and make sure each garment was bagged and hung. Even though there were signs the Signora was tiring, the tremble in her hands more marked and her whole body starting to droop, everything had to be done properly. By the time they turned off the lights, she looked exhausted.

'It was time that I came back here,' she said, closing the metal door and locking it carefully. 'I have been guilty of avoiding this place.'

'That's quite understandable,' said Belle.

'No, it isn't.' The Signora's tone was steely. 'To give up has never been the Ginaro way.'

They stood together in the lift in silence, then walked back through the office and returned the key to the receptionist. Belle wondered if the Signora really wanted her assistance or if she felt the need to give her some sort of job, control her like she did everyone else.

They drove directly back to the *palazzo* and when they arrived the Signora announced that she was feeling tired and would have lunch up in her room. She looked frail as she walked up the stairs, one careful hand on the rail, white gloves held tightly in the other.

Watching her go, Belle wasn't sure what she was meant to do now. There had been no more arrangements made. Was lunch to be eaten with the rest of the family? The dining room was empty and in the salon the only sound she could hear was the ticking of a large ormolu clock. Belle wandered through into the orangery where she sank into one of the rattan chairs and stared out of the window. She had come to Italy feeling like a faded version of herself and now it seemed as if Enrico's mother wanted to rub away at what was left. Dress her in their clothes, keep her busy. Could Belle get lost here? Disappear completely?

'Belle!' It was Perla, fresh-faced and smiling. 'How did it go with Nonna Gilda in the archive?'

'It was fine ...' said Belle, roused from thoughts that were only getting darker. 'Although it's a strange and soulless place, isn't it?'

'I have never been,' admitted Perla, sinking into a chair and throwing her bare tanned legs over one arm. 'I would like to see it but she has never offered.'

'I think she hasn't visited it herself much since Luciana became ill.'

'Probably not.' Perla had her phone in one hand and was scrolling as she spoke. 'Lots of things changed after Luciana's diagnosis; at least that is what Pietro says.'

'You never met his mother before she got sick?'

'By the time I came here, she was already beginning to decline. Pietro talks about her often though. They were close; she understood him.' Perla's face clouded. 'Slowly, she changed until one day she was gone altogether.'

'Very cruel,' agreed Belle, feeling the weight of this family's sadness, heavy as her own had been.

'Poor Pietro, but soon we will have our own family.' The clouds lifted from Perla. 'And he will be happy.'

'I hope so,' said Belle, knowing from experience that happiness came and went.

'I was hoping to find you,' continued Perla, back to her usual sunny self. 'I am having lunch by the pool and thought you might like to join me.'

'I wasn't sure whether everyone ate lunch together,' said Belle.

'Only on Sundays. Everyone is too busy in the week. I hardly see Pietro since he started this job.' She sounded plaintive now.

Ironically, Belle had spent more time chatting with Enrico when she was living on the other side of the world than she did now staying in his house. She missed the long-distance intimacy of those Zoom calls when they had focused entirely on each other without any distractions.

'Let's have lunch by the pool then,' she agreed, glad for the company. 'Do we need to let someone know?'

'I will tell the maid. After lunch we will relax, swim, enjoy the sunshine. You can get changed and I will meet you in the loggia.'

Up in her room the new clothes were already waiting on a rack, wrapped and bagged like the garments in the archive had been. Belle steered around them to the wardrobe to find her bikini and an old silk kimono she liked to wear as a beach wrap. If the Signora found her lounging by the pool in an unapproved outfit, she probably wouldn't be impressed, but Belle didn't care.

The loggia ran along one side of the pool, all graceful pillars, soaring arches and welcome shade in the heat of the day. She found Perla supervising the setting of a table, issuing orders to the maid. A black cat streaked through and a tabby watched from one corner.

Flowers were placed on the table and monogrammed linen napkins. A jug of sparkling water and freshly cut lemons. A glass of Prosecco for Belle. It felt like an occasion.

'Do you always lunch so stylishly?' she asked Perla.

'Not every day, but I like to make things special if I can.' She was photographing the table with her phone, nimbly hopping up on a chair to get the best angle. 'For my Instagram. You should follow me.'

'I don't bother much with social media,' admitted Belle.

'Really?' Perla looked askance at her. 'But you will like my page. Take a look, at least.'

'Now?'

'Yes, yes,' urged Perla.

Reaching for her phone, Belle discovered that *@perla_stylish_life* already had tens of thousands of followers. Snapshots of a glamorous world were punctuated with selfies, and photographs of Perla in a series of outfits from the Casa di Ginaro range. Belle noticed how many likes each shot had received.

'You're an influencer,' she realised.

Perla's smile glowed. 'Not really, but I enjoy making things look nice and taking pictures.'

The chef had produced photogenic food, plating it all up beautifully, but Perla demanded more. She asked Belle to twirl a fork in her spaghetti and hold it high above the bowl. She got her to hold a salad of juicy red tomatoes and torn bread soaked in olive oil up against the silk of her kimono. And then slice into a trimmed artichoke, stuffed with parsley, crisp breadcrumbs and melting pecorino. It was astonishing how much effort she put into ensuring each shot looked perfect.

'I can only do this at lunchtime,' Perla explained. 'At dinner Nonna Gilda says it ruins her enjoyment of the food.'

'It does rather delay the moment of being able to eat,' said Belle.

'Once you have eaten, all you are left with is dirty dishes.' Perla picked up her fork and speared a piece of tomato. 'The beginning when it all looks perfect, that is the best part of a meal.'

The spaghetti sauce was bright with seafood and citrus, the artichokes tender except for a crunch of breadcrumbs; the salad tasted like summer. As Belle was eating, the large tabby cat continued to watch them unblinking and another cat, this one ginger, walked beneath the table and rubbed against her legs.

Belle kept noticing more and more cats in the *palazzo*. A white one had stalked through the vestibule that first afternoon when they were waiting for Pietro. A silver cat with dazzling green eyes had been in the kitchen the next morning. A fawn-coated kitten had mewled at her when she left her room today. She was fairly sure she hadn't seen the same one twice.

'Are they pets or strays?' she asked, as the ginger cat leaped up on the chair beside her.

'Both,' said Perla, glancing at the animal but not trying to shoo it away. 'They are rescued by Nonna Gilda. All of Ostuni knows she will care for them, and so they bring them here. Katarina is supposed to be trying to find them homes, but I think there are too many cats and not enough people who want them. And so, they stay.'

'How many are there?' asked Belle, astonished by this evidence of a softer side to the old Signora.

Perla shrugged. 'Who would know? They aren't meant to come inside, except the kitchen to be fed, but of course they always do and Nonna Gilda never stops them.'

Belle had never lived with an animal in the house before she met Ari. She had grown to love his old dog Waru, but hordes of cats she wasn't so sure about.

'Who feeds them?' she asked.

'Mostly Katarina. She puts on the flea treatment even though they scratch her, and she takes them to the vet if they are sick. Nonna Gilda says she is an angel,' Perla added with a roll of her eyes.

The ginger cat sprang from its chair onto Belle's knee, turned a circle, then settled down. She stroked it cautiously, in case it got the urge to bite or scratch, instead feeling the tremble of its purring beneath her fingers.

It was difficult to believe the old Signora had such a soft spot. Still here were all these rescued animals, proving that there was more to her than Belle had thought.

'Even Enrico doesn't know how many there are,' said Perla. 'Sometimes he complains and tells Nonna Gilda, *no more*, but she never listens.'

'She must really love cats.'

'If she doesn't save them, then who will? That is what Nonna Gilda says. But yes, I think perhaps she likes cats more than she likes people.'

'It is Katarina who does all the work though?' Somehow Belle wasn't surprised about that.

'She likes to be the angel, the one who takes care of everything, because then everyone admires her.' Perla sounded bitter. 'This is why she does so much charity work.'

'Weren't you meant to be helping with that today?' Belle asked, taking a sip of Prosecco.

'I am always meant to be helping.' Perla didn't bother trying to hide her resentment. 'This morning I had to put hundreds of invitations in envelopes. Katarina could email them, that would be faster. But no, she has to get them designed and printed then spend hours writing in them with her special pen and I am meant to be her assistant. I only escaped today because we had arranged to have lunch.'

Belle gave her a sidelong look. She didn't remember any lunch arrangement. 'Had we?'

'Well maybe not, but I had to say so otherwise I was going to die of boredom,' Perla complained. 'You don't want that do you?'

'It would be terrible,' Belle agreed, dryly.

'Besides, I couldn't leave you to lunch alone. You are a guest and it is my duty to look after you; that is what I told her.' Perla sounded pleased with herself. 'And so Katarina is still inside, writing invitations and being an angel. And we are out here, having a good time.'

'Will you go back and help her again later?' asked Belle.

Perla smiled at the idea. 'Definitely not. I wouldn't dream of it.'

Belle thought that Perla might be selfish but she couldn't help admiring her determination to rebel. In this household, ruled by tradition and the old Signora, it would take a certain strength to carry on living however you wanted.

Once they had finished eating, they moved to loungers beside the pool, Belle shaded by an olive tree, Perla soaking up the sun.

'It is good to relax,' she said, with a contented sigh, closing her eyes.

It wasn't long before Belle felt restless. She took a couple of dips in the pool and stroked a long-haired cat that walked by, leafed through an Italian fashion magazine, then was ready to move again. Judging by the gentle snuffling sounds, Perla definitely wasn't.

Belle considered trying to follow her example. But snoozing in the afternoon seemed a bad idea for someone still trying to adjust her body clock to a new time zone. Also those clothes were up in her room, waiting. Belle needed to unwrap them, take a look, maybe try a few things on and decide whether or not she would wear them.

'Perla?'

The younger woman groaned in reply.

'I need your help.'

'OK but not now, I am relaxing.'

'What if I told you there are some new clothes in my room.'

Perla's eyes snapped open. 'What clothes?'

'From the Casa di Ginaro range, for me to wear while I'm here.'

'Just a few?' Perla wanted to know. 'Or many?'

'Loads … a whole rack.'

Sitting up, Perla clapped her hands. 'Exciting!'

'I suppose so.' Belle felt a definite lack of excitement.

'What are we waiting for? Let's go and see them.'

In a frenzy, Perla tore off the garment bags, strewing them around the room, exclaiming in delight over most items and tutting her disapproval at a few.

She insisted Belle tried on every single garment. 'Many of these pieces I have never seen before. They must be samples of new designs.'

'What if they're not my style?' asked Belle.

'Then you find a way to wear them in your style,' decreed Perla, pausing to photograph Belle dressed in a loose linen top with bright butterflies embroidered on it. 'This one is perfect on you.'

Belle was resistant to the idea of surrendering to the Ginaro family's uniform. 'I don't know,' she said, staring into the mirror and seeing that the outfit did suit her.

'Nonna Gilda expects it,' Perla pointed out. 'Everybody in this family dresses in clothes from the collection. This is her rule. No one goes against it.'

'Never? Not even Enrico?' It seemed extraordinary that one frail woman could hold so much sway, and everybody accepted it was going to be that way. Maybe this was an Italian thing, respect for the older generation. Perhaps Enrico was the kind of guy who liked to keep his mother happy. Nonetheless, Belle found it strange.

'He may have but not while I have lived here.'

'Wouldn't you prefer to wear your own things?' she asked Perla. 'Be free to have your own style?'

'I look good in these clothes, don't I?' She stood beside Belle and assessed her reflection. 'Before, I couldn't afford to buy things like this; now I can have as many as I like. It is a dream come true.'

'You really love clothes,' observed Belle.

'Of course; don't you?'

'I like them, yes, but still I'm not sure about these.' Belle stared at the rail filled with garments.

'They are beautiful and they are free, so what is the problem?' asked Perla, sounding exasperated. 'And Nonna Gilda will be pleased. It is much better to do what she asks. Or at least make her think that you are.'

10

The Stars Are Different

Perla had torn through her room like a cyclone, scattering frocks, tops, trousers and garment bags. Once she left, Belle was faced with the prospect of tidying up. She started packing some of her own clothes into her suitcase, to make way for the new things that it seemed she would be wearing but, quickly losing heart, cleared a space to sit on the bed, and typed out a message to Greg.

> FaceTime later? Nothing serious, just some weird shit with the Italian royal family.

Greg would be sleeping still so Belle didn't expect to hear back from him but she felt better having sent the message. She needed to talk to someone from her own world before she got too lost in this one.

There was nothing wrong with the Casa di Ginaro clothes, they were stylish and well made. It was the feeling of giving up a part of herself that Belle chafed against. Her mother had changed so much to please another person. She still dyed her hair because Rod didn't think she should go grey. She learned to cook foods he loved but never ate much herself. Rod liked her to be slim, to wear shoes with heels and smart casuals. After he moved in with them Belle didn't think she ever again saw her mum dressed down in jeans.

So tonight, she might wear the butterfly top, paired with her own slouchy linen pants, but that didn't mean she was going to blend in with this family.

There was a discreet knock on the door and assuming it must be the maid, Belle called out for her to come in; then saw Katarina's face crease with a frown as she peered round and found the room in disarray.

'What happened here?' Katarina asked.

'Signora Ginaro has lent me a few things to wear and I was sorting through them.'

'I see.' Katarina seemed to be stifling a smile. 'May I help you?'

Without waiting for a response, she came in, tidying as she moved through the room. Garments were slipped back onto hangers and hung in the wardrobe in a colour-coordinated row or folded neatly into drawers. In no time at all order was restored.

'Perla and I got a bit over-excited opening things and trying them on,' explained Belle, feeling judged. 'I'm not normally quite that messy.'

'Oh, Perla was here,' said Katarina, as if that explained everything.

'She was helping,' said Belle. 'There are a lot of clothes.'

Katarina assessed the butterfly top that Belle was still wearing. 'This looks perfect on you. You are ready then? I came to fetch you. We are to meet a little earlier than usual this evening. Nonna Gilda wants us to gather in the salon for an *aperitivo*, although I am not sure why; it isn't usual.'

'I think she wants me to look at the plans for the display room,' Belle explained.

Katarina seemed taken aback. 'But why?'

'She thinks I might be able to help.'

'Why not ask me?'

'Perhaps she needs a fresh perspective,' suggested Belle.

'The display room was meant to be Luciana's project. I thought it had been forgotten about, that Nonna no longer cared about it.'

'Apparently she still cares,' said Belle, tying up her hair with a bright scarf, even if it was a mismatch with the butterfly top.

'I would have stepped in and taken over.' There was concern in Katarina's voice. 'I suppose she thought she couldn't ask any more of me.'

'You do seem very busy,' said Belle, wary of treading on her toes.

Katarina shrugged. 'Being pregnant saps my energy, especially now it is so hot.'

As she was speaking a cat came slinking through the door that had been left ajar. It stalked across the room and Belle watched it stop and stare around, as though seeking the most comfortable spot, before leaping onto the bed.

Katarina was quick to shoo it off and chase it out of the room. 'I am so sorry. They are not supposed to be inside, but what can I do?'

'It's fine,' said Belle, who didn't mind the cats too much, although it occurred to her that if they were semi-feral, they might not be house trained. 'Unless they are likely to pee everywhere?'

'We spray with peppermint oil to try and stop them.'

'Ah, that explains the minty smell. I thought it was some sort of cleaning product.'

'So long as that is all you can smell.' Katarina wrinkled her nose. 'Don't let them into your bedroom. There ought to be some boundaries.'

'Do they go into Signora Ginaro's room?' wondered Belle.

Tiredly, Katarina nodded. 'They are always in there. I make sure the housekeeper cleans and sprays with peppermint every day.'

Belle smoothed on a lipstick that was barely a shade brighter than her own lips. 'Now I am ready,' she confirmed.

'In that case come down and I will make you a gin and tonic or a Negroni, in fact, any cocktail you want within reason. When I was at university I worked in a bar.'

'Is that where you met Gianni?' asked Belle, following her out the room and shutting the door firmly behind her so no cats could invade.

'No, Gianni was a friend at university. We met at a party and from the beginning I knew we were right for each other.' Katarina's wan cheeks glowed faintly at the memory.

'That sounds romantic,' said Belle. 'I felt the same way about my husband Ari. Have you been together ever since?'

'We dated on and off for a while,' said Katarina, leading her down the stairs. 'It took Gianni a little longer to decide that I was right for him.'

In the salon, a drinks trolley had been set up. Belle decided on a Negroni and Katarina mixed it with the same quiet efficiency she had brought to tidying the messy room. She was almost too restrained, this young woman, and Belle wondered what it would take to get her to open up a little more.

'It must have been unnerving coming here for the first time to meet Gianni's family?' she ventured.

'Not really,' said Katarina. 'He made sure I knew what to expect and his parents were very kind.'

Passing the cocktail to Belle, she began to polish the remaining empty glasses with a soft cloth, even though they were already sparkling.

'There were signs that Luciana was unwell even then,' Katarina remembered. 'She kept calling me by the name of Gianni's previous girlfriend. And once she took me for a walk to show me round Ostuni and became so disoriented that I had to use Google maps to get us home. Luciana had lived in this town her whole life so at the time I thought it was strange, but I didn't understand what was happening.'

'It's easy to miss those earlier signs,' said Belle, having wilfully ignored them herself. 'Especially if you don't know a person well.'

'I hadn't known her long when she began to deteriorate.' Katarina set the sparkling glasses down in a row. 'We brought our wedding forward so she could attend and, of course, she never knew about the baby. She would have been a wonderful nonna.'

'I'm sure she would have been,' said Belle, picturing how it must have been when Luciana was still here, changing perceptibly day by day, slipping away from her family, becoming a stranger. 'How hard for you all.'

'Hard, yes,' Katarina frowned at the memory. 'Gianni refused to give up hope, spent hours and hours researching treatments, looking online, talking to so many different doctors, until in the end I think he knew as much as the doctors themselves but, of course, there was nothing to be done. He found that difficult to accept.'

Belle could imagine it. To give up wasn't the Ginaro way, as the Signora had told her that morning.

'Everyone struggled. Pietro was inconsolable, Enrico too, and I have never known Nonna Gilda to be like that ...' A door slammed and they heard the echo of male voices. Katarina's face lightened. 'They are home.'

Belle turned as Enrico came striding in, smiling at the sight of Katarina at the cocktail trolley. 'My daughter-in-law is making Negronis. This is going to be a good evening,' he declared to his sons, following close behind.

'It has been a long day,' said Gianni, shifting a cat that was nestling in some tasselled satin cushions so he could perch on an uncomfortable chair.

'Every day is long.' Pietro kicked off his shoes and stretched out on a gold-trimmed chaise longue. 'Except at the weekend.'

'This weekend we are going sailing,' Enrico reminded them. 'The whole family together.'

'Not the whole family because Perla won't come.' Pietro sounded certain. 'Nobody will get my wife onto a boat.'

'I won't come either,' said Katarina. 'I am sick enough on dry land, so I am very sorry but no.'

'I am sorry too, but I understand.' Enrico sounded disappointed. 'Perhaps Belle and I should go together, like last time.'

'No, no, we want to come,' Gianni assured him.

'We are looking forward to it,' agreed Pietro.

'I thought we might head north, towards Polignano a Mare and maybe stop somewhere to eat lunch. Or do we take a picnic? What do you think?'

'Whichever you want, Papa,' said Gianni.

'Isn't there a restaurant in a sea cave in Polignano a Mare?' asked Belle, who had seen enticing pictures when she was researching the area online. 'I suppose it's much too touristy though.'

'We can be tourists if you like,' Enrico told her. 'Why not? This is a free day and we can do whatever we like with it.'

Katarina was still mixing drinks when the old Signora made her entrance, rigorously lipsticked and powdered. Shaking her head at the offer of a cocktail, she unfurled a roll of papers she was carrying and set them down on a desk. 'My display room,' she announced. 'These are the plans that Luciana and I commissioned.'

At first Belle wasn't sure what she was looking at. The design seemed to be for a large room, divided into a series of smaller spaces.

'I'm sorry, but where is this exactly?' she asked.

'In the room that is presently my archive, of course' said the Signora, as though it was obvious.

'Down in the basement?' Belle couldn't conceal her

surprise. 'Why have a display room there? Who will be able to see it?'

'Our family, whenever we choose to visit,' said the Signora.

'But you said that Casa di Ginaro is important to the history of this town. Perhaps other people would like the chance to view your collection.'

The Signora looked nonplussed. Her forehead creased deeply. 'Other people?'

'I imagined that it would be like a gallery or museum, open to the public,' explained Belle. 'You would share the story of your family, display photographs of them and perhaps some of yourself wearing the items that are on show.'

'And let strangers enter our building and roam around the basement?'

'Couldn't it be in the foyer of the Casa di Ginaro building? Just a few display cases, and you would change the exhibits every week.'

'Things would get damaged,' the Signora argued. 'The light ... the air.'

'No, no,' Belle reassured her. 'You can use UV blocking glass and control the temperature in each display case.'

'Who will change the exhibits each week?' The Signora seemed determined to find objections. 'That girl on reception can't be trusted even to arrange a few magazines on a table.'

'I will do it,' offered Katarina.

The Signora sank down on a couch, absent-mindedly stroking the cat that climbed immediately onto her lap. 'You are an angel, *cara* but you do so much already.'

Enrico had shrugged off his light linen jacket, thrown it over a chair, and rolled up his sleeves. 'I think we should consider this idea,' he said. 'There is enough space in the foyer, and it would be nice for the staff to see the collection every day as they go in and out.'

'We already have these plans.' His mother wasn't easily won over. 'It was how Luciana thought it should be done.'

Belle stayed quiet. She didn't want to be seen as challenging the wishes of Enrico's late wife. It wasn't her business what they did with the archive and possibly she had said too much already.

'Why not give it some thought?' suggested Enrico, weighing in on her side again. 'Nothing is set in stone. The plans can be re-done.'

'The foyer ... I don't know,' his mother murmured, carefully rolling up her documents.

'I like the idea,' said Enrico. 'Actually, I have often thought that we should do something similar.'

His mother glared at him. 'You never said so.'

He shrugged. 'It was your and Luciana's project. I didn't want to interfere.'

'You believed she and I were doing things the wrong way?' The old Signora bristled.

'Mamma, there is no wrong or right, only different ideas that are worth considering and what Belle has suggested makes sense to me.'

The atmosphere in the room felt charged by more than Negronis. The others had fallen silent, and Belle saw them exchanging glances.

'I am very glad you have told me this, Enrico.' The old Signora sounded anything but. 'And I will consider it of course.'

After that the conversation shifted as they sipped their Negronis. They talked about fabric shortages and staff changes, problems with deliveries and glitches with the website. Sometimes they spoke in Italian, and their voices were raised as though they were disagreeing. If the Signora offered an opinion, they fell silent and listened.

Then Enrico put down his half-finished drink and helped his mother up. Arm in arm, they moved towards the dining room, the others following, as if there had been some signal that Belle had missed to say it was time to eat.

Everyone took their customary seats at the table and waited for Perla who came rushing in late, talking on her phone, hurriedly slipping it in a pocket when the Signora glared at her. She didn't apologise or offer any excuse, merely said, 'I suppose it is seafood tonight?' and wrinkled her nose.

The Signora nodded and, as Perla sat down, her expression was long-suffering.

A feast of seafood followed. Belle tasted raw fish singing with fresh lime, smelled the earthy tang of black garlic in a bowl of spaghetti and clams, then savoured tender flakes of sea bass with crisped Senise peppers that filled her mouth with sweet smokiness.

'On a Wednesday we always eat like this,' Katarina told Belle, picking disinterestedly around the edges of her plate.

'Mamma's favourite,' added Gianni. 'She loved seafood. She looked forward to Wednesdays.'

'On her birthday, we would have lobster,' said Pietro. 'Always, every year. At the restaurant by the tower in Miramare da Michele.'

'My husband loved seafood,' said Belle, who with every piquant bite of the white fish *crudo* and every tender flake of sea bass thought how much Ari would have relished this meal. 'One of his cousins goes kite fishing off the beach near our home and quite often would drop us off a feed of snapper.'

'You must have a good life in New Zealand,' remarked Gianni, warming very slightly. 'They say it is beautiful. I plan to see it some day, when life is not so busy. Katarina and I will tour where *The Lord of the Rings* was filmed.'

Enrico shot a look at his elder son. 'You never told me this is something that you wanted.'

Gianni gave an expressive shrug. 'It is on my list of places to visit.'

'What else is on this list?' his father wanted to know.

'We are planning to go to Disneyland; the one in Florida,

when our children are old enough to enjoy it,' Gianni told him.

'Perhaps you should travel somewhere now, before the baby arrives?' Enrico suggested. 'Take this opportunity while you have it.'

Belle wondered if he was thinking about the trips he and Luciana had hoped to take and how he regretted missing out on them. Perhaps he didn't want his son to have the same regrets.

'They call it a babymoon,' she put in. 'Lots of couples take them, apparently.'

'A babymoon?' Gianni sounded amused. 'I have too much happening at work and Katarina is busy too. In August we will go to the villa as usual. The list can wait.'

Belle had never bothered making lists. She found life more interesting if she let opportunities open up then decided whether to take them. That attitude had brought her and Ari together; it had carried her all the way here. Again she felt the differences between her and this family, and the distance dividing her from Enrico, even now with them in the same room.

'Do you have one of these lists also?' he asked his younger son.

Pietro glanced at Perla. 'I don't know, do we?'

His wife glanced back at him, with a quick raise of her eyebrows. 'Everyone has plans, don't they?' she said, without elaborating.

As soon as dinner was finished, the Signora retired to her room. Belle imagined her up there watching television in bed, with cats curled on her covers. It made her more likeable, this unexpected love of animals; still Belle couldn't help noticing that whenever she left a room, the atmosphere seemed to lighten.

Without her there Gianni seemed less stern and Katarina

not as guarded. Pietro started larking about, making his father smile, and Perla pulled out her phone, checking for anything she may have missed over dinner. It was as if everyone felt free to be themselves again.

'Papa, this evening shall we drink our *digestivo* in a bar?' Perla suggested. 'Instead of in the garden?'

'A bar, why not?' agreed Enrico. 'It will make a change.'

Together, trooping through the cooler evening air, they discussed the places they preferred. There was a debate about which bar had the best gelato and where Katarina might find a hot chocolate. At Perla's urging they plunged into the maze of lanes leading to the oldest part of town. She took them to a bar hidden in a narrow street, with beanbags for seating, dark corners lit by flickering candles and the insistent beat of the sort of music Belle didn't normally listen to.

Not long after they sat down, groups of her friends began to appear. It was much the same crowd she remembered from her first day in Ostuni. Again Perla and Pietro seemed like king and queen of their own little court, only now Enrico was here too, in charge of ordering the drinks for this young and glamorous set. He knew their names, kept glasses topped up and was, thought Belle, an easy host.

'It is good to see Signor Ginaro with a smile on his face,' said a voice in English, and Belle looked up to find Mia, wearing a scarlet dress so short that it exposed a large and colourful butterfly tattooed on her upper thigh.

'We match,' said Belle, touching the butterflies embroidered on her top.

'I love it,' Mia sat down beside her, reaching for an espresso Martini from the tray-load that had been delivered to their table, then leaning in closer, touching the fabric. 'This one is from the new collection, yes? We don't have it in the shop yet.'

'How are things going there?' wondered Belle.

Mia's expression was pained.

'That bad?'

'I tried asking Gianni again if I could transfer to another city, but no it is impossible,' said Mia, raising her voice to be heard above the music, which suddenly seemed a notch or two noisier. 'There are no openings and he cannot say when there might be.'

She looked like a child dressed in her older sister's clothes, sipping her mother's drink, vulnerable and very young. Belle wished she could offer some useful advice. It was tough to be at the start of your life and yet not know how to get it started. She had been that way herself; she was again now.

'I'm sure something will come up.' Even to her own ears, the words sounded lame.

'I hope so because that shop is so boring and I don't think ...' Mia paused and looked more closely at Belle, eyes narrowing. 'What has happened with your make-up?'

Belle hadn't defined her eyes and shaded her face. There hadn't been time, and besides she couldn't be bothered.

'Not even a little lipstick?' Mia sounded disappointed.

'I put some on earlier, but it must have worn off. Does it matter?'

'It matters,' Mia put down her drink. 'Come with me, we will fix this.'

'Actually no ...' Belle began, because she didn't need more making over.

'Please,' Mia appealed. 'It won't take long and we can talk in the bathroom; it won't be as loud there.'

Her beanbag was so low and squishy that Belle needed a hand to climb out of it and Mia held onto her as they weaved past candlelit tables filled with groups of well-dressed people.

'This place is so expensive,' she told Belle. 'We wouldn't come here normally but Perla knows that Signor Ginaro will pay the bill so she is taking advantage. All those cocktails, it will cost what I earn in a week.'

In the bathroom at least the thump of the music was dulled. Belle leaned on the edge of the sink as Mia began unpacking a surprisingly large amount of cosmetics from her small, blingy bag.

'One day I will come to the *palazzo* and show you how to do this. You may need to buy a few things; I will tell you what, OK?' she said, setting to work.

'How do you know so much about make-up?' Belle wondered.

'YouTube, of course,' Mia said, as if it was obvious. 'I watch it and then practise on my own face. It is good to try with someone else for a change. I made you look prettier last time, didn't I?'

'You did,' agreed Belle.

Other women came in and out to use the toilets. Some chatted with Mia about the products she was using, as they reapplied their own lipstick and teased their hair. Even if they had been speaking English, Belle suspected it would have sounded like a foreign language to her. Apparently thanks to YouTube, these girls were experts in grooming.

'Have you ever thought about doing this for a living?' she asked, as Mia applied liner to her eyelids with a steady hand.

'You mean in a shop like Sephora?'

'I was thinking more as a hair and make-up artist in magazines or the film industry.'

Mia began lengthening her lashes with a curved mascara wand. 'Everything is about who you know, and I don't know anyone.'

'But you know me and that's what I used to do, work on movies.'

'Seriously?' Mia paused. 'With famous people?'

Belle nodded. 'Sometimes, yes.'

'Then who?'

She listed a few names that the younger woman might have heard of and at the mention of a couple, she looked semi-impressed. 'I didn't do their hair and make-up though,' Belle said.

Mia laughed at that. 'Thankfully.'

'But I do have some contacts so I could find out about the best courses to apply for … if you'd like me to.' Belle didn't want to seem pushy.

Mia was dusting shimmering powder onto her cheeks. She met Belle's eyes in the mirror. 'You would do that for me?'

'Of course,' Belle told her. 'I didn't manage to get a job in the film industry without someone helping me.'

'So they would pay me for playing with make-up.' Mia sounded entranced by the idea.

'It's more hard work than glamour,' Belle warned her. 'But you have talent so it's worth a try.'

'You think I have talent? No one has ever said that before. Always I am the one who is bad at everything.'

'You're not bad at this.' Belle examined herself in the mirror and saw that again she had been transformed into a more glamorous version of herself, flaws smoothed and corrected. 'I expect you'd learn to do special effects make-up too.'

Mia made a squeaking sound. 'That would be so cool.'

'Let me see what I can find out.'

By the time they made it back to the table, Gianni and Katarina had gone home and the tray had been emptied of espresso Martinis. Even Perla had one in her hand which seemed unwise since she was pregnant, but it was hardly up to Belle to say so. She found Enrico sitting as far as possible from the speakers, that were relentlessly pumping out music, and she sank into the beanbag beside him.

'You disappeared,' he said. 'I thought you might have left with Gianni.'

'Mia has been beautifying me,' Belle explained. 'Apparently despite my great age, I am clueless when it comes to applying make-up.'

Enrico laughed. 'Maybe that is because you don't really need to wear any?'

'Mia would disagree. She's going to come and give me a lesson.'

'You don't mind?'

'Not really, she's fun.'

'These young people.' Enrico looked around at them. 'They are so different to the way I remember myself at their age.'

'What were you like?' Belle was curious.

'Less sophisticated, not as confident, and like Gianni I took life very seriously.'

Belle looked round at the slim-hipped, floppy-haired boys and scantily-clad girls. Most likely, like Mia, none of them were as confident as they seemed.

'At that age my future was already carved out,' Enrico continued. 'The *palazzo*, the business, even my marriage really because I met Luciana when we were very young.'

Belle wished she had encountered Ari much earlier. All the time she was dating other men, he had been out there. She felt cheated of the years they could have spent together.

'I envy them, with so much life ahead, so much possibility,' admitted Enrico. 'They must see me as very old. Since I lost Luciana, it is often how I see myself.'

Belle hadn't heard him talk that way before, although many times, when they were chatting on Zoom, he had seemed sad and lonely.

'I keep asking, have I had the very best of life already?' Enrico paused, as though trying to shake off his bleaker thoughts, then apologised. 'Here we are together, out having a good time, and I am spoiling it.'

'No, you're not,' Belle reassured him.

'I have hardly seen you since you arrived. It should have been possible for me to escape work. Normally Gianni is happy to take over but this week he seems to need my help. I have neglected you.'

'It's been fine,' Belle assured him. 'Perla and Katarina have been looking after me.'

In one corner a DJ was setting up his decks and it seemed like the bar was about to get even noisier.

'Would you like another drink?' asked Enrico. 'Or shall we leave the young people to their party?'

'Let's head home,' said Belle, preparing to haul herself out of the beanbag again. 'This place is starting to make me feel old too.'

They slipped away unnoticed by Perla and Pietro, who were up and dancing. It was a relief to be out in the quiet, dark streets where the white stone buildings were glowing in the moonlight.

'Ostuni is pretty at night; a fairy-tale town,' Belle remarked.

'You are glad you came?' asked Enrico. 'Being in Italy is helping?'

Belle could have lied, given him a polite *yes, thank you*. But she had always been honest with him.

'I miss Ari in a different way here. At home I see him everywhere and there is a reminder of him in everything I do. It's like a thousand sharp pinpricks of grief every day.'

'I know that feeling,' he murmured.

'Here I get distracted for a while, then suddenly it comes back, like a wave crashing over me, so much sadness.'

'In time those waves might become smaller and the gaps between them longer,' said Enrico.

'I'll never stop missing Ari though,' she said with certainty.

'I don't think that you would want to.'

'You're right,' Belle realised. 'I would hate to stop missing him.'

They were nearing the *palazzo* now and Belle wasn't ready to go inside. She wanted to delay the moment, keep walking and talking, and make the most of having time alone with him.

'It's such a lovely evening,' she began.

'But it is late,' Enrico replied. 'And I have an early start.'

Just as they reached the *palazzo*, he stopped her. 'You are right, this is a beautiful night. We should make the most of it.'

And so they walked on through empty streets, their footsteps echoing, until Belle was hopelessly lost, finally emerging onto the town's ramparts and looking out over a view of bright lights in an inky black sky.

'The stars are different here,' said Belle, tilting her head. 'It's a reminder of how far from home I am.'

'I hope that soon you will feel at home,' said Enrico.

Belle hesitated, then reminded herself this was her friend and she could be open with him. 'Your sons, are you sure they don't mind me staying with you?'

The question seemed to surprise him. 'Why would they mind?'

'Our friendship ... how we met ... they might not really understand ...'

'Young people meet each online all the time,' he pointed out.

'But they don't expect us to act the same way they do. To them we are old, remember.'

'Even old people need friends,' said Enrico, lightly. 'And my sons are very happy to have a guest. Tomorrow Gianni has suggested taking you with him to Lecce. We have a shop there and he needs to drop by, so you can take a look around the city. Then on Friday Pietro is hoping to spend a morning with you in Alberobello. And at the weekend we will all go sailing together, as planned.'

There was no one else in sight, only Belle and Enrico walking the wide stone-flagged avenue that curved round the edge of the town. She wondered if moments like this one were what his sons were trying to avoid. Was Gianni taking her to Lecce because he wanted her company? Did Pietro long for the chance to go sightseeing with her? Perhaps she was being uncharitable, but what if actually they were doing their very best to occupy her time so she didn't spend it with their father?

Turning to walk back through streets washed by moonlight, Belle remained uncomfortably aware that his sons might not be quite so pleased as Enrico imagined.

11

Too Many Cats

Wandering through the streets of Ostuni late at night with Enrico, she had missed two calls from Greg. By the time they got back to the *palazzo* Belle only wanted to collapse into bed and fall unconscious. Greg must have been on her mind though, because she had strange anxious dreams about him. As soon as she opened her eyes, she reached for her phone.

'Ah, Princess Belle,' Greg said, answering her FaceTime call.

'Queen Belle actually.'

'Did you just wake up?' He raised a wine glass. 'I'm having a much-needed drink.'

'Drinking alone?' That wasn't like him. 'Why?'

'I'll share my news once you've told me yours. What's going on?'

'Nothing major really.' Easing out of bed, Belle turned her phone towards the wardrobe so he could see the rail of clothes. 'They've lent me all this stuff and I'm expected to wear it. My own things aren't on brand apparently.'

'They look nice though,' said Greg. 'Are they?'

'Yes, they're gorgeous.' Belle pulled out a couple of frocks and a jacket, holding them up so he could see. 'Wildly expensive.'

'And the problem is?'

'I don't know.' Belle flopped down on her bed again,

leaning back on the pillows. 'It feels as though they're trying to take me over. And I don't like it. Tell me I'm being ridiculous.'

For a moment all she could see was a part of his ear. She heard a sound that must have been Greg topping up his glass then he came back into view. 'You're being ridiculous.'

'Should I get over myself then?' she asked. 'Wear all this stuff?'

'To me it seems the easier option. But then I wouldn't say no to fancy free clothes right now.'

That wasn't like him either, thought Belle. When he wasn't wearing jodhpurs, Greg lived in checked shirts and denim.

'Why the sudden desire to update your wardrobe?'

'I can't go out on a date looking this rough, can I?'

'You're dating again?' Belle was pleased. 'Tell me everything.'

'There isn't much to say. So far I've just had one boring coffee date.'

After his boyfriend walked out, Greg had been heartbroken. Belle recalled how worried Ari had been and wished there was some way he could know that his friend had turned a corner.

'Time for me to get back out there though,' Greg told her. 'I'm ready.'

'That's great. It's been a while, after all.'

'What about you?' he surprised her by asking. 'Ari wouldn't have expected you to be on your own forever, you know.'

She looked away from the screen, not replying.

'Belle?' he pushed, gently.

'I'm not ready,' she said, still not meeting his eyes. 'It's too soon.'

'It's more than two years.'

'I don't need reminding,' she said, sharply.

'All I'm saying is that Ari wanted you to be happy.'

'I know that.'

Belle wished people wouldn't keep on making assumptions. She knew that Greg meant well, but to think about being with anyone but Ari felt like a disloyalty. She couldn't replace him in her life; she didn't want to.

Saying goodbye, getting Greg off the phone as quickly as she could, Belle braced herself against another wave of sadness. Perhaps two years was a long time but it never felt it. And they had been two strange years of lockdowns and loneliness, of being at home but feeling lost, of needing what she couldn't have. Two years from now would Belle feel any different than she did right now? She couldn't imagine it. She couldn't even say where she would be by then.

Right now, she was here with plans for the day ahead. She was going on a trip to Lecce with Gianni. Maybe this would be a chance to get to know him better, find out what kind of man lay behind that solemn exterior. Perhaps Belle would warm to him more than she had already. If she was going to stay with this family, then she needed to make the effort.

Climbing out of bed, she approached the cavernous wardrobe, and stared inside at all those beautiful clothes.

'Oh, stuff it,' she said to herself, pulling out a dress patterned in a bold print of oranges and lemons, and tossing it on the bed. 'I'll wear the damn things.'

Still she reached for Ari's greenstone pendant and slipped it on beneath the fabric, feeling it warm against her skin.

Downstairs she found Gianni in the kitchen, watching Katarina feeding a small cluster of cats that were milling round her legs.

'Good morning,' said Belle, picking her way between them towards the coffee pot. 'I hear we are heading to Lecce today?'

'I need to go for work and thought you might like to come along,' said Gianni, a little brusquely.

'It is such a lovely city,' added Katarina more warmly, as

she scooped kibble into a row of bowls, the cats purring and mewling around her. 'The history, the architecture, I adore it.'

'Are you coming too?' asked Belle, hoping so as she helped herself to some fruit from the food that had been left out.

'I don't feel too well and besides there is too much to be done here.'

'Couldn't you take a day off?' Belle suggested. One day this young woman was going to become the matriarch of this *palazzo*; she would be the old Signora who made the rules, but right now her life seemed mostly hard work and duty.

'I have to find homes for some of these cats.' Katarina cast an exasperated look at the animals that were crowding round their feed bowls now. 'Perla is meant to be helping me take photographs and post them online but ...'

'She must have had a late night,' said Belle. 'Why don't I stay and help?'

'You can't miss a chance to see Lecce.'

'Tomorrow then? Honestly, I'm happy to give you a hand. This seems like a lot of cats for one person to handle.'

'Too many cats,' said Katarina, grimly.

Belle had expected to be whisked off to Lecce by Enrico's driver but instead Gianni led her through the garden, down some steps and to a gate set in the wall. Behind it was the small garage that housed his sporty low-slung Maserati, a gleaming white car he was clearly proud of.

'A twenty-first birthday gift from my father,' he told Belle. 'I expect he will give the same to Pietro.'

Belle tried to recall what she had been given when she turned twenty-one. Perhaps a cheque so that she could buy whatever she wanted. There certainly hadn't been much fuss made.

'What a lovely gift,' she said, sliding into the plush red leather passenger seat.

'My father is very generous,' Gianni told her, starting the car and letting the engine purr, before backing out of the garage carefully.

On the drive along the *autostrada* to Lecce, he questioned Belle about her business. How long had she been running a gallery? What sort of art did she sell there? Did business tend to be good?

'It's a very small place,' she told him.

'But you could expand?'

'I suppose so if I wanted, but I don't have any plans.'

'You don't want to grow?' He shot a sideways glance at her. 'Why not?'

'It's fine the way it is.'

Gianni seemed to be digesting that, as the car flashed by olive groves and glimpses of the sea. Then he asked, 'Who is looking after your business while you are here?'

'No one; I've closed the gallery, at least for the time being,' said Belle. 'It's never very busy over winter anyway.'

'You have stopped trading? Completely?' He sounded concerned.

'Yes, I may open it up again, or I might not. I'm taking some time to decide exactly what I want.' Belle knew she was fortunate. She had savings to live on and the house was mortgage-free. Lots of people weren't in the position for this sort of breathing space.

Gianni drew the obvious conclusion. 'You are thinking it is time for you to retire?'

Belle definitely couldn't afford that. 'No, I need to do something, I'm just not sure what.'

'You have no idea what the future holds?'

'Not really,' said Belle.

'No plans at all?' His voice had an odd note, and Belle thought he seemed to be struggling with the idea.

'The plan is to spend the summer here, and figure it out,' she explained.

'That doesn't seem much of a plan to me.'

They continued for the next kilometre or so in silence. Gianni put his foot down and she heard the rumble of the Maserati's engine. He drove fast, like everyone here, but wasn't a reckless driver. And when he spoke again, Belle could tell that his mind had been occupied by their earlier conversation.

'Do you have goals?' he wanted to know. 'Not only for work, for your life?'

'Only to be happy.' Glancing at his face, Belle saw that he was frowning. 'Isn't that what everyone wants?'

'But happiness takes work. Like everything else, it needs planning.'

'How do you plan happiness?' Belle wanted to know.

'I have created a goal matrix,' Gianni explained, with more enthusiasm than she was used to hearing in his voice. 'It has headings for work/life balance, relationships, business aims, personal development, the type of leader I want to be, and I review it every six months.'

'A matrix?' said Belle, who had never heard of such a thing.

'Yes.' He was warming to his theme. 'For example, my work goal has been to learn about every aspect of the business, so when I take over, I will understand it inside out.'

'Do you plan your personal life too?'

'Of course. I aim to have a large family and for that I had the goal of finding the right wife. It is a matrix; it all fits together.'

'It doesn't sound very romantic,' observed Belle. 'What about love, surely that played a part?'

'Yes, but it was important to love the sort of woman who would fit in with my family and that we wanted the same things, so our marriage would be happy.'

'You always have a strategy.'

'Always,' he agreed.

'What if something unexpected happens?'

'Then I have to review the strategy,' said Gianni, as though it was obvious.

Was this truly what Enrico had been like at the same age, wondered Belle. He had said so but she couldn't imagine it. Gianni was burdened with staggering amounts of certainty. Life might dent that as he went along, suffering failures and disappointments like everyone did. He was bound to change to some degree. Even so, in his fifties would he be the type of man his father was? Somehow, Belle doubted it.

In Lecce they valet-parked the flashy car at a hotel and went their separate ways: Gianni to the shop where, apparently, he had some sort of staffing issue; Belle to walk streets filled with buildings carved from soft golden limestone.

She wandered past a long parade of shops then turned a corner and unexpectedly came across an immense basilica. She then strolled along narrow, stone-flagged streets that opened up to reveal more glorious baroque churches. Belle peered into the entrance courtyards of palatial buildings and wondered what sort of people lived there, looked up one moment at intricately carved stone statues, and the next at washing hanging from balconies overhead.

She loved exploring like this, soaking in the sights, with no list of must-sees dictating where she went, no guide book filled with facts and figures, just another corner then another, and the surprise of what lay around them.

When she was tired and hot, she stopped at a bar, escaping the sun at a shady table beneath some trees at the centre of an elegant piazza. The waiter suggested a Caffè Leccese and Belle said yes, even though she had no idea what that might be. An iced coffee arrived, sweetly spiked with almond milk syrup, and sipping it Belle gazed at the ornate façade of the church that dominated one whole side of the piazza. She listened to Italian voices, and smelled old stone warmed by dry heat. It might mean another hour stuck in a car with Gianni, still she was glad to have come here.

They had arranged to meet at a café near the Casa di Ginaro shop. Apparently, it was famous for its *pucce*, which Belle discovered was a local street food. Sourdough flatbreads, baked crisp and stuffed with whatever she might want. Fontina cheese melting over roasted cherry tomatoes, little balls of aubergine with mint, sweet caramelised onions, thin leaves of cured meat. After her long walk, Belle was ready to eat, biting into the sour crust hungrily, tasting smokiness from the wood-fired oven and the richness of *capocollo* salami, savouring the creamy cheese and the sharp bite of mint.

Gianni seemed distracted as he ate, studying his phone and sighing. 'Just as I fix one thing, another comes along,' he muttered, throwing down the phone. 'I need to get back. There is a problem at the shop in Ostuni.'

'The one that Mia works in?'

'Used to work in.' Gianni was obviously exasperated. 'Apparently she has walked out. Mia is a friend and this was a good opportunity for her but she is unhappy because I wouldn't transfer her to the shop in Rome. I told her to be patient, but no.'

'I suppose she has goals,' Belle couldn't help saying, although she hoped that Mia hadn't been too hasty.

Gianni drove faster on the way home, the engine roaring as he sped along. They weren't even halfway through the journey, when he cleared his throat.

'My father ...' he began, his tone level and brisk. 'He has had a very difficult time.'

'I know that,' said Belle, already tensing.

'My mother was everything to him. Her loss is something he will never recover from.'

'I understand,' Belle assured him. 'Absolutely.'

'Papa is a very kind man. Generous with everyone, not only his sons. If he can help another person, then he will. Sometimes they take the wrong message from this.'

Belle couldn't blame this young man for being protective of their father. But she needed Gianni to understand that she wasn't there to take advantage.

'Enrico has been very kind to me. A good friend ...' she began, reaching for the right words.

'He is a good friend to many people.' Gianni was gripping the steering wheel, his face stony and Belle realised that a person who always had a goal in mind was going to find it difficult to believe she almost never had one. A young man with a matrix wouldn't understand an older woman who was drifting through life. Trapped next to him in the passenger seat of the low-slung car, suddenly there didn't seem enough air to breathe.

'What Enrico and I have is purely a friendship, I need to make that very clear.' Every time Belle said the words, they seemed to sound less convincing. 'It's all we want from each other.'

'A friendship,' Gianni repeated, and she sensed that he wasn't convinced.

'I lost someone too,' Belle reminded him. 'My husband.'

'I know that and I am very sorry for your loss,' said Gianni, automatically, making Belle grit her teeth.

'Thank you,' she forced out.

It wasn't difficult to see how the situation could be mis-read. Here was a woman who had met a wealthy man online. She flew from the other side of the world, closing her business, and abandoning her life. It wasn't unreasonable to assume that surely, she must want something.

'I came here to escape,' she told Gianni, because it was the truth. 'Home was so sad. You must know how that feels?'

He nodded, but said nothing.

'I don't have any other plan in mind,' she promised. 'Not a single one.'

Gianni glanced away from the road, briefly meeting her gaze. 'I can help with that.'

'A goal matrix?' she asked, half-joking.

He was staring at the road again. 'For you, an action plan.'

That was when Belle knew for sure that she and Gianni would never understand each other.

Once he had dropped her off at the *palazzo*, Gianni went to the office for the rest of the afternoon. Belle's relief at getting away from him felt almost physical, a heaviness lifting from her shoulders. Hopefully he would feel that his duty was done and he didn't need to spend more time with her.

She let herself into the *palazzo* with the key that had been provided, still feeling a bit like an intruder. The place was silent and seemed empty. Presumably the Signora was upstairs taking her afternoon rest and Katarina was at her desk busy with charity work. It seemed that Belle had the remainder of the afternoon to herself and a sudden sense of freedom made her feel lighter still.

She might go back to the cathedral while she had the chance or fritter away time people-watching outside a bar. First though, she headed downstairs to the kitchen for a glass of water.

Katarina was there, sitting at one end of the long table, head sunk in her hands. She startled when Belle came in.

'You're back,' she said, straightening. 'I didn't hear the door.'

'Is everything OK?' Belle asked.

'Yes,' Katarina replied, then slumped in her seat again. 'No, not really. The cats are driving me crazy.'

There were scratches on her arms and Belle noticed they looked raised and red; very new. 'Photographing them didn't go well?' she guessed.

'It is impossible. I think they prefer not to be adopted. Life here is too good.'

'I imagine it's difficult to make a cat do anything if it doesn't want to,' said Belle, who'd never had one herself, but had shared flats in places where people did.

'They are a nightmare,' replied Katarina. 'At this rate I will never find homes for any of them.'

There wasn't a cat to be seen in the kitchen, only the pervasive scent of peppermint as a reminder this was where they had been.

'When you want them, they are gone. If you try to bribe them with food, they won't eat. I hate cats,' said Katarina, then she shook her head. 'Please don't tell Nonna Gilda I said that.'

'It seems unfair that you are the one who has to deal with them all,' said Belle, taking a glass from the cupboard and filling it with water.

'Who else will do it?'

'I offered to help and I meant it,' said Belle, dismissing the idea of a relaxing few hours alone. 'I'm sure if we go hunting then we'll find some cats.'

'You don't mind?' asked Katarina, sounding more hopeful.

'It might even be fun.'

She gave a hollow laugh. 'I doubt it.'

Belle might not know much about cats but when Katarina explained how she had been going about the process, even she could see what had gone wrong. Surely you couldn't expect any animal to pose in front of a backdrop, be still and look photogenic. No matter how organised a person you were, and how clear the plan you had in mind, the cats weren't likely to co-operate.

'We should try sneaking up on them,' Belle suggested to Katarina. 'Take a photograph while they're sleeping in the sunshine or stalking through the grass.'

'That won't look right,' she tried to argue. 'I need the

exact same background for every shot, so the page on the adoption website looks tidy.'

They were suited to each other, this girl and Gianni, with their love of order and planning. Belle could imagine how they would go through life together, trying to keep everything under control. Maybe it was what they needed to be happy, but it wasn't going to work right now.

'Let's try it my way for a bit,' she suggested.

'OK,' Katarina agreed, reluctantly.

They started in the gardens because some of the cats were always hanging about there. Sure enough, as they moved along its pathways, they found a black cat curled up inside a wide stone urn on a plinth. A handsome long-haired ginger was asleep on one of the loungers beside the pool. A tabby was hunting lizards on a wall. Some cats fled before they could take a shot, but others stared unblinking into the camera.

When they sat down, a few came closer, slinking out of the shadows of the loggia, rubbing round their legs and purring when Belle stroked them.

'You are a cat whisperer,' said Katarina, photographing a marmalade-coloured one that had sprung up onto Belle's lap.

She stroked its soft, warm fur for a moment, then lifted it back down to the ground. 'Surely we have enough photographs for your website by now?'

'Enough pictures yes, but we need words to go with them. Descriptions of their different personalities.'

'Do cats have different personalities?' Belle wasn't convinced. 'And if they do, how will we know what they are?'

They both watched the marmalade cat prowling around Belle, eyeing her knee, as though considering another leap upwards.

'That one seems friendly,' said Katarina. 'The others, I don't know. Still, we need to make them sound like animals people will want to own.'

Katarina worked in the music room, surrounded by guitars propped on walls, old violin cases, a dusty French horn and the even dustier baby grand piano, all instruments that no one ever played anymore. Her desk was clean and orderly though. There were no random piles of paper or books, no spare hair ties or dirty coffee cups, just a computer, a fresh notepad and a single pen.

She brought over another chair so Belle could sit beside her. Then they loaded up the pictures and tried to compose captions, finding ways to describe each stray.

'I think this black cat looks lazy and sweet,' decided Belle.

'That is the one that scratched me,' Katarina pointed out.

'OK, what about lively and full of fun?'

Katarina giggled, and started typing, translating Belle's words into Italian. 'The tabby might be quite sweet. I am pretty sure it has never tried to attack me.'

Belle sensed problems lay ahead for the adoption plan. If someone chose a cat then it would need to be found and somehow constrained until the person came to fetch it. That was assuming there were many potential new homes for these semi-feral creatures. She didn't mention her misgivings to Katarina.

'You mustn't tell Nonna Gilda that I am doing this,' the young woman confided now, clicking on a picture of the long-haired ginger.

'She doesn't know yet?' Belle was surprised.

'I couldn't mention it. What if she refused to let me? It is easier this way.'

'She may notice some are gone though.'

'No, no I won't touch her favourites. And Nonna Gilda will keep finding new cats, so it won't matter if some of the old ones are no longer here.'

'I won't say anything,' Belle promised, and was rewarded with the trace of a smile.

She was starting to see glimpses of the real Katarina, the person behind the barriers she had put up.

'Is there anything else I can help you with?'

'Maybe there is . . .' Katarina paused, then asked tentatively. 'Could you help me with Perla?'

'Perla, how?' Belle hadn't expected that.

'You are her friend, she likes you. But she doesn't like me,' Katarina said, flatly. 'She seems determined not to. And it is starting to cause problems for Gianni and Pietro.'

Belle hadn't missed the tension between the two. 'That's awful, but I'm not sure what I can do.'

Katarina shut down her laptop and closed the lid. Again, she seemed to be choosing her words carefully. 'I have tried with Perla. When she first came here, I did my best to help her fit in and learn to be a part of this family. But she wasn't interested. Today it should have been her helping me.'

'Perhaps she had other things to do,' offered Belle, although she suspected those things might have been enjoying a long lunch and an easy day.

'Perla likes having the Ginaro name, she enjoys all of this.' Katarina nodded towards the frescoed walls of the music room. 'But she doesn't understand that it takes work to be a part of it. All of us do so much, while she does nothing.'

Belle wasn't entirely without sympathy for Perla. Surely, she had a right to lead the life she wanted.

'The problem may be that she isn't interested in your charity work,' she explained, trying to be tactful. 'Perla does love fashion though. That's why I suggested she might help with the display room. But Signora Ginaro didn't seem to like that idea . . . or any of my ideas, in fact.'

'I liked your idea for the archive,' Katarina told her. 'It makes sense to have it exhibited in the foyer.'

'You didn't say so at the time.'

'No.' Katarina straightened her laptop on the desk, and placed the pen and notebook squarely beside it.

'Why not?' Belle wanted to know.

'It wasn't my place.'

'You are Gianni's wife. Surely you're entitled to say what you think.'

'That is not how it works in this family,' said Katarina.

After getting on so well all afternoon, it would be a shame to end on a disagreement. But Belle was concerned that Katarina believed she had to be passive. This was Italy, not the Dark Ages.

'In that case perhaps this family needs to change,' she said, and instantly Katarina's barriers were back up.

'You are a stranger here,' she said, tightly. 'You don't understand how things are done.'

'True,' conceded Belle, who had never felt more of an outsider.

'If Nonna Gilda had wanted my opinion she would have asked for it. Instead she asked you.' Fleetingly Katarina's eyes flashed with annoyance, a micro-expression that was there then gone.

'I'm not sure why,' said Belle, honestly.

Katarina stared at her. 'Neither am I.'

She had been doing her best to get to know this young woman, but if Belle had made any headway, now it seemed lost. Katarina got to her feet, her face closed, her shoulders stiff.

'I'm sorry if I ...' Belle began.

'Thank you again for your help this afternoon,' Katarina cut in. 'I will let you know if there is any interest in the cats.'

She turned on her heel and, watching her go, Belle stood in the music room. She looked round at the instruments that the Ginaro family had collected over the years, and the yellowing sheet music stacked inside a large glass cabinet. This space was vast and Katarina seemed to be the only one who ever used it. It must get lonely sitting in here day after day while her husband was busy ticking off goals on his matrix. And it must be difficult making a space for herself in this family, fitting in, being who they wanted.

Belle glanced down at the desk. The rigid order of it bothered her. Shifting the laptop ever so slightly to a more careless angle, she ruffled the pages of the notebook and moved the pen.

Before walking out of the music room, she ran her fingers over the keys of the piano and the notes rang out, shattering the silence.

12

Secrets And Lies

Pietro was always late, that was what everyone kept telling Belle. So, when he didn't appear for breakfast at the time they had arranged, she assumed she was expected to hang around in the vestibule. They were meant to be spending a morning in Alberobello, a town known for its many *trulli*, the cute whitewashed stone buildings with conical roofs. Belle was keen to go there, imagining Pietro would be an easier companion than his elder brother, but she didn't see that as a reason to wait until he bothered to appear. Instead, she downed a glass of pomegranate juice, watched a sleek cream cat stroll the full length of the kitchen table, then quietly let herself out of the *palazzo*.

Belle headed towards the older part of town. She wanted to lose herself in narrow lanes, go slowly and soak up the atmosphere. If she ended up at the cathedral then she would take a look inside, but perhaps her feet would lead her in a different direction altogether; she didn't really mind.

Walking through the piazza, she spotted Mia sitting outside a bar. She was clad in a skimpy orange dress, her dark glossy hair spilling over her shoulders, and even at this hour, her eyes were smoky and her lips glossed. The girl waved at her.

'Belle, Belle,' she called, both hands in the air.

'Don't tell me off for not wearing enough make-up,' Belle said as she approached the table.

That morning she had managed only tinted sunscreen and a dab of lip balm. Then she had chosen the plainest palest shift dress from the Casa di Ginaro collection, matched it with her scuffed old Birkenstocks, tied up her unbrushed curls with a scarf and worn Ari's greenstone.

'I heard you left your job,' she said to Mia.

'Yes and I wanted to thank you. What you said to me, it changed everything.'

'I didn't say you should walk out.' Belle sat down beside her. 'I meant to consider your options, not do something rash.'

Mia's hand was in the air again but now she was waving to attract the waiter's attention.

'Why would I waste any more of my life doing something I hate and am no good at?' she asked.

'Gianni is furious,' Belle told her.

Mia lifted her chin. 'I don't care.'

'What will you do now?'

'This is why I wanted to thank you ...' Mia broke off as the waiter approached. She ordered coffee and a *pasticciotto* then tried to decide if she also needed a granita, conducting a long conversation in Italian with the waiter, switching to English to check what Belle wanted, then back into her own language.

'You wanted to thank me,' Belle reminded her, once she had finished.

'Yes, yes, because after I walked out of the shop, I went straight to see the stylist who did your hair and told her that she needed me. At first, she didn't agree, but finally I convinced her.'

'You'll be working in the salon?'

'Doing make-up for her clients.' Mia beamed. 'Also sweeping up hair from the floor and cleaning the washbasins, but every job has its drawbacks.'

Belle stifled a smile. She hoped there wouldn't be too much sweeping.

'I will learn about styling so when I apply for make-up courses, they will see I have experience,' Mia said, brightly. 'Then, some day, I will get out of this boring town.'

'You have a plan,' observed Belle.

'Do you think it is a good one?'

'It definitely seems better than staying in a job you don't like, even if it has inconvenienced Gianni a bit.'

'I told him he should hire Perla.'

'Would she want to work in the shop?' Belle couldn't imagine it.

'She was always saying that it couldn't be so bad,' Mia said, shrugging one shoulder. 'Now let her find out.'

'But if she's pregnant ...' Belle stopped in her tracks, hoping she hadn't broken a confidence.

'Pregnant? I don't think so,' Mia scoffed. 'Perla may have told you so, but she says all sorts of things.'

'She said it was still a secret.'

'This is what she does.' Mia smiled at the waiter who was approaching with a loaded tray, then added matter-of-factly, 'She tells some big story, it is all a secret, no one must know, and that is because everything is in Perla's imagination.'

'Why would she lie?' Belle didn't know what to make of it.

'Who knows?' Mia shrugged again. 'She has told me so many lies about her family, her life, her plans. Sometimes I think that even she imagines they are true.'

Belle was struggling to understand. 'What does Pietro think?'

'He adores her, does whatever she wants, believes anything, but Pietro is not always so smart.'

Belle drank an iced Caffè Leccese and ate a light dome of sponge filled with pistachio cream, while she tried to adjust to this new view of Perla. Of all the Ginaro family, she had been the warmest and most welcoming. Was she really not to be trusted?

'Ask her again about the pregnancy, see how she responds,' suggested Mia. 'She tells so many stories that she forgets what she has said and to who.'

'I really don't want to believe this,' Belle admitted. 'I like Perla.'

'I like her also,' agreed Mia, digging a spoon into her almond granita. 'But I never take her very seriously.'

Leaving the bar, Belle walked on through Ostuni, losing herself in the labyrinth of cobblestoned lanes, climbing staircases, passing beneath arches, catching glimpses of shimmering sea and bright sky, then finding herself somehow almost back where she had started. Belle's mind went round in circles too. Was everyone being unfair to Perla?

The real niggle was the pregnancy. Perla had mentioned it once, the very first day, then never spoken of it again. Why confide that sort of news to a stranger when you hadn't told your family? It bothered Belle.

Winding through the streets, she climbed upwards, until she reached the Byzantine cathedral with the distinctive rose window, squeezed between old buildings, clinging to the hilltop. Belle pushed open its heavy oak door and stepped inside. While she had never been religious, she liked the restful feel of sacred spaces. Here the air was heavy with incense and silence. Sitting in one of the pews, closing her eyes for a few moments, she touched the greenstone round her neck.

Perla wasn't her problem, decided Belle, none of the Ginaro family were. She was here only for the summer, passing through their lives, not staying.

Opening her eyes, it struck her that the cathedral's interior wasn't entirely unlike the *palazzo*. Painted ceilings, soaring columns, showy grandeur; in a Catholic church, this wasn't unusual, but in a place where you lived day after day – washed, ate, slept, came together with others – surely it would start to shape you? Suddenly she was glad of her own ordinariness, glad to have grown up in a plain townhouse not a palace, to have lived in flats with mould on the walls rather than valuable artworks; it seemed easier to be ordinary.

Belle had seen enough of the cathedral's interior. Back outside, she found that the morning was warming and the small piazza beginning to bustle. Perhaps she would walk around the town's ramparts, then find a peaceful spot to have lunch, take the whole day slowly and spend it alone.

Eventually she found her way to the edge of Ostuni and paused atop its defensive wall, looking out over the view – such a wide expanse of flat land and sea, so much space it was dizzying. Standing there, Belle thought about her life with Ari. How small it had been, how simple and contained, even at the beginning. Now life felt more like this view; so much space it was impossible to fill and all she saw was emptiness.

Turning away from the scenery, Belle retraced her route, walking down the steep hill paved with smooth, slippery flagstones, the muscles in her calves complaining about so many steps. It was fine to wander aimlessly through a new town, to explore its possibilities, but Belle wasn't sure a woman in her fifties should be taking the same approach with her future. She might only be passing through the Ginaro family's world, but where was she going afterwards? Perhaps she did need a plan. Even Mia seemed to have one now.

As Belle was walking across the piazza, thinking she might choose a little *trattoria* and treat herself to something delicious for lunch, she heard the tinny horn of an approaching Vespa, and a man's voice calling her name.

'Belle, I have found you.' It was Enrico, astride an orange scooter, his head squashed into a helmet that looked a size too small.

'Hello,' said Belle, in surprise as he pulled into the kerb. 'I thought you were at work.'

'I heard Pietro let you down this morning,' he remarked,

with a shrug, as if it was only to be expected. 'And that you hadn't gone to Alberobello. So, I decided to take a lunch break, and thought you might like to join me. I have been calling but you didn't answer.'

Belle glanced at her phone and realised she had put it on silent mode in the church then must have forgotten to change it. 'Sure,' she agreed. 'Where shall we go?'

Enrico offered her a helmet, covered in colourful flowers, that had been strapped onto the handlebars. 'Climb aboard and I will show you.'

'Is this your Vespa?'

'It belongs to Gianni but he never uses it, not now he has his car. I am sure he won't mind me borrowing it.'

It was a bit like mounting a horse, thought Belle as she swung a leg over the seat and settled into it. Except here Enrico was sitting in front of her and she could feel the heat coming from his body. As they accelerated onto the street, she leaned into him for balance, aware this was the closest she had been to any man, since Ari.

'OK?' he called back, perhaps sensing that she had tensed.

'I've never ridden one of these before.'

'Don't worry, I have. It was a long time ago, but I haven't forgotten.'

They sped out of the town and wound down through groves of olive trees. Nearing the coast, the roads became sandy and bare aside from low-growing scrub. The Vespa was at full throttle now, racing along and Belle was clinging to Enrico, too alive with adrenaline to feel awkward.

Ahead was a sign pointing to a lido and he followed it, slowing as they turned into a car park. Parking beneath a shade cloth, he waited until Belle had dismounted, then climbed off himself, removing his helmet, hair ruffled and a smile on his face.

'That was fun. For a while, I forgot I am a man in my fifties. I went back to my boyhood.'

'I'm amazed you survived,' Belle told him.

'Was it so bad?'

'No, it was fun.' Her heart was still rushing, although whether that was down to the thrill of the ride or his unfamiliar closeness, Belle wasn't certain. 'I enjoyed it.'

'Good, because that is how we are going home again, later,' Enrico said, as they walked together towards the cluster of low buildings that edged the sand.

This lido was more like a plush resort, with a cocktail bar as well as rows of padded loungers lined up beneath parasols on a broad beach. The restaurant was set back, situated on a deck but still with views of blue water beyond.

The sea was impossible to avoid here, not sheltered by steep dunes and towering pines like it was at home. Belle didn't love it like she once had; but this was Enrico's sea, not Ari's, so she couldn't hate it either.

They were shown to a table for two and the waiter brought over water, a basket of crunchy breadsticks and a couple of menus.

'Why don't you order?' Enrico suggested. 'I have been eating the same things for too long. This time I would like to be surprised.'

'You'll have to translate the menu for me.' It was short but all in Italian.

Enrico read it through, not only listing the ingredients, but describing each dish, the flavours and textures it was likely to have.

Belle chose the dishes that intrigued her rather than the ones she was certain to like – spaghetti with white wine and sea urchin roe, scallops with salted lemon, red prawn tartare, and tender mussels blanketed with cheese and breadcrumbs.

'Did you come here with Luciana?' she asked him, as they waited for their drinks to arrive.

'We ate out very often. It would be difficult to find a place nearby that we hadn't visited.'

'You must see her everywhere then, like I do Ari at home.'

'It happens less than it used to.' He smoothed his ruffled hair with one hand. 'Perhaps because she was shut away, not in the world, for the final part of her life. The last time I ate here, it was with my sons and my mother. And so, the memories of the other times begin to fade. When I think of Luciana I remember the rest home, the way it smelled, the other people there, the kindness of the staff and the sense of desperation.'

'Oh, Enrico.' Belle at least had been spared all that. And knowing how much Ari would have hated it, she supposed it was at least something to be grateful for.

'I am sorry,' Enrico said, with a shake of his head. 'Here I am again in a beautiful place with you and speaking of sad things.'

'There's no need to apologise. We've always been able to talk about the sad things.' Those unflinching conversations had been what kept Belle going. 'There were times, when you and I spoke, and it was such a relief to let the words out, everything I had been thinking and feeling.'

'It was exactly the same for me,' Enrico said, softly. 'Our Zoom calls were often the best part of my day.'

'You couldn't speak to your family like that ... or your friends?' Belle remembered what Katarina had said that morning in the kitchen. That he had better people than her to confide in.

'For my sons I needed to be brave, my mother is too old to be burdened, and my friends were Luciana's friends too ...' he broke off, shrugging.

'And it was easier to talk via a computer, just us, no interruptions,' Belle guessed.

'Now we can speak person to person, this is easy too and it shouldn't always be about sadness.'

Before she could respond, the waiter came over bearing

their cocktails, a blend of gin, elderflower and Prosecco that Belle had thought sounded refreshing.

'It is good to have you here.' Enrico held up his glass. 'You are exactly how I imagined you would be.'

Belle didn't think she could say the same. Enrico looked like the man she had met online, sounded like him too, but she was still getting to know what he was really like.

'It's good to be here.' She clinked her glass against his.

The waiter served swirls of spaghetti swimming in deep white bowls. Digging in her fork, Belle took a taste and found the brightness of lemon and parsley and the sweet brininess of sea urchin roe.

'You like it?' asked Enrico, watching her eat.

'Mm.' Belle's mouth was singing with the newness of the flavours. 'And I really wasn't sure if I would.'

'In that case why order it?' he asked, curiously.

There had been other pasta dishes on the menu, a spaghetti with yellow tomatoes and clams, a tortelli filled with pecorino cheese, a rigatoni with langoustine. All had sounded safer.

'I wanted to try something new,' Belle explained. 'That's why I came here after all. Like you I've been doing the same things for too long.'

'*Va bene*,' he nodded. 'And how is it going, this trying new things?'

'Well you took me on a Vespa ride; that was interesting.'

Enrico laughed. 'Not as interesting as it would have been on the Vespa that I rode when I was a teenager, believe me. It was ancient and there was always something broken, but my father insisted I needed to learn how to fix it myself. By the end it was almost tied together with string. You are right, it is amazing I survived.'

'I didn't have any transport at all when I was younger,' Belle recalled as she soaked a crust of bread into the slick of briny sauce. 'I used to hitch-hike most of the time, which seems so risky now when I think about it, but never worried me at all back then.'

'Where did you hitch-hike to?'

'Anywhere I could find work for the summer. I'd pick grapes in one place and hops in another, and I'd be happy so long as I had enough money to pay for my dinner and a bed for the night. Looking back, those were good times, simpler.'

'Was everything really simpler then, or does it only feel that way?' Enrico wanted to know.

'I'm not sure,' said Belle. 'I look at these young people now, Perla and Mia, their lives don't seem very simple at all. Maybe ours weren't either, and we just didn't realise.'

'Maybe,' said Enrico, as the waiter set down a plate of mussels, warm cheese oozing over glossy black shells. 'Life is certainly complicated now. But this idea of trying new things, it is interesting, I like it.'

Since Belle had done the ordering, she insisted on settling the bill, brushing off his attempt to argue. She hadn't paid for a thing since the day she arrived, and it didn't sit well always to be the one doing the taking.

'You are very generous, thank you,' said Enrico afterwards, as they strolled along the beach together.

Shoes in one hand, Belle splashed through the shallows of the low waves lapping the shoreline. 'I'm staying in your house, wearing your clothes,' she said. 'Lunch seems the least I can do.'

He glanced at the pale lilac shift dress she was holding up with her other hand to stop the hemline trailing in the water. 'Do you mind?' he asked. 'Mamma didn't tell me what she was planning. I hope you didn't feel obliged to wear them.'

'I don't feel entirely myself,' Belle admitted. 'But I'm not really sure if I can blame the clothes for that.'

Enrico looked at her questioningly.

'I've been feeling a bit adrift,' she admitted, hitching the dress higher and wading out a little deeper. 'Who am I now that Ari has gone? That's what I keep asking myself.'

They were walking a wilder stretch of the beach, backed by low dunes covered in marram grass, towards another lido in the near distance. The sea was cool on Belle's bare legs and the sand gritty beneath her feet.

'You are who you always were,' Enrico told her.

'No, I don't think so. My life altered completely after I met Ari.'

'We all make compromises, shape one another over the years,' Enrico pointed out. 'I am certain that Luciana changed me.'

Belle had left her job, moved into Ari's house, even started riding horses. She had been happy to rush headlong into the life he offered. Now it dawned on her that she might have done the exact same thing she had always resented her mother for, reshaped herself completely.

'I thought that Ari was the one losing himself,' she said, staring out towards the nothingness of sea and horizon. 'What if really it was me?'

'Then I suppose now you must find yourself again.'

When she turned, Belle saw he was studying her. 'But how?'

'Give it time.'

'It's been two years already.'

'And now you are here, trying new things, seeing new places. Maybe that will help.'

'I hope so,' said Belle, thinking of her mother and her tidy, repetitive life. She had seen herself as so different, surrounded by her clutter of art and books, freer and more bohemian. But maybe she had been following in her mother's footsteps all along, repeating the same pattern. The idea was unsettling; it disoriented her. Belle thought it was like one of those trick pictures, where you think you are looking at one thing, and it turns out to be quite another.

'Everyone feels like they've lost themselves sometimes.' Enrico was reassuring.

But now viewed from a distance it all seemed clearer. Belle had seen less of her own friends and spent more time with his. Stayed out on the coast and avoided her usual haunts in the city. Put her husband at the centre of her life. She had chosen all that; Ari hadn't asked her.

'How do you lose yourself?' she wondered, trying to make sense of it. 'How does anyone do that?'

Enrico replied, without missing a beat. 'Very easily I think.'

As they walked on together, Enrico pulled off his own shoes and rolled up his trousers, joining her in the water. They splashed onwards with the sea breeze in their faces and the sun on their skin. Just before reaching the next lido, they turned and started walking back without needing to say anything.

Beside the Vespa again, Belle pushed her sandy feet into her Birkenstocks and accepted the floral helmet from Enrico who smiled as he passed it over. 'You may be wearing our clothes, but you still look like yourself,' he promised.

Riding back to Ostuni, still holding onto him, as rows of olive trees blurred past, and the road rose towards the cluster of white buildings on the hilltop, Belle wasn't sure who she was anymore, or even who she wanted to be.

Reaching the *palazzo*, they left the Vespa in another cave-like garage hidden in the wall, this one full of mountain bikes and sea kayaks. Enrico had some work to finish and Belle decided to spend what was left of the afternoon by the pool. Hardly anyone used the loungers or seemed to swim there. It was like a scene set for a movie but the actors hadn't arrived yet.

She collected everything she might need for a couple of hours slumped in a sun-lounger: sunscreen and a hat, a book and a couple of magazines. Then went and found a spot beneath the shade of an olive tree.

As she lay in the peaceful garden, eyes closed, Belle thought about Ari. After waiting so long to find one another, she had been ready to give herself fully to their life together. He made her happy. She had never let herself consider that one day she might be without him. She relied on him being there.

She wished Ari was here now, lying on a lounger beside her soaking up the sun. When she opened her eyes, Belle almost expected to see him, but there was no glimpse of his figure caught from the corner of her eye, sitting with his feet in the pool or pottering in the garden. He wasn't here, except viewed in a rear-view mirror, as she moved on and left him in the distance. He was a memory.

This was what Enrico had been talking about, realised Belle. Memories faded, she couldn't stop it happening, and soon she would see Ari less and less. The thought had tears coming to her eyes, and before Belle knew it, she was crying properly, helpless with grief.

'Belle, Belle.' It was Enrico. 'What has happened? Who has upset you?'

'No one ... it's just ... sadness,' she managed.

He sat on the edge of the lounger, his body turned towards hers. 'Another wave of it?'

As Belle nodded, he moved a hand to her face and very gently wiped some of the moisture from her cheeks with his fingertips. 'I felt the same. Work was impossible, and so I came to find you again. It is better to be sad together, than alone, yes?'

They stared at each other for a few seconds, she with her face swollen and red, his clear but troubled. Then without thinking Belle fell into him, pressing her face into his shoulder, feeling the warmth of his skin through the linen of his shirt, smelling the light woodsy cologne he wore, sensing the steady pulsing of his heart.

Other people had touched her after Ari's death, but Belle had never really wanted them to. This time it was different.

When they eased apart, Enrico moved to the lounger beside her, lying down and closing his eyes against the sun filtering through the olive branches. Belle watched him, chest rising and falling, wondering if he had fallen asleep.

Then he stretched out a hand and she reached to take it. They lay there together, palm pressed to palm, listening to the sounds of the garden, to birds and cicadas singing, as the sun shifted in the sky and the shadows lengthened, and a pure white cat prowled around them.

13

All At Sea

Belle woke in a heavy mood that wasn't lightened by the thought of going sailing. The prospect of being trapped out on the water with stern, disapproving Gianni was far from appealing. Packing a small bag full of essentials, she wished it was just her and Enrico heading off together again.

Dressed in linen shorts and a scoop-necked top, she made her way downstairs. Perla was the only one to be found in the kitchen. She was swathed in an embroidered linen robe, hair piled artfully on her head, taking selfies from different angles as she held a cup of coffee.

'Good morning,' she said, without glancing away from the screen.

'Where is everyone?' Belle asked.

'They went to the marina already. I think there was something they needed to take care of.' Perla sounded entirely disinterested. 'The driver will come back for you soon, I am sure.'

'You're not coming along,' observed Belle. 'I suppose it might not be much fun ... you know, with your pregnancy.'

Perla looked at her now, eyes squinting. 'I am sorry, with my what?'

'Your pregnancy,' Belle repeated.

'Katarina is the one who is pregnant, not me.'

'You told me on the day I arrived, remember?' Belle

insisted. 'You said that you were waiting for the right moment to announce it.'

'You must be mistaken,' Perla was checking her image on
the screen again. 'You were jet-lagged, your brain was in a
fog that day, remember?'

Belle was very certain she hadn't imagined it. They had
been standing in the vestibule, waiting for Pietro, when Perla
had unexpectedly confided the news.

'So, you're not expecting a baby,' she clarified.

'Of course not.' Perla's voice rang with impatience. 'Me
and Pietro plan to have some fun before we start our family.
If you thought that I said that, then you misunderstood.'

Belle was disappointed. She had wanted Mia to be the one
telling lies. Now she thought back to other conversations
with Perla, wondering what was real and what fabricated.
As she made a fresh pot of coffee, she kept an eye on her,
still photographing herself, moving around to find different
lights and backgrounds.

'We could ask the driver to take us somewhere else,' Perla
suggested, putting down her phone at last. 'What about
Lecce? We can go shopping. There is a place I think you will
love, full of clothes that are colourful and fun.'

'Thanks, but I don't need more clothes,' said Belle.

'Alberobello then? Pietro forgot yesterday that he was
meant to be taking you. We will find some shops there too.'

'I promised to go sailing,' said Belle.

'But you don't really want to?'

'Not really,' she admitted.

'Why do it then?' asked Perla.

'For the same reason that Pietro is doing it; to make Enrico
happy.'

Perla unclipped her hair and it tumbled over her shoulders.
She picked up her phone again. 'I don't think that is why
Pietro is going. Or Gianni either.'

Belle stared at her. 'What do you mean?'

Perla gave a careless shrug. 'I think they don't want you spending too much time alone with their father.'

That was what Belle had suspected, but hearing it said out loud, she was taken aback.

Perla pouted at the screen, held it at arm's length, and snapped a shot. 'Where did Enrico take you yesterday?'

'We just had lunch at the beach,' said Belle. 'And spent some time here by the pool.'

Perla tilted her head and took one last shot. Then she poured her cold coffee into the sink and helped herself to a fresh cup from the pot Belle had made. 'Gianni thinks he can control everything, even his father.'

Belle stared at her. Yes, Perla told lies, but surely not all of the time.

'The boys believe all he needs is family,' she continued. 'But why shouldn't Enrico find love again?'

'We are friends ...' Belle tried to insist, yet again.

'But you want more than that surely? You want all of this.' Perla held her arms wide. 'Who wouldn't want it?'

'Nothing I say is going to make any difference, is it?' Now Belle was dreading the day ahead even more than she had been.

If there had been any way to get out of this sailing trip then she would have jumped at it. Only Enrico was keen to have her there, his sons resented her presence. Unless Perla was lying; and there was really no way of knowing.

On the way down to the marina, as the driver whisked her through the olive groves, Belle tried to decide if it might be better to leave Ostuni. It was a short car ride and she had no answers by the time she arrived. Approaching the elegant old yacht, she saw the three Ginaro men on its deck. Pausing, she watched as they busied themselves with whatever tasks were necessary before setting sail. Even from that vantage point she could tell Enrico was happy to have his sons on board.

He looked up and saw her, raising his arm to wave, the smile on his face even broader. As the two younger men followed his gaze, neither of them was smiling. They didn't want her there, thought Belle, and it was a bad feeling not to be wanted. Still, she waved back and walked past the rows of small motor boats towards the larger vessel moored beyond them.

The boys might not enjoy sailing much but they knew what they were doing. Gianni manned the helm as they motored out of the marina, then Pietro got busy hauling up the sails. Belle was ill-at-ease, the one who didn't belong.

'Are you OK?' checked Enrico, sitting beside her. 'Do you need anything?'

'I'm fine,' she told him, thinking that Gianni's gaze kept flicking towards them as he steered the boat into deeper water, sure she wasn't imagining it.

The weather was overcast, but Enrico assured her that soon the sun would burn away the fine layer of cloud, the sky would be blue and the day perfect. They had brought a picnic and would be following the coastline north towards Monopoli and Polignano a Mare.

'Papa, is there coffee?' called Gianni.

'Yes, we have two flasks, do you want a cup?'

His son nodded. 'And some *biscotti*?'

'I would love some too,' said Belle, who hadn't touched her breakfast after the conversation with Perla.

The swaying of the deck didn't slow Enrico as he climbed down the short ladder that led to the cabin. Through the doorway Belle could see his head as he moved around the galley. She watched him and sensed Gianni's eyes on her, watching too.

It was Gianni who broke the silence. 'I have been thinking about your action plan. I have brought along some ideas for us to brainstorm.'

'You mean today, while we're out sailing?' asked Belle, taken aback.

'Why not take this opportunity of having time together?'

'Action plans aren't really my style.' Belle was more direct than usual, shorter on patience. 'That's not how I do things.'

'You are not prepared to give it a try?' Gianni's voice was laced with disapproval.

'Thanks, but no, definitely not today.' If Belle made a plan, it had to be her own, not something he had thought up for her.

If Enrico was aware of the shift in atmosphere when he returned with the coffee flasks and a package of home-made *biscotti*, then he showed no sign. He poured hot drinks for everyone then settled on the squab beside Belle.

'The breeze is picking up,' he remarked.

Belle sipped her coffee, worried that every interaction between them was going to be studied and noted. A whole day of this would be exhausting.

At least the view was distracting. Narrow beaches dipped between crevasses in the rocks, towering cliffs were topped with crooked buildings, fishing boats bobbed in harbours. Belle focused on the scenery and tried to block out everything else.

'I never tire of this trip,' said Enrico. 'I must have made it hundreds of times.'

'Mamma loved it,' remarked Gianni. 'She said that of all the places you sailed, home was the most beautiful.'

'She was right, but there are many places that we never got to, and they must be beautiful too.'

'There is some amazing sailing where I live,' said Belle, who had been out with friends once or twice. 'The Hauraki Gulf has beautiful islands, vineyards to visit, a bird sanctuary.'

'I would like to experience that,' agreed Enrico.

'You should come,' Belle encouraged him. 'Probably we could charter a yacht. I can find out.'

'It would be good to travel again,' he replied. 'I could escape the winter for a few weeks, stop somewhere on the way.'

Enrico was talking as though this might really be a plan and Belle imagined having him in New Zealand. She would take him to all the places she loved, the wild beaches and the bush walks, and was certain he would love them too.

'Yes, come,' she urged. 'Come for a decent length of time so we can do a boat trip through Fiordland, and maybe a Great Walk or one of the cycle trails.'

'Papa would never stay away from work for that long,' insisted Gianni, sounding certain.

'You are always telling me that you can take care of the business,' Enrico pointed out. 'Besides, a person can work from anywhere these days.'

Gianni shifted uncomfortably on his feet. 'Take the helm, Papa. I need to go down below. All that coffee.'

He stayed down there for a while, leaving Enrico to steer the yacht while Pietro came to sit beside her, lolling on the squabs, feet up on the table.

'This is not how I imagined I would be spending my twenty-first birthday,' he complained. 'My plan was to party.'

'Oh, I'm so sorry I had forgotten,' Belle admitted. 'Happy birthday.'

'Tonight, there will be a special family dinner,' Enrico reminded her. 'And after that my son can party for as long as he likes.'

'Oh, we will be partying,' Pietro promised. 'Don't expect to see me and Perla for the rest of the weekend.'

'I imagine we will cope without you,' Enrico replied, dryly.

Pietro grinned. 'Do you want to come, Papa? You could dance all night with us.'

'OK.' Enrico smiled back. 'Your Nonna will be keen to join us too.'

'Now that I would like to see.' Pietro's grin widened. 'Nonna Gilda shaking it on the dance floor.'

'She might surprise you.'

'Nothing Nonna Gilda did would surprise me. She is a legend,' said Pietro.

Moving to the bench opposite, he lay down on the squab, stretching over its full length and yawning as he rested his head on a cushion. 'Since I am going to party all night I will take the chance for a rest now,' he declared.

'Sure, don't worry about us,' said Gianni, emerging from the cabin.

'You can manage,' said Pietro, with another lazy yawn.

Enrico smiled indulgently at both of them. He adored his sons, that was obvious. He might be prepared to leave his work to travel to the far side of the world, but Belle wasn't convinced he would ever want to leave Gianni and Pietro for long. She liked seeing their closeness; still she envied it a little.

If ever she'd had a bond like that with her own father, Belle couldn't remember it well. She was a little girl when he died and all that was left were a few photographs as proof he had pushed her on a swing at a local park and helped her build sandcastles on the beach every summer. He was a bear of a man, that much she recalled, and he liked to read her stories. In the reel of scenes that played in her head, he was often laughing. Belle hoped she had brought him the same kind of joy Enrico's sons seemed to bring him.

They traced the coastline in the yacht until Enrico decided it was time to moor up in a quiet bay where they would eat lunch and have a swim. It was much the same routine as their first sailing trip together, except now his boys were there too, Pietro leaping from the deck with a yell and divebombing into the water, Gianni executing an elegant dive as he followed.

Belle took the more sedate route, down the ladder, bracing for the chill of the water as she lowered herself in, and staying close to the yacht while the three men raced each other to the shore.

Gianni won, reaching the beach first, with Enrico closely following, while Pietro trailed behind. They stood on the sand together for a while, then headed back towards her, more slowly now, laughing and chatting. While his sons climbed the ladder to towel themselves dry, Enrico swam to her side.

'That was the first time Gianni has beaten me,' he said, more with pride than dismay.

'He is a good swimmer,' Belle observed, floating on her back in the buoyant water, star-fishing her legs and arms.

'I taught him myself when he was very young, and Pietro too, although he never listened or tried as hard as Gianni. The day that Pietro beats me too, I will know I am in trouble.'

The boys were laying out lunch on the table, and calling for them to come and eat.

'Are you ready to go up?' asked Enrico, as Gianni shouted down again, saying he and Pietro were hungry and were going to start without them.

'I guess so,' agreed Belle, and looking up saw Gianni staring back at her.

It was an elaborate picnic. Delicate leaves of swordfish carpaccio spiked with citrus, creamy ricotta cheese wrapped in prosciutto, a Panzanella salad of soft sweet tomatoes and crisp sour crusts, and small puffs of pastry filled with mozzarella and béchamel sauce.

Enrico sat at the table, a son on either side of him. Belle was alone, while he was surrounded. She wondered if the boys intended her to feel excluded or if she was reading too much into every little thing now.

Once everyone had finished eating, they set sail again, heading south to be home in time for Pietro's celebration. Before dinner there were to be drinks in the salon, vintage champagne the family had been saving for this occasion. Between then and now, Belle would only have a little time to herself.

Should she stay or was it better to go? Reaching the marina, she remained in two minds. As they were driven back to the *palazzo*, and Belle thanked Enrico for another wonderful day, then went upstairs to shower the salt from her skin, the same thoughts kept circling through her mind. The boys might not want her here but their father did. So what did she want?

Belle was lying on her bed, staring at the ceiling, lost in indecision when she heard a soft knock on her door. She was in no mood for Gianni and his action plan. She didn't have the patience for Perla or the energy for Katarina. And she thought it was very unlikely to be the old Signora.

'Yes,' she called out, tentatively.

'It is me, Mia.' The door opened and a glossy dark head appeared around it. 'I have come to do your make-up.'

Belle tried to be discouraging. 'Thanks, that's kind, but I'm fine.'

Ignoring her, Mia wheeled in a large make-up case, one with little drawers and special sections for tools that Belle mostly couldn't identify.

'I did my first proper job today, a bride and three brides-maids.' She beamed with pride, as she opened up the make-up case. 'Even though I am exhausted now, I wanted to come and help you just like I promised. I will show you exactly what to do and the products you must buy. And you will look beautiful for Pietro's birthday dinner.'

Mia moved a chair to face the window. Then she beckoned Belle over. 'Quickly, and I can tidy up your hair too.'

Belle yawned and swung her legs off the bed. Perhaps a little make-up would give her a lift. Besides she needed to talk to someone and Mia knew this family.

'You were right about Perla,' she began, as foundation was dotted onto her face and blended carefully with a brush.

'No pregnancy?' guessed Mia. 'Just another of her stories.'

'I always thought the first rule of lying was that you don't tell people things when you're bound to be found out.'

'There are rules of lying?' Mia was brushing an iridescent powder over her cheeks. 'In that case Perla hasn't heard of them. She says whatever comes into her head.'

'How am I supposed to know when it's a lie and if she's telling the truth?' Belle asked.

'It is not always easy even for me, and I have spent a lot of time with her.'

An extraordinary number of products were being layered onto her face. Mia must have bought more make-up as well as a fancy case to store it in. As she worked, she kept making Belle note down the essentials and insisted she must invest in them herself.

'What else has Perla said?' Mia asked, slicking something onto her eyelids. 'Maybe I can tell you whether it's true or not.'

With her eyes closed it seemed easier to say. 'This morning she claimed that Gianni and Pietro don't want me here. They believe I'm chasing after their father. And they don't like me being alone with him.'

There was a moment's silence as Mia thought about it. 'This might be true,' she decided.

Belle's heart sank. 'I should leave if I'm not welcome.'

'But Enrico has welcomed you, and he is the head of the house, not Gianni or Pietro,' pointed out Mia.

'I don't want to cause problems between him and his sons.'

'If you go away Enrico will be sad again. He has been more cheerful since you arrived. Anyone can see that.'

Mia made Belle open her eyes, so she could coat on mascara, then brushed away the extra powder she had applied beneath them to catch any dusty particles of eyeshadow that might have fallen.

'Pietro and Gianni think only of themselves. As children, they were the same. Their mother spoiled them,' she said, as she worked.

'Perla told me you are in love with them both,' Belle recalled.

'She did?' Mia paused, lip gloss in one hand, brush in another. 'I know that was a lie.'

'Why say it then?'

'For effect, to be interesting, or maybe she really does believe it. Who can tell with Perla?'

Once Belle's lips were glossed, Mia plugged in a heated brush, so she could tackle her hair.

'If you would like a break from the family, you could visit the villa at the beach. It is beautiful there.' Mia began to spiral the hot brush through her hair. 'The place will be empty as they mainly use it at the height of the summer.'

'If I went to the villa that would please Gianni and Pietro.'

'Maybe they need to get used to not always being pleased,' reasoned Mia.

Belle thought she might have a point. Was she really going to let herself be chased away by these boys who always got what they wanted? If Enrico was happy to have her here then surely that was what mattered.

She chose something to wear from the crammed rail in her wardrobe, a deep burnt-orange dress with crimson embroidery, and hung the greenstone round her neck. Once dressed, Belle examined her reflection in the mirror. She looked fine but even so this was the last time she would let anyone play with her appearance. Enough was enough.

'Have you decided? Staying or going?' asked Mia.

'I may stay, at least for a while,' said Belle, realising it was what she wanted.

'You have come so far and it would be a shame to leave so soon,' agreed Mia.

After she had packed up her make-up and left, Belle stayed at the window staring out at the cluster of whitewashed houses, with the glossy tiled domes of churches rising above and the sea and the sky beyond. Was it really Ostuni she didn't want to leave? Or was it Enrico?

A feeling flooded her, a warmth she recognised, a sort of longing she hadn't expected to have again. *We are just friends*, she reminded herself.

14

Small Moments In Time

The salon could be a gloomy space but this evening fairy lights were strung through it and music was playing. A magnum of champagne had been left in an ice bucket beside a long white platter covered with delicate fingers of toasted bread topped with caviar, anchovy and aioli.

Belle was early and the first to appear. She occupied herself browsing the artworks on the walls, mostly gloomy portraits of stern-looking people, a few landscapes, all displayed in showy gold frames. Maybe some of them were valuable, Belle couldn't tell, but still she preferred her walls at home, covered in Ari's sensual seascapes and art made by his friends.

Before long the others appeared. First Gianni with Katarina, next the Signora armoured in another of her formal jackets, then Enrico looking lightly tanned from his day on the yacht, and finally Pietro and Perla making a late entrance, arm in arm.

The champagne was opened and flutes filled. Enrico gave a speech, mostly in Italian, ending with a toast.

'To my son Pietro,' he said, raising his glass. 'Happy birthday. *Tanti auguri.*'

'*Tanti auguri,*' they echoed.

Belle was aware of being an outsider at an intimate occasion and, while Katarina was busy passing round the caviar toasts, Gianni made sure to confirm it.

'Usually, these birthday celebrations are only for close family. This is the first time we have included a stranger,' he told her.

'I'm honoured then,' said Belle, lightly. 'Although I hope I'm not such a stranger now.'

'I must thank you for helping Katarina with the cats,' he added, rather stiffly. 'Already there is interest in one.'

'Oh, that's good. Which cat?'

'I think a long-haired one. Katarina did tell me but ...'

'There are so many cats,' Belle finished for him.

Once the champagne bottle was empty, they went through to the dining room and found a festive table, with lit candles. Gifts were given before the first course, jokey things mostly, although with a flourish his father presented Pietro with the key to a car.

'Promise me you will drive it carefully,' said Enrico, handing it over. 'Don't make me regret this.'

Pietro dismissed his concern with a laugh, slipping the key into his pocket. 'Of course, Papa.'

Belle would have been impatient to see the vehicle this key belonged to, or even wanted to take a drive, but Pietro didn't seem in any hurry. He and Perla were seated side by side, their faces young and beautiful in the soft gold evening light and the radiance of the flickering candles.

They ate burrata cheese, soft mounds of mozzarella seeping cream as they cut into them, the richness tamed with peppery rocket leaves. Then short ribbons of pasta served with tender clams and nutty chickpeas. Finally a dish of herbed swordfish with a piquant salsa of green olives. As always, the conversation shifted in and out of Italian as they forgot that Belle was there and then remembered again.

Finally, there was a birthday cake, layers of liqueur-soaked sponge and creamy lemony ricotta with a blizzard of white chocolate shavings on top.

'No candles,' declared the Signora, as the cake was placed

in the centre of the table. 'Since you are not a child anymore, Pietro.'

'No candles, what a pity,' murmured Perla.

Enrico produced a dusty bottle of Moscato and poured each of them a glass of the sweet, velvety wine. They held their glasses in the air, toasting Pietro again.

'Our next celebration will be when I become a father,' observed Gianni, putting his glass to his lips.

Perla glanced at him. 'Actually, no it won't.'

'And why is that?' asked Gianni, an edge in his voice.

'Because the next party will be for our farewell, mine and Pietro's.'

'You are leaving?' The Signora turned to her youngest grandson. '*Perché?*'

Pietro looked to his wife and she encouraged him with a nod. He gazed around the table, clearing his throat. 'Now that I am twenty-one and will inherit the money Mamma has left me, we have decided to go travelling.'

'Your mother meant for you to invest that money for your future,' Enrico said, worriedly.

'We want our future to be an adventure.' Pietro exchanged a smile with Perla.

'Do you intend to travel until the money runs out?' Gianni asked, his tone critical.

'Maybe,' said Pietro, untroubled. 'We can find work if we need to. Or I will sell the sports car that Papa has given me. I am not stressing.'

'Where are you intending to go?' asked Enrico, more curiously.

'First New York then California. After that we will head south, Mexico, and probably Peru.'

Pietro was holding his wife's hand now and the frosting of diamonds on her wedding band glittered in the candlelight.

'But Perla is meant to be helping in the Ostuni boutique

now that Mia has left, and getting some work experience,' said Gianni.

'I don't want to do that,' said Perla, sweetly but firmly. 'And I won't.'

'You are making a mistake,' Gianni told her, turning to Pietro. 'Both of you.'

Pietro released Perla's hand and rested his arm across her shoulders. As she leaned into him, he muttered something in Italian that seemed to antagonise his brother.

'When the money runs out, will you come back here asking us for more?' asked Gianni.

'We won't need to,' Pietro promised. 'We will be fine; you don't need to worry about us.'

'I am not worried,' replied Gianni. 'I wouldn't waste my time.'

Enrico tried to calm the situation, but his boys were at each other's throats and nothing he said made a difference. The conversation shifted to Italian and all Belle could understand was that it was getting angrier. She glanced across the table at Katarina who only raised her eyebrows.

Then the Signora scraped back her chair and got to her feet, gripping the table for balance.

'There should have been candles after all,' she rasped. 'It seems that you are not yet an adult.'

The room was silent as she left. They stared at each other for a few moments, then Perla stood, and Pietro followed.

'Our friends are waiting,' he said. 'It is time for us to party.'

'Enjoy the cake,' added Perla and, taking his hand again, together they walked away.

The rest of them stayed at the table, dotted with half-drunk glasses of wine, the remains of the cake at its centre. Belle thought that Enrico looked shattered. She felt the uneasiness of being a part of this family's drama, but not a part of the family.

'That was not the evening I expected,' Enrico said, heavily. 'Perhaps we should take our cake and drinks outside and see if we can improve what is left of it?'

'I won't eat another bite,' said Gianni, staring at the mess of ricotta and sponge on his plate.

'Me neither,' agreed Katarina, who hadn't managed much anyway. 'I feel sick and a little dizzy, I need to lie down.'

When it was just the two of them, Enrico let out a hiss of breath. 'I hate it when they argue but it seems to happen more and more.'

'That's a pity,' said Belle, who as an only child had sometimes longed for a sibling to play and fight with. 'But I suppose all brothers do.'

'As boys they were inseparable, the best of friends, running through these rooms, playing noisy games.' Enrico shook his head. 'That doesn't seem so long ago, and now they are both men and not such friends anymore.'

Belle thought Pietro had plenty of reasons to resent his brother. Gianni was going to inherit almost everything, he would be the head of the family. It would be surprising if there wasn't some conflict.

'My sons are men and one of them is leaving home. Life moves on.' Enrico reached for two clean forks, picked up the cake platter and tucked the bottle of Moscato under his arm. 'Meanwhile we have the rest of an evening and I need some air, will you come and join me?'

Belle nodded in agreement and, collecting their glasses, she followed him.

Outdoors it was still, with barely a breeze. Enrico lit the brazier and they sat in front of it, taking forkfuls of cake and sips of wine, as the sky darkened and the night settled in.

'Maybe it is not such a bad thing for Pietro to go travelling,' Enrico decided. 'He may benefit from getting away, experiencing some of the world. What do you think?'

Belle considered the question for a while before replying.

'I don't think it matters. If they are determined to go then they will, whatever anyone thinks.'

'Still, I worry,' said Enrico.

'Of course, you do. I expect your parents worried about you.'

'I was the sensible one like Gianni, I gave them fewer reasons to worry.'

'You and Gianni don't seem particularly similar to me,' admitted Belle.

'In some ways we are though.' Enrico stared into the fire. 'I know how he can be at times, but Gianni has a good heart. Both of my sons do. The problem is they are so different in every other way.'

'Is Pietro more like his mother?' wondered Belle.

'Pietro is not like anyone. He is entirely himself and his mother doted on him. If Luciana were here then I think she would tell me not to worry so much, to let him go and have his adventures.'

'Ari would say the same. He was a believer in people following their dreams and never really much of a worrier.'

'*Va bene*, I will try to take their advice. As you say, I cannot stop my son. He has Luciana's money now, and he and Perla are adults, whatever my mother might think.'

He moved to put more wood on the fire, watching as the flames caught and crackled. 'The house will be quieter and emptier without them.'

'You'll have a grandchild soon.' Belle reminded him. 'And it seems like Gianni plans to fill this place with children.'

He smiled at that. 'My son may change his mind after a few sleepless nights.'

Belle could visualise Enrico as an older man, sitting here as another generation splashed in the pool or played music too loudly. She imagined him content, leading the life he was born for, with his family around him.

He left the fire and came to sit beside her again, his

expression thoughtful. 'Gianni must envy his brother at times. The freedom he has, all the adventures that lie ahead for him.'

'But Pietro won't have the wealth that Gianni will inherit,' Belle pointed out.

'He won't have the problems either. All of this – the house, the business, the Ginaro legacy.' Enrico looked towards the dark shapes the olive trees made. 'It isn't always easy.'

Belle hadn't considered it that way. Being the eldest son in this family had seemed like an advantage, but perhaps having it all wasn't everything.

'Has it been difficult for you?' she asked him.

'At times, yes.' He turned and his eyes met hers. 'I have had a good life, a privileged one, but it was a life that chose me. Now I find myself wondering who is Enrico, what did he want, just like you seem to be wondering who is Belle.'

'We've been on different journeys and have arrived in the same place,' Belle realised.

'I think so.'

'Couldn't you have said no to working in the family business, left it to your sister and done something different?' Belle couldn't imagine being railroaded into a life she didn't want.

Enrico stood and paced back to the fire, his face glowing in the heat as he shifted logs with a long metal poker and the flames flared brighter.

'I thought it was my duty. My parents always told me I was to care for what my family had created until it was time to pass it on to the next generation. And I was proud to be the one to do that.'

'Now the next generation seems ready,' Belle pointed out. 'This may be your chance to choose something else.'

'What would I choose?' Enrico put down the poker and stared into the fire. 'I am a widower, getting old, maybe it is too late.'

'You could go travelling,' Belle suggested. 'Find some beautiful places, have adventures.'

'Alone?' He sounded doubtful.

'With a friend.'

'With a friend, yes, that is more appealing.' He turned and gazed at her. 'Would you come travelling with me?'

Belle remembered all those destinations she had fantasised about visiting – luxury safari lodges in the Masai Mara, houseboats in Kerala, glamping in the Galapagos Islands. Places that had always seemed out of her reach.

'I'd love to,' she said, thinking it was still a dream, but now Enrico was dreaming too.

'We don't need to go far to find beautiful places,' he told her. 'In Otranto on the coast, there is a cathedral with the most exquisite mosaic floor. Monopoli is charming and in the historic centre there is a restaurant I am sure you would love. And you can't miss Martina Franca at night-time. We can make a start here in Puglia.'

'I'd like that,' said Belle, wondering if his sons would insist on coming too, hoping they might not. Alone with Enrico, she felt like she could breathe better, even here in this *palazzo* that felt so oppressive.

They stayed there as the fire collapsed into glowing embers, side by side but not quite touching, and somehow Belle was aware of every breath Enrico took. In the distance they heard music playing and the sound of other people's voices. It seemed this was a night for parties and Belle visualised Pietro in a bar surrounded by friends, dancing and laughing, as she and his father sat in their circle of light.

Sleepily heading upstairs, later than either of them had in-tended, with a whispered goodnight, Belle watched him go. They were friends, that was true, but alone in her room, leaning back against the door, she was forced to admit that there were moments, little gaps in time, split-seconds, when she felt something else too.

It had always given her a lift to see a message arrive from him. Whenever her phone pinged, she hoped that it would be his name she saw on the screen. Now Belle thought this must have been happening for months, with every new message, with all the hours and hours of talking late at night and early in the morning, the feelings stirring up then settling down again. She just hadn't recognised it.

She slept only for short stretches that night and whenever she woke the same thoughts ran through her head. She loved Ari still, so she couldn't love Enrico too.

Well before dawn, she gave up trying to rest and, sitting in bed, scrolled through photographs of Ari on her phone. A shot of him astride his horse, sitting in his favourite chair, picking lemons off a tree. If he hadn't gone surfing that day, he would still be doing all those things. And Belle wouldn't be here in Italy.

As the sun rose, she moved to the window and watched it touch the white buildings and paint the sky pink. When her phone rang and she saw it was Greg, she answered at the last moment.

'Good morning.' His voice was warm and bright. 'Or actually good evening for me.'

'Is it a good evening?' Belle saw that he was dressed in a tight dark top, rather than his usual well-worn plaid. 'Are you heading out somewhere?'

'About to, yes,' he confirmed.

'With a guy?' she pressed him. 'Someone you met on a dating app?'

'Someone I know, he's a local, owns the beach café.'

Belle hardly ever visited her nearest café in Muriwai. It was usually packed with day-trippers and beachgoers, so the service was slow. She searched her mind, and found the haziest recollection of a tall man, about a decade younger than Greg, who might have been its owner.

'I may know who you mean. Fair hair, nice eyes? Did he ask you out?'

'Not exactly. He came over for a riding lesson and I hope you don't mind, but I put him on Tama. The only other beginner's mount on the property is Jake and he's lame at the moment.'

'No, that's fine,' said Belle, pleased that Ari's horse was getting some attention. 'I take it the lesson went well, if you're going out for a drink with him?'

'For dinner,' Greg corrected. 'At the Hunting Lodge.'

'Ah, it went *that* well.'

Possibly it was a trick of the light, but Belle thought Greg was blushing. 'I thought I should check with you about Tama,' he said, quickly. 'In case Matt books another lesson or I decide to take him out for a hack some time.'

'You like this guy,' realised Belle.

'I've seen him around, I've always liked him,' Greg confirmed. 'But hey it's only a dinner.'

'You look great,' she told him, and this time Greg definitely blushed.

He asked how it was going in Italy and Belle murmured evasive answers. Everything was fine, nothing new to report, weather hot, sun shining. Greg stared out from the screen, listening.

'You don't look so great,' he observed when she had finished.

Belle rubbed her eyes. 'I've only just woken up, and didn't get much sleep in the first place.'

'Are you sure everything's fine? Has something happened?'

'No.' Belle looked away from the screen.

'Do you want something to happen?'

She glanced back at him. 'What do you mean?'

'You're not getting bored?'

'I'm just a bit tired this morning.'

'Maybe try and get a bit more sleep then. It's still early isn't it?'

'I'll try,' she said, knowing there was no chance. 'Have a good time on your date. Let me know how it goes.'

After he had rung off, Belle rested her head against the window. She hoped things worked out with the guy from the beach café, that Greg didn't get his hopes up and his heart broken, although she worried that he might. It seemed to her that love was something you always lost in the end; one way or another.

It was Sunday, which meant Belle had been in Italy for a week. She knew enough about life in the *palazzo* to expect another long lunch in the garden. Needing some time to herself first, she tiptoed downstairs, careful not to wake anyone, and slipped through the front door.

Belle made her way slowly to the old town, taking a meandering route, turning down streets that looked interesting. Eventually she came across an empty bar with a couple of outdoor tables where she settled down in the morning sunshine.

Enrico and Ari occupied her mind, as she sipped a coffee and nibbled on a custard-filled *pasticciotto*. They were such different men. One was slender, the other had been stocky. One liked to talk, the other didn't waste many words. One cared about clothes, the other couldn't have cared less. How could she have feelings for both of them? It was impossible.

The waiter intruded on her thoughts, coming to clear the table and stopping for a chat. Where was she from? Did she like Puglia? He asked all the usual questions that people have for tourists but only when he learned she was a guest of the Ginaro family, did he show signs of genuine interest.

'I was at school with Enrico and Luciana,' he told Belle, wiping down her table. 'It was sad what happened. They say she had violent rages towards the end. No one expected that for Luciana. She was always so sweet and kind, the prettiest girl in our class, everybody liked her.'

He moved away and Belle was left thinking how much Enrico must have been through. Despite that he always had time to listen to her problems. He remembered what she said, from one conversation to the next. He was a man who drove a Vespa slightly too fast while laughing. Who held her hand as they swam underwater and into a sea cave. And held her again while she cried.

'Do you want something to happen?' Greg had asked earlier on. He was being flippant but even so, it was a question Belle thought she might need to ask herself.

15

Perla's Stylish Life

Two cats were sitting in the sunshine on the doorstep of the *palazzo*. As Belle approached, they seemed to stare at her accusingly. One was a tabby that sometimes jumped on her lap and she stopped to stroke it, feeling the warmth of its fur and the tremble of its body as it began to purr.

There was something comforting about stroking a cat and Belle was still there when Perla came trailing barefoot along the street unsteadily, high-heeled sandals clutched in one hand, mascara smudged beneath her eyes, hair wild.

She sat down on the step, beside the cats, and her head fell back against the door. 'Oof what a night, I am a wreck,' she complained.

'Are you only just coming home?' Belle had partied fairly hard at times in her youth but usually by dawn the party was over. 'Where is Pietro?'

'He is still with his friends but I have had enough, I can't even walk a step further.' Pushing the cats off the step, Perla lay down in the space where they had been. 'I will have to stay here.'

Belle was surprised that Pietro had left his wife to walk home alone in such a state. 'What have you been drinking ... or taking?' she asked.

'Too much of everything,' Perla murmured in reply, eyes closing.

'You can't sleep here. Come on, let me get you upstairs.'

'Leave me, I am fine.' Perla shook off her hand as Belle tried to help her up.

'You most definitely aren't fine. You need toast and tea, and your bed.'

'Toast and tea?' Perla laughed as if it was the funniest thing she had heard in her life. She kept on giggling.

'Now you're just being annoying,' said Belle, standing hands on hips, exasperated. 'Get up or I'm going to abandon you here and half the town will see you slumped like an old drunk and they'll never stop talking about it.'

'Don't be horrible,' wailed Perla, but at least she got to her feet, leaving the shoes where she had dropped them.

Belle picked them up. 'Where is your bag?' she wondered.

'I don't have a bag, only my phone, but where is my phone?' Perla looked around as though she expected to see it.

'You must have lost it.'

'Oh no, I can't have lost another phone ...'

There was every chance she would slump down on the step again, so Belle grabbed her arm and steered her through the front door.

'My phone,' Perla repeated, plaintively. 'I have to find it.'

'Later.' Belle was stern. 'Right now, we need to get you into bed.'

'You are being horrible to me again.'

Chivvying her upstairs, Belle kept hoping someone would appear and take over, Gianni maybe, even the maid, but no one came to her rescue. Somehow, she got Perla to her room, which was strewn with clothes and empty glasses, the bed barely visible beneath the tumble of her and Pietro's belongings.

Belle swept everything onto the floor, as Perla was tugging off her skimpy, strappy dress and dropping it where she stood.

'Tea and toast.' She giggled again, falling face-forwards onto the bed.

'You're a mess,' Belle observed.

'Yes, I am, this is true, but I had such a good time. You should have come with us, Belle, you should have come and partied.'

'Judging by the shape you're in, I'm very glad I didn't.'

'You stayed to eat cake with Enrico.' The girl rolled onto her back, arms flailing for the covers. 'And Katarina and Gianni.'

'It was lovely cake,' said Belle, tugging the covers over her.

'It was awful cake,' insisted Perla. 'So are Katarina and Gianni, awful, awful.'

'No, they're not.'

'You don't know, nobody knows.' Perla threw off the covers and tried to sit up.

'Stay in bed,' Belle told her.

'Nobody knows, nobody knows.'

'What don't they know?'

'That Gianni is having an affair with Mia.'

Belle dismissed this instantly as another of Perla's stories. 'Of course he isn't,' she said briskly. 'Now why don't I go and get you that tea and toast, or at least a glass of water.'

As she left the room Perla was half singing, 'Tea and toast, tea and toast', her latest lie apparently quite forgotten.

Belle might have done her share of partying, but she couldn't recall ever coming home in the sort of state Perla was in. Fortunately, the girl had made it back, without her phone, any cash or even a credit card apparently, weaving through the streets barefoot in that clinging dress. Thankfully this was a small, safe town.

Katarina was in the kitchen, preparing to feed the cats, a large sack of kibble on the counter, clean stainless-steel bowls stacked beside it. She looked up as Belle appeared.

'Is everything OK, you look worried?' she asked.

'Actually, I'm cross,' Belle told her.

'Who with?' asked Katarina, distracted by scooping biscuits into the bowls, as cats appeared from every direction and eddied round her feet.

'With Pietro for letting his wife stagger home on her own, drunk and probably also high ...'

Katarina seemed unmoved. 'That is very normal, it happens all the time.'

'And now I've been left to deal with her,' finished Belle.

'She will be fine. Let her sleep it off somewhere,' advised Katarina. 'I have found her in the garden, on the floor in the salon, several times on loungers by the swimming pool.'

'Today you almost found her on the doorstep.'

Katarina laughed at that. 'She is always fine. That is the thing with Perla.'

'I promised to take her tea and toast.'

'You are kind, but by now she will be completely unconscious.'

Katarina put bowls brimming with cat biscuits down on the ground in an orderly line, then washed her hands and dried them carefully before starting to make coffee. Her eyes looked tired, her skin pale, but she moved around the kitchen quickly and efficiently.

'You would like some breakfast?' she asked Belle.

'Thanks but no, I went out and ate earlier.'

'It is a beautiful morning.' Katarina, glanced through the window to confirm it. 'And very hot already. I think it would be cooler to have lunch inside today, but Nonna Gilda prefers to eat in the garden.'

The cats were swarming round the bowls now, tabbies and gingers, a skinny black, a fluffy grey, a couple that were the colour of marmalade. One was missing an eye, some had frayed ears or bald patches, others were sleek and cared for.

'Gianni told me you'd had some interest in adopting,' said

217

Belle, thinking there seemed to be even more cats than usual.

'There are people coming tomorrow to see a tabby and a long-haired grey.' Katarina bit her lip anxiously and Belle wondered why she didn't seem happier.

'That's good isn't it?'

'Yes but it would be better if Nonna Gilda wasn't here when they arrive and I don't know how to manage that. Almost the only place she ever goes nowadays is the hairdresser, and her appointment this week is for Wednesday. I know because I made it myself.'

Belle could see that it wasn't going to be easy to dislodge the old woman from her *palazzo*. 'Does she have any friends that she visits?'

'Not really. She was closest to Luciana. They spent a lot of time together.'

Again Belle found herself feeling almost sorry for this older woman that she didn't really like much. 'She must be lonely now, then. If she hardly ever goes anywhere or sees anybody.'

'It wasn't always this way,' Katarina told her. 'Gianni says before she retired from the business Nonna Gilda went into the office every day. Now mostly she stays here watching television in her room.'

Belle thought about the archive. It hadn't been mentioned again and she had assumed that the Signora, having been frosty about her idea, must have put the entire project aside again.

'What about trying to get her back to the office tomorrow,' Belle suggested. 'To look at the foyer and consider how it might work as an exhibition space.'

Katarina seemed unconvinced. 'Why would she want to do that?'

'Because you're going to tell her that you really like the idea and she should think about it. Some day you'll be in charge of that archive; your opinion should count. Besides, it's your chance to get rid of some of these cats.' As Belle spoke a couple were stalking each other, moving slowly, fur ruffled. One made a low growling sound and the other hissed in reply.

'I suppose I could try.' Katarina chewed at her lip again. 'You will accompany her there?'

That hadn't been in Belle's mind but Katarina looked so hopeful. 'Sure, if you can convince her to go.'

She was rewarded with a smile. 'I will do my best.'

Even though she continued to vow that it was a complete waste of time, Katarina helped make up a tray for Perla – a glass of orange juice, a cup of coffee, some *biscotti*, headache pills.

When she took them upstairs Belle found Perla fast asleep, exactly as predicted. She left the juice and headache pills on her nightstand then stood at the window, drinking the coffee rather than waste it and eating one of the *biscotti*, admiring the view of the sea, shimmering in the distance.

The room smelled faintly of stale wine and cigarettes. Perla was snoring loudly, lying on her back, mouth open, hair tangling over the pillow. Reaching for her phone, Belle tapped on the Instagram icon. Photographs of the night before had already been posted on *@perla_stylish_life*. They must have been taken early, before her make-up was smudged and her dress got stained. Thousands of her followers had liked them. They wanted to know where her outfit came from and what was in her cocktail. They told her she was beautiful, admired her glowing skin, the natural soft curls in her hair, even her lipstick shade.

Belle moved her gaze back to Perla, noticing a silvery line of drool leaking from the corner of her mouth. She wondered what all those followers would think if they could see her now, and for the first time she almost understood Perla's lies, because it was all a lie really, a version of her life only loosely connected to reality, how she wanted to be seen.

The sun was blazing; however, as Katarina had predicted lunch was served outside. At least they were in the relative cool of the loggia, at a table covered with fine linen from the Casa di Ginaro collection, and with a centrepiece of pale pink moth orchids floating in a large crystal vase.

As her glass was filled with effervescent blush wine, Belle watched Enrico. For a moment she imagined there was only the two of them there, drinking wine, eating lunch, talking. But the Ginaro family couldn't be shut out for long. Their voices roused Belle from her thoughts. It seemed that the Signora was cross because Pietro hadn't appeared for lunch.

'I will send the maid to fetch him,' she announced. 'He needs to show some respect.'

'Mamma, no, he and Perla must have been out half the night, let them sleep,' said Enrico.

'This is his birthday lunch,' the Signora insisted.

It was possible that Pietro hadn't even made it home yet, but Belle didn't say so, instead staying quiet, sipping her wine, listening to them argue.

'He knew he was expected here, didn't he?'

'Yes, Mamma.' Enrico sounded calm but Belle sensed that his patience was strained.

'I suppose he imagines that we are going to lecture him about these plans he and Perla seem to have made,' said the Signora. 'Travelling instead of getting on with his life.'

Somehow Enrico kept his patience. 'Many young people take time out to go travelling. There is no reason why he shouldn't do this if he chooses. As for Luciana, she only wanted her sons to be happy.'

'Pietro does whatever he wants, he always has,' muttered Gianni as, beside him Katarina stared at her plate, not eating.

'That is not fair,' argued Enrico. 'Not true, at all.'

'It is very easy to spend money that you never had to earn,' pointed out Gianni.

Even the cats were making themselves scarce. Belle wished she could do the same. She had no desire to sit through another Ginaro argument.

And then unexpectedly Pietro appeared, looking rumpled in the same clothes he had been wearing the night before, eyes hooded and bruised with shadows.

'I am starving,' he announced, treating them to his most charming smile as he took a seat at the table.

'You are late,' his grandmother replied, stiffly. 'And where is your wife?'

'Perla is sick, she must have eaten something that didn't agree with her.' Pietro was already piling his plate full of pasta baked with marinated tomatoes and *stracciatella* cheese.

'At least you have an appetite,' observed the Signora.

Her anger subsided as she watched him eat and her face was transformed by a fonder expression. Almost everyone at the table seemed to relax along with her; everyone except Gianni.

'Did you treat your friends to cocktails, pay the bill everywhere you went?' he asked his brother.

'It is good to be generous,' Pietro replied, loading a fork with pasta.

'If you have the money, yes.'

'I have money,' pointed out Pietro. 'Well, I will very soon.'

Sitting between them, Enrico held up his hands. 'No more fighting, please. Can we enjoy our lunch?'

Gianni wasn't to be deterred. 'You haven't won Super-Enalotto, you know. Mamma's legacy is no jackpot. When you have spent it, then it is gone.'

'Relax, OK.' Pietro dabbed tomato sauce from the corner of his mouth with a napkin. 'Perla is working on something exciting.'

'Perla is working?' Gianni seemed sceptical.

'Yes, in the digital space,' confirmed Pietro. 'She has

thousands of followers on Instagram. Have you seen her page?'

'I don't have time to waste staring at my phone all day like she does,' Gianni said, dismissively.

'Perla is becoming an influencer.' Pietro sounded proud. 'Lots of brands want to collaborate with her. Once we start travelling, more opportunities are sure to open up.'

Katarina had pulled out her phone and was tapping on the screen. She passed it to Gianni, who stared, eyes narrowed. 'Why didn't we know this?'

'Because none of you think about anything but yourselves,' Pietro said, matter-of-factly.

'I knew about it,' admitted Katarina. 'I follow Perla on Instagram.'

Gianni looked up from the screen. 'You didn't tell me.'

'No.' Katarina looked uncomfortable. 'I didn't think to.'

'You are only interested in yourselves, just like I said,' added Pietro, his head bent over his plate.

'I am interested.' The Signora held out a hand for the phone. 'Show me this page.'

'Nonna,' her grandson started to explain. 'Instagram is a social media website where people ...'

'I know that, Gianni,' she interrupted, testily. 'I may be old but I am still living in the world with you. I have heard of Instagram.'

The Signora studied the screen for a few minutes, arched her brows, then nodded. 'Very nice.' Pietro was wiping a crust of bread round his plate to soak up the last of the crushed tomato sauce. 'Remember when that pink dress sold out on the website and no one could understand why? Almost certainly that was Perla. I took the picture of her wearing it in Alberobello. Often I am her photographer.'

Now everyone had a phone in their hand and was scrolling, Belle included. She found the image that he must mean. Perla was holding hands with Pietro, who was mostly out of shot, and was turning back towards him with a smile. Beyond her was a row of *trulli*, the distinctive stone buildings with conical roofs that were dotted through the nearby valley. Her dress was vivid pink against the whitewashed walls.

'It was a lot of work actually,' Pietro continued. 'The light needed to be right, the angles, Perla wasn't happy until everything looked perfect.'

'It is true that dress did sell out,' Enrico reflected.

'Because it was beautiful,' said Gianni.

'Because people want to look like us,' said the Signora. 'They want the life we have, like I have always told you.'

Belle wondered how many young women had that same bright pink dress hanging in their wardrobe and dreamed of looking as perfect in it. *Perla's Stylish Life*; it might just be another of her lies, but it was an elegant one.

Gianni was frowning at his brother. 'Why didn't you mention any of this to us before?'

'I did but you weren't listening. You and Katarina only ever want to criticise Perla. You hate to hear anything good about her.' Pietro had finished his food and was leaning back in his chair. 'I am still starving. Is there more?'

'Of course, *caro*.' The Signora rang the small bell that she kept beside her wine glass. 'I will have the maid bring it for you.'

Katarina was gazing down at her plate. All she had done was push the pasta round it with a fork. Belle felt sorry for her sitting through these long lunches, when she had so little appetite. Most likely she felt like she had to be there; that it was a part of being a member of this family, of fitting in. Did she ever envy Perla's freedom to be herself and do what she wanted?

'But we do have a social media plan.' Enrico turned to Gianni. 'You are looking after this, yes?'

'We use an agency, they are very good.'

'They are doing a terrible job,' argued Pietro. 'Casa di Ginaro is not even on TikTok yet.'

'It is not our market,' Gianni insisted.

'Perla says that is changing. She knows much more than this agency you are relying on. You should talk to her.'

'We should,' Enrico agreed. 'I am very interested in hearing what Perla has to say.'

Katarina looked up from her plate. 'I have watched some of her videos on TikTok.'

'Sometimes I help her shoot those,' said Pietro, as the maid placed a second helping of pasta in front of him. 'It is what we are doing when everyone thinks we are wasting our time.'

Katarina added hesitantly. 'They are clever.'

'My wife is clever.' Pietro looked up from his food. 'That is what none of you seem to realise.'

Still watching and listening, Belle said nothing. Even if she were a part of this family, would she feel free to speak her mind? Might she quietly go her own way like Perla seemed to; or hold herself back like Katarina did? The questions ran through her mind, as Enrico tried to calm things. And Belle couldn't really imagine being like either of them.

'Nobody is doubting Perla's intelligence,' Enrico was saying. 'I don't know why you would think that.'

'Not you Papa, but Gianni. Nothing she does is right in his opinion.'

Gianni's face tightened. 'That isn't true.'

'Yes it is.' Pietro sounded bitter. 'You have never liked her. Right from the beginning you made it obvious.'

'Enough,' protested Enrico, his impatience evident now. 'No more fighting at the dinner table. I cannot stand it anymore.'

Both of his sons gaped at him as he raised his voice so loudly that it echoed round the loggia. They can't have been used to being shouted at.

'We will discuss the social media plan tomorrow at the

weekly meeting,' Enrico said, his tone more level. 'For now, Gianni, you need to spend some time analysing what this agency has been doing. I expect a report in the morning.'

'But Papa, I ...'

'And Pietro, will you please let Perla know that we would like her input?' continued Enrico.

Pietro nodded. '*Si, si* Papa.'

He fixed his gaze on his youngest son. 'Don't say yes to me then forget to do it.'

Pietro shifted in his seat, awkwardly. 'Perla isn't well, so ...'

'She has a hangover,' said Enrico. 'I believe she has survived them before? Tomorrow I want you both at that meeting. I don't expect to be let down.'

'I don't let people down.' Pietro was defensive.

'But you do; all the time. Just the other day you promised to take Belle to Alberobello and then didn't turn up.'

'That wasn't my fault. Perla needed help with something she was working on.'

'It isn't good enough.' Enrico wasn't to be placated.

Belle had never seen this side of him. He was so steely that for a moment even she found herself gaping. But he was the head of a business, she reminded herself, a person used to taking charge, and must always have had this steel in him, just didn't show it unless he had to.

'You owe Belle an apology,' Enrico told his son.

'I am sorry,' said Pietro, sheepishly. 'We can go another time.'

Alberobello with its picturesque *trulli* all grouped together. People had told Belle it was a touristy place, heaving with souvenir shops and usually crowded, still every visitor to Puglia needed to see it.

'Yes, of course,' she said, politely.

'Not this afternoon though,' Pietro added, quickly, in case she had any idea of it.

Belle imagined all he wanted was to sleep. Now that he had eaten, Pietro's eyes seemed lidded and heavy, and sweat was beading on his face. 'Another time is fine,' she told him.

'But we could go this afternoon for a quiet stroll.' Enrico suggested. 'A drink in a bar, maybe a gelato.'

'It is much too hot,' said Pietro. 'We would be better to stay here, rest ...'

'I will be resting in this heat,' agreed the Signora, dropping her napkin beside her plate, and getting to her feet.

'So will I,' added Katarina. 'If you are ready then let me help you upstairs, Nonna.'

She took the older woman's arm and Belle watched them go, Katarina slender seen squarely from behind, the Signora smaller and stockier, leaning against her slightly.

'And I suppose that I must work,' said Gianni, a frown etched on his face. 'Since apparently I have a report to prepare.'

'I suppose you must,' said Enrico, and he smiled towards Belle, any trace of sternness dissolving. 'Just you and I then, if you would like to join me. A quiet stroll. Maybe a gelato.'

They travelled to Alberobello in Gianni's low-slung sports car, but there was no arriving at a fancy hotel and tossing the keys at a valet, as his son had done in Lecce. Instead, Enrico found a space in a car park and they followed a flock of people walking towards the *trulli* zone.

The town was very touristy, as he had warned, with busloads of sightseers, but nevertheless Belle found herself enchanted by the whitewashed huts crowned with conical roofs clustered along its winding stone streets. Among the hundreds of these peculiar fairy-tale houses, many were souvenir shops, with their owners sitting outside, trying to tempt shoppers inside. Others seemed to be people's homes, with laundry drying on lines outside and the sounds of televisions coming from open windows.

'I used to dream of living in one when I was young,' Enrico admitted, as they strolled past the *trulli* side by side.

'Instead of the *palazzo*?' Belle was surprised.

'I imagined it would be nice, all of us close together in a small home, rather than spread out in such a large one.'

'I thought you loved your house?'

'I do, of course … still, a *trullo*, they have thick walls so are cool in summer and cosy in winter. Many have been modernised and they are beautiful inside. The *palazzo* is such a demanding building, always something needs maintaining; in a *trullo* you would have a simpler life.'

They stopped so Enrico could photograph Belle against a background of magical *trulli*, covered in swathes of jasmine. Then he suggested trying a selfie and, with their heads closer together, held his phone at a steep angle above them.

'I have watched Perla do this,' Enrico explained. 'There is an art to getting a good one.'

It was a really terrible photo, decided Belle later on, sitting at a bar and looking through them. Taken so close, their age showed starkly on their faces, and both of them were squinting unattractively into the light.

'Unfortunately, we will never be influencers,' she told Enrico.

He glanced at her screen. 'I don't know about that; I think we look good together.'

Belle examined Enrico's face in the selfie then looked at him sitting beside her, amused at the sight of it.

'Maybe I need to ask Perla for a few more tips,' he conceded. 'I can always improve.'

He was a friend; Belle repeated the words in her mind like a mantra, knowing that to the busloads of tourists walking past they must seem like a couple, dressed in their stylish pale linen, sipping craft beer and laughing together.

'I'm going to delete this selfie,' she told him. 'I'd hate for it to get into the wrong hands.'

'It is the only shot we have of us together,' Enrico objected.

Belle touched the trash can icon. 'Gone,' she told him. 'From all my devices.'

'We can take another,' he said, lightly.

As the sun faded, Alberobello sparkled with lights, the tourist hordes seemed to thin and the evening air cooled. They ordered more drinks and grazed on small plates of fat green olives and marinated white anchovies.

'This is nice.' Enrico leaned back in his chair, running a hand through his short-cropped hair, making it stand on end. 'Much more relaxing than lunch, certainly. My family always seems to be arguing these days, but then I suppose most families do.'

'Mine almost never argues,' Belle told him, truthfully.

'How do you manage this miracle?'

'It's easy not to fight with people when you hardly ever see them.'

'They live far from you?' guessed Enrico.

'Not really, they're in the city so only forty minutes away, but we're not close, we never have been really.'

Enrico gave his head a shake as if trying to clear his mind and process this thought. 'So now that Ari is gone ...'

'I'm on my own.' Belle finished for him. 'But that's fine, I'm used to it.'

'I can't imagine a life without family,' he said thoughtfully, seated across the table from her, beer in hand, hair spiky.

'I can't imagine a life with one,' she countered.

Probably he would assume there had been some sort of falling out. The truth was undramatic and less easy to understand, not a break-up but a quiet withdrawal.

'My mother and I are very different,' Belle explained. 'She and my stepfather are a tight unit, they don't really need me.'

'But when you lost Ari, surely they supported you?'

'They tried to, in their own way, but they never really approved of him. Ari was so much older than me ... and not exactly their sort of person.' In fact, Belle's mother had made it plain that she didn't understand her choice of husband. Any remaining ties loosened after that and they saw almost nothing of each other, aside from the occasional duty visit around Christmas time or birthdays.

'It must have been very lonely for you,' said Enrico.

'I suppose yes, it has been at times,' agreed Belle, watching people drifting past: tour groups, families with children, couples hand in hand – everyone with somebody. 'But often it felt like I wanted to be lonely.'

'I was raised to believe that family is the most important thing,' Enrico told her. 'Mamma drummed it into me. *If we don't have each other then we have nothing*, is what she would always say.'

Belle thought of the old Signora, in the echoing halls of the *palazzo*, surrounded by cats. 'But your mother seems quite lonely even if she is surrounded by family. Don't you think?'

'Lonely?' Enrico considered the idea. 'I think perhaps it was a mistake for her to retire. She is a shrewd woman and very smart; she loved being a part of the business, lived and breathed it.'

'Why did she stop working then? Surely she didn't have to?'

'She got older and decided it was time for me to take the reins. The archive was to be her retirement project.'

'Then Luciana got sick.'

'She did.' Enrico nodded slowly. 'And I think you are right, now Mamma may be a little lonely.'

'She has the cats for company,' said Belle.

Enrico groaned. 'Those cats. Are there more of them, even since you arrived? I think there may be.'

'Quite possibly.'

'The cats started arriving when Luciana became unwell. It

calmed her having a cat on her knee, and then later for my mother they seemed to help fill the space where she used to be.' Emotions chased across Enrico's face; concern, sadness, regret.

Family was everything to him, the most important thing, and his love for them went bone-deep. Belle felt it now as they walked back to the car through streets lined with *trulli*, past seething restaurants and bars. She was more and more aware of the love that was everywhere. In every home they passed, love between husbands and wives, parents and children. Love in the clasped hands across restaurant tables, and the couples hand in hand, and the man dropping a kiss on the cheek of the baby daughter he held in his arms. Other people's love: it might as well have been in the air, Belle almost felt like she was breathing it.

Driving back to the *palazzo*, towards Ostuni brightly lit against the darkening sky, Enrico beside her and deep in his own thoughts, Belle could feel it still.

16

Love And Loneliness

Belle had left her curtains open as she liked being able to see outside when she opened her eyes in the morning. Watching now through the window as the sky lightened, she noticed it was raining very lightly, misting the glass, until even her view was clouded. Before long the sky blued, the sun beat down again and the window cleared. It was set to be another scorching hot day.

When Belle got out of bed, she almost tripped over some shopping bags she had dumped on the floor the night before. More new clothes had been sent from the Casa di Ginaro collection, too many clothes, dresses and tops, trousers and skirts, summer jackets. By the time it was all unpacked, her room looked more like it belonged to Perla. Amid the clutter, one item stood out; a scarf, long and wide, a generous piece of fabric shot through with shades of aquamarine. It was the sort of thing that might have caught Belle's eye if she were out shopping. She had a fondness for scarves and this one was pretty.

The single clever trick she had was knowing how to wear a scarf. She could wind it round her neck and it would somehow look better than when another person did the same. Often, she tied one in her hair. On cold nights at home, she liked to sleep with an old pashmina round her shoulders. She had silk scarves and cashmere, bright ones and dark, a vintage Hermès square, and several chunky handknits she had bought in thrift stores. The last thing Belle needed was more scarves; still she liked this one.

Looping it round her neck and slipping Ari's greenstone back into her pocket, she checked in the mirror. The scarf looked good on her.

Belle wore the aquamarine scarf down to breakfast although Katarina was too distracted to notice.

'I talked to Nonna Gilda,' she said, setting eyes on Belle, and seeming agitated. 'She has agreed to visit the archive with you this morning to consider installing a display in the foyer.'

'Did you tell her that you like the idea?'

'Yes, yes I did. She wanted me to join you but I must stay here ... the cats.'

'Of course,' said Belle, supressing a sigh, as a tortoiseshell cat curled around her bare legs and a kitten mewled at her plaintively. She wasn't exactly thrilled at the thought of another morning spent at the archive with the Signora.

'Hopefully two of them will be gone by the time you both get back,' added Katarina. 'For now they are shut up in the orangery.'

'Everything is organised then,' said Belle.

'This is my talent, organising.' Katarina was brushing stray pellets of cat kibble into a dustpan. 'I am not creative like you and Perla.'

'But I'm not really creative,' Belle told her. 'I wish I was.'

She looked up in surprise. 'You have a gallery.'

'It is full of other people's creativity. I only arrange things.'

Tipping the mess of cat biscuits into the bin, Katarina shrugged. 'Then you are more like me, an organiser.'

'Perla is an artist in her way,' observed Belle. 'And artists are not always easy to live with.'

'Your husband was an artist, yes?' said Katarina, reaching for the Moka pot and a canister of coffee.

'Ari always said that if I'd known him as a younger man then I might have found him difficult.' Belle had never really believed it. 'By the time we met, he wasn't painting, so I suppose he wasn't really an artist anymore.'

'Neither is Perla; almost everyone posts photographs on Instagram, it is hardly the same.' Katarina was spooning coffee grounds into the Moka, her back turned to Belle. 'Yesterday Gianni was cross with me for not mentioning her page to him. Always she comes between us, causing trouble. Now she is taking Pietro from his family.'

The Moka pot hissed as she lit a gas jet beneath it. She retrieved ice from the freezer and reached for a bottle of almond milk syrup, everything about her quietly efficient. Belle thought it hardly seemed surprising that she and Perla didn't get on. They were as different as the brothers they had married.

'Pietro said we are only interested in ourselves.' A frown flickered over Katarina's face. 'That is so unfair.'

Belle didn't want to get caught between the different factions of this family. She didn't want to be a part of it.

'They are the selfish ones, not us,' said Katarina, bitterly.

The Moka pot gurgled, signalling that the coffee was ready. Katarina poured treacly black espresso over cubed ice and laced it with almond milk syrup, then put the cup in front of Belle who breathed the steam appreciatively.

'It might be good for Pietro and Perla to have some time away,' she suggested, doing her best to be diplomatic.

'Good for them, maybe,' said Katarina, her frown deepening. 'But they will be leaving everything to us, just as always.'

Belle waited for the Signora in the peppermint-scented vestibule. She appeared at the same time as her driver arrived to collect them and nodded approvingly, although whether at their promptness or at the aquamarine scarf tied artfully around Belle's neck, she wasn't certain.

'*Siamo pronti*?' the Signora asked.

'We're ready,' Belle confirmed.

They made the short trip without any attempt at conversation. Only when they arrived at the Casa di Ginaro building did the Signora turn and say, 'I suppose you are surprised to be here with me again?'

'A little,' agreed Belle. 'I didn't think you liked my idea for the display very much.'

'Not at all,' the Signora said, frankly. 'But since we have come, we may as well discuss it further.'

The reception area was as spacious as Belle remembered, a mostly empty room, floored with shining marble. The moment they appeared, the receptionist hurried over and began fluttering around. Did Signora Ginaro need a glass of water? Would she like to sit down?

Shrugging her off, the Signora turned to Belle. 'This part of the building is the face of our brand and it is very traditional.'

'It might be the entranceway to any number of other companies,' Belle pointed out, looking at the acres of marble, high ceilings and mirrored walls. 'It doesn't say Casa di Ginaro. When you step through the doorway you can't even tell this is a fashion house at first.'

The Signora was very still, only her eyes moved as she cast them round the room. 'Maybe Katarina is right, and it is time for change. Tradition is important, yet we must also move with the times.'

The receptionist looked crushed. Did Signora Ginaro still not like the flower arrangement? Would she prefer a stack of books rather than a pile of magazines? Might it be better if the furniture was configured in a different way?

'I am not opposed to change.' The Signora interrupted. 'But whether we are talking about the style of a room or the cut of a jacket, it must be the right change.'

'There are so many options. You could display a series of

images, have a video wall ...' Catching the Signora's pained expression, Belle wavered for a moment then decided she had nothing to lose by speaking her mind. 'Personally what I'd like to see is the clothes exhibited here. There is something sad about them being locked away in that dark room, all wrapped up in dust covers. I understand that textiles need to be treated carefully but if no one can ever look at them what is the point?'

Belle paused for a response, but the Signora only gave her a cool stare.

'A renovation?' the receptionist began, hesitantly. 'The entrance foyer has been exactly like this for as long as I have worked here. Only the flowers and the magazines ever change. Nothing else.'

The Signora sighed heavily and, staring into space, repeated, 'I am not opposed to change.'

By the time the driver appeared to collect them, there was a plan of sorts. The designers who had come up with the original concept for the display room would be given the chance to offer new ideas. Everyone had agreed this was a first step, not a commitment. It couldn't do any harm to consider the possibilities.

Settling into the back seat of the car, the Signora turned to Belle. 'That was an interesting morning. Do you think we have given her enough time?'

Belle didn't understand at first. 'I'm sorry? Who?'

'Katarina, obviously. Have we been out of the house for as long as she wanted?'

'So, you know ...?' Belle began, slowly.

'That she is adopting out some of the cats, yes of course.'

'And you don't mind?'

'There will always be cats,' said the Signora, as the driver was pulling away from the kerb. 'Old ones will go and new ones will come.'

'In that case then, I think maybe we should give Katarina a little longer,' suggested Belle.

'*Va bene*,' agreed the Signora, calling to the driver, 'Bar Pausa please Luigi, we will stop for a coffee.'

Being out and about in Ostuni with the Signora was like going on a royal walkabout. Even the few steps to reach the bar from where the driver had dropped them involved stopping several times to exchange pleasantries with people who knew her. Then the waiter rushed over to wipe down a table that already seemed perfectly clean and adjusted the sun umbrella to be sure they were properly shaded. Most people crossing the piazza at least nodded a greeting or called *buongiorno*, others paused at their table to comment on how well the Signora was looking and ask after her family.

'I have lived here all my life.' The Signora's gaze drifted around the piazza, then settled on Belle. 'Unlike my grandsons, I never longed to travel. Everything I need is in Ostuni and I miss it when I go away, even to the villa.'

'It's a lovely town,' murmured Belle.

'You like it here.' The Signora's eyes seemed to search her face. 'But you miss home?'

'I miss the way it used to be, when my husband was there,' Belle admitted.

'It is very hard to lose a husband, I know that. I was also young to be a widow. At least I had my daughter and Enrico. You are alone.'

Belle didn't need reminding, 'I have friends,' she said, although really since Ari died there had been mainly Greg and Enrico.

The waiter brought out their coffee along with a dish of sweet, crunchy almond biscuits. Belle reached for one and nibbled on it, finding it tasted of vanilla and candied fruits.

'Friends aren't the same as family,' the Signora insisted. 'Not at all.'

Quietly, Belle disagreed. Friends could be loyal. After Ari got sick, it had been Greg and Enrico that she relied on. Without their friendship, Belle knew she might have foundered.

'Family is everything,' finished the Signora. 'That is my philosophy.'

Belle didn't bother to argue. 'Did you never want to share your life with anyone else?' she asked instead. 'After you lost your husband?'

For a fraction of a second, Belle thought she might have gone too far. Then the Signora blinked.

'I have a good life.' Her face firmed into a frown; she sounded cold as stones. 'Could any man make it better? Change has to improve things, as I told you earlier, otherwise there is no point in it.'

'Love isn't always so logical though,' Belle pointed out. 'It's not like redesigning a room. You can't always control it.'

'I disagree.'

Belle looked at the Signora, dressed in linen that somehow never seemed to crease, wearing lipstick that didn't smudge, with hair that a stiff wind wouldn't dishevel. She was prepared to believe this woman imagined she could influence most things.

'My husband was a romantic man.' The older woman's expression lightened and she half-smiled at the memory. 'He believed we were meant to be together, fated for each other. The truth is I chose him.'

'But you were in love?' Belle assumed.

'We were well-matched and I was happy,' said the Signora. 'He was a good husband, kind and hardworking as I knew he would be. I was careful and chose well.'

Belle remembered seeing Ari across a room and knowing that they had belonged together. Her feelings tended to lead her places. They had brought her all the way here. She was as unlike this carefully controlled woman as it was possible to be.

When the driver came to collect them, Belle decided to walk instead. The sky had cleared, the sun was shining and, saying goodbye to the Signora, she set out to lose herself in Ostuni, following streets she hadn't been down before, taking a left turn where she remembered last time going right, exploring lanes so narrow she could stretch her arms to touch the walls on either side.

Despite her best efforts, Belle kept passing places she recognised. The bar where she had eaten breakfast, a shop window she remembered browsing in, a show of flowers she had stopped to admire before.

She passed people gathered at benches and tables in a piazza, kissing cheek to cheek as they met on the streets, crowding into shops. It was still novel seeing so much life going on around her.

After Ari's death she had severed so many connections. Then lockdowns came along and made it easier not to re-connect. There had been days when Belle had spoken to no one but Greg and Enrico, whole weeks even. She had chosen loneliness.

Now she walked by the Casa di Ginaro shop and further on came across the salon where Mia worked. Belle peered in and there she was sweeping the floor, jabbing the broom resentfully at a drift of fallen hair, while the stylist was busy with a client. Looking up and seeing Belle at the window, she gave her trademark one-shouldered shrug. Belle felt sorry for her. She had suspected there would be too much sweeping involved in this job and not enough applying make-up.

Mia was the only person she knew in Ostuni that wasn't part of the Ginaro family, the closest thing to a friend that she had made here. And perhaps because the edge of loneliness felt sharper than usual, Belle reached for the door and pushed it open.

As the bell rang with a *ching*, both women glanced over, the stylist questioningly, and Mia more hopeful.

'I was hoping you might be able to fit me in for a blow-dry,' said Belle.

Mia said something in Italian and the stylist shook her head emphatically. 'I am very sorry, but she is fully booked,' she apologised.

'I was thinking you might do it, actually.'

'I am just the trainee. She lets me shampoo, but not blow-dry.' Mia screwed up her face.

'But I'd like you to do it,' said Belle.

'Really?' Mia cheered instantly. Abandoning her broom against the wall, she hurried to fetch a cape and towel.

'It's only a blow-dry,' said Belle smiling at the stylist. 'I'm sure it will be fine.'

The woman looked at her blankly then went back to trimming her client's hair.

'She doesn't understand English,' Mia reminded her, settling Belle at the washbasin.

As she rubbed shampoo then conditioner into Belle's hair, massaging her scalp with firm fingers, she told her about the make-up courses she had been applying for, the places she preferred, the ones that seemed less appealing.

'You have been busy,' remarked Belle, moving from the washbasin to a chair stationed in front of a mirror.

'I am making big plans, but still nothing is really happening yet.'

Mia combed the knots out of her hair, roughly dried it off, then started working on a smaller section with a large round brush. 'It is frustrating.'

'Perla and Pietro have been making plans too.' Belle had to raise her voice to be heard above the blow-dryer. 'Did you hear? They are going to travel the world.'

'That won't happen.' Mia sounded definite.

'They're saying it will.'

'Have they even booked flights?'

'I don't know about that,' admitted Belle.

Mia gave a derisive snort. 'Why would Perla go to some foreign place where no one knows her? Here, she is a Ginaro. In the rest of the world, she isn't special.'

'Do you really think this is another of her stories?' That hadn't occurred to Belle.

'I think she loves living in a *palazzo*. It is her dream come true.' Mia twirled the brush, creating a smooth loose curl. 'Wouldn't anyone want to live there?'

'Not me,' said Belle.

'Truly?' Mia stared at Belle in the mirror. 'You don't like it?'

'It's not really my style.'

'But why? The *palazzo* is so beautiful. The finest house in all Ostuni, the biggest pool, the best view ... luxurious.'

'A home should be a place that you're at ease in,' explained Belle. 'And I never feel completely at ease there. It's ostentatious.'

Mia tilted her head, confused. 'I don't know that word.'

'Everything is about showing off,' Belle explained.

The girl's face cleared. 'Yes, that is why Perla likes it.'

The stylist was darting curious glances at them. 'Are you sure she doesn't understand English?' Belle checked.

'Hardly a word.' Mia released another bouncy curl and smiled with satisfaction. 'But perhaps she is surprised at how good a job I am doing. I did tell her but she wouldn't listen.'

'Maybe now she'll let you do some blow-drying?'

'If she has any sense she will.' Mia unclipped another damp section of hair to work with. 'Hopefully I won't be here too much longer though. I intend to leave Ostuni and travel to new places. It isn't just a story I tell to make myself more interesting.'

As her hair was being tamed, Belle kept thinking about Perla, full of drama and stories. Her life was such a performance. While it was possible that she intended to go travelling, equally she might have said it for effect. Who would know? Perhaps not even Perla.

'I never know what to believe. She even told me that you and Gianni were having an affair.'

'An affair, Perla said that?' Mia's smile dimmed. She held the nozzle of the dryer away from Belle's hair. 'Who was there at the time, only you?'

When Belle nodded, she seemed relieved. 'If Perla says that kind of thing in front of Katarina there will be trouble. Gianni will be furious.'

'Mia, is it true?' Suddenly Belle had a feeling it might be.

'That depends,' she said and resumed blow-drying, focusing on a single section of hair, lips pressed tight.

For a few moments neither of them said anything. Belle watched until Mia looked up and their eyes met.

'*Va bene*, I will tell you how it is. Me and Gianni, we grew up together, he was the first boy I kissed and, yes, later we took things further. When he came back from university in the holidays, always we were with one another. Then he brought Katarina home and that was when I knew that I was the girl he slept with, not the one he wanted to marry.'

Mia released the final curl and ran her fingers through Belle's hair to loosen it. 'I wanted him to love me. Then I could have lived in the *palazzo*, worn the latest clothes from the collection, been one of them. Instead, here I am sweeping up hair.'

'You wanted to be a part of the Ginaro family, like Katarina and Perla?' Belle checked.

She nodded. 'It was what I dreamed of, growing up. I always imagined I would.'

'Mia, you don't want a life like that,' Belle promised. 'You can do all sorts of things ... lead your own life.'

'I am not sure which direction to take or even how to get started.'

Belle didn't tell her that you could feel like that at almost any age. 'You need to get out of this town,' she said, instead.

Mia gave a quick one-shouldered shrug. 'I know it.'

Back at the *palazzo*, Belle went looking for Katarina. She wasn't at her desk in the music room and down in the kitchen there was only the maid, clearing up after lunch.

'Katarina?' Belle asked and the maid waved a soapy hand at the window, pointing towards the garden.

She found the young woman stretched out on one of the loungers beside the pool, eyes closed and fully clothed, shaded by a sun umbrella. One hand was resting on her belly and on her bare arm Belle saw the raised red welts of fresh scratches.

'Oh dear, did this morning not go too well?' she asked.

Opening her eyes, Katarina sat up, still holding her belly with one hand, now rubbing her lower back with the other.

Belle dropped down onto the lounger beside hers. 'Did you get rid of any cats?'

'Yes, yes the tabby was perfect and those people loved her. The long-haired grey one though, I don't think she wants to leave the *palazzo* because she put up a struggle.' Katarina held out her arm as evidence. 'The family chose another instead. I am praying that they never decide to bring either of them back.'

'You need some sort of gauntlet,' said Belle, staring at the scratches. The cats seemed to go wherever they chose, springing through open windows and slipping through doors left ajar. Surely that wouldn't be an ideal scenario with a new baby in the house. 'Actually what you need is a proper cat sanctuary. A separate building where they could be until they are rehomed. Is that a possibility?'

'It would be a lot of work and I am too hot and tired, even

to think.' Katarina fanned herself with one hand. 'I have had enough of everything today. I came outside hoping for a breeze, but no. Now I am just lying here. I can't move.'

'Why not have a dip in the pool?' The water looked tempting, as always.

'I don't have my bathing suit.'

'I could go and fetch it for you,' Belle offered.

'I don't even know if it fits me anymore.' Katarina breathed an exhausted sigh. There was a sheen of sweat on her skin, and she looked as pale as ever. 'It's so hot ... too hot.'

'There's no one here, let's just jump in,' Belle suggested.

'Naked?' asked Katarina, astonished.

'I'm wearing a bra and knickers, aren't you?'

Katarina giggled. 'We shouldn't.'

'Why not?'

'What if somebody comes, one of the gardeners or the maid?'

'There's never anyone out here.' Swinging her legs off the lounger, Belle removed the aquamarine scarf and stripped off her clothes. 'I'm going in.'

The water wasn't cold exactly but still it was refreshing. In high-waisted knickers and black T-shirt bra, Belle swam a few strokes. A few moments later, she heard another splash and found Katarina treading water beside her.

'Ahh yes, that is good.'

'Total heaven,' agreed Belle, not giving a second thought to her ruined blow-dry.

'Nonna Gilda wouldn't approve.' Katarina's eyes darted round the poolside as though the Signora might emerge from the shrubbery any moment and catch her floating there in an ivory silk bra and briefs.

'Doesn't she take a rest in the afternoon? I think we're safe,' Belle reassured her. 'Besides, she was young once. Maybe she swam in her underwear.'

Katarina giggled again. 'Can you imagine it?'

'Not really,' Belle admitted, flapping her arms and legs to swim a slow length as Katarina wallowed. 'What would she say if she did see us?'

'She doesn't need to say a thing, she just gives you that look, it is enough.'

'Terrifying.' Belle submerged herself completely then surfaced, pushing the wet hair out of her eyes.

'Nonna Gilda can also be very kind though.' Katarina insisted.

'You mean with the cats?' Belle swam to the end of the pool, pushing off the wall and drifting back again.

'With her family too. She is good to Gianni. Whenever he gets stressed at work, it is always her he talks to.' She lay on her back and floated, the mound of her belly rising above the waterline. 'My poor husband, he works so hard and he will always have to.'

'He inherits it all in the end, doesn't he?' Belle still thought that was unfair.

'He will inherit staff whose livelihoods depend on him, a *palazzo* that needs constant maintenance. It will be Gianni who takes care of his father when he is old. He is the responsible one ... oh *merda*.' Katarina broke off, staring over Belle's shoulder, everything about her face reflecting dismay.

When Belle turned, she was half expecting to see the old Signora glowering at them, but instead there was Perla, standing on the edge of the pool.

'You are swimming in your bras?' Perla looked particularly lovely, bare-legged in a short, floaty boho dress, hair falling round her shoulders.

'Please don't take any photographs,' begged Katarina, eyeing the newly recovered phone in her hand.

'I don't think any of my followers would want to see you like that.' Perla's lips curled in amusement.

'Why don't you join us?' asked Belle. 'Come for a swim.'

'Yes, why not?' echoed Katarina.

'In my underwear?' Perla turned to leave, then seemed to think better of it. Impulsively she tossed down her phone, peeled away her dress and stood for a moment by the pool in a lacy bright yellow bra and skimpy matching briefs.

'But this my followers might be interested in,' she said, before executing an elegant dive into the water.

Perla was laughing as she surfaced. Katarina smiled too. Together the three of them bobbed in the pool, nobody argued, there were no barbed comments, the two wives almost seemed to like each other.

It wouldn't last long; Belle had been here long enough to realise that. But as the sun warmed her shoulders and the water cooled her body, she enjoyed the moment for as long as it did last.

The truce held until dinnertime and the mood at the table was curiously festive. Enrico opened Prosecco, Gianni lined up flutes and even the Signora looked less forbidding than usual.

Accepting a glass of bubbles, Belle asked, 'Are we celebrating something?'

'We are celebrating the future of Casa di Ginaro,' Enrico told her.

He looked brighter and lighter tonight. Sipping her Prosecco, Belle's eyes swept along the table and she saw that almost everybody did. Even the two brothers weren't at odds this evening.

As they drank the bubbly wine and ate fennel-studded *taralli* biscuits, Enrico explained why.

'This morning we had a meeting and decided to make some changes at Casa di Ginaro.' His gaze shifted to Perla. 'First of all we have appointed our first brand ambassador. Perla will also be looking after our social media from now on.'

Lit with a shaft of sunlight, leaning into Pietro's shoulder,

Perla looked delighted. This might have been what she had wanted all along.

'My wife is clever,' Pietro murmured, dropping a kiss onto her head and holding her tightly.

'What about your travel plans?' asked Belle, assuming they had been forgotten.

'I will be travelling a lot for photo shoots,' Perla explained, airily. 'And it will be necessary for Pietro to come and help set up the images; it is a very big job and I can't do it on my own.'

Katarina's lips tightened slightly and from the expression on her face, Belle guessed this had come as news to her too.

'It is not the only change,' Enrico continued. 'I have also decided the time has come to think about succession. For now, I will be overseeing the company, but Gianni will start taking on more responsibility.'

As he spoke Enrico caught Belle's gaze and held it. Then he smiled, a softening in his eyes.

'I have spent a lifetime working and there are other things I would like to do. Besides it makes sense to make this change while we have Mamma here to guide Gianni, the way she guided me. No one knows this family or our business like she does.'

The Signora accepted the compliment with a brisk nod. 'I thought I had retired, but apparently I have as much to do as I ever did,' she only half-complained.

'This time was always going to come some day,' finished Enrico. 'Now it is here.'

The Signora raised her glass. 'To the future,' she said.

Enrico touched his flute to hers. 'And to the past, to all the people who made Casa di Ginaro what it is today.'

'Congratulations,' said Belle, looking around the table at the faces of the Ginaro family, seeing how pleased they looked. Gianni would have more power now. Perla more importance. Pietro could still go travelling. Belle was happy for each of them, but happiest of all for Enrico, who was looking in her direction still, his eyes almost black in the evening light.

'Soon you will be able to go sailing every day if you want to, Papa,' said Gianni.

'You can travel,' added Pietro 'Visit the places you always wanted to see.'

'I can,' Enrico agreed, smiling at his sons. 'I will have more time and freedom. At the moment this is all so new that it feels hard to believe, but eventually I will get used to the idea. Our lives are going to be different.'

The Signora rang the bell to call for the first course and the maid hurried in with crisp zucchini flowers and salty rolls of pork *bombetti* stuffed with melting cheese.

Katarina didn't eat much, but that wasn't unusual, so nobody remarked on it. Neither did she look as happy as the others, Belle noticed. She had smiled along with them, raised her glass to toast the future, echoed her congratulations, but then her smile had faded. Nothing was going to change for her, except that her husband would be working longer hours just as a baby came along. No one had offered her anything she wanted.

The next course appeared and Katarina's quietness continued. As they ate, Gianni cast a sidelong glance at her. 'What is wrong? Are you feeling ill?'

Katarina only shook her head. 'Not really, no more than normal.'

She managed a few crackers from the cheese platter that followed, sipped water from her wine glass, but Belle didn't hear her voice amid the chatter of the others, even as they slipped into Italian.

Once the meal was finished and the Signora stood, ready to go up to her room, Katarina got to her feet also.

'No,' she said, the word sounding loudly, then covered her mouth with her hand.

Everybody stared and the Signora took a step backwards as if she had been struck. 'What is the matter with you, Katarina?'

'You cannot leave me here in this house with all these cats ...' A sob caught in her throat.

'There are too many cats, Nonna,' said Gianni, putting a hand on his wife's arm, trying to calm her.

'It has gone too far,' agreed Enrico, looking troubled.

'You can't expect me to find homes for them all.' Katarina's eyes were wild. 'It is impossible.'

'We took these cats in and so we have a responsibility to care for them,' said the Signora, firmly.

'It was you who took them in and I am the only one that cares for them. I have had enough. I don't even like cats. They don't like me.'

'What are you suggesting?' The Signora stared at her intently. 'We shut them out and leave them to fend for themselves? Or have them all put to sleep?'

'No ...' Katarina faltered.

Seeing the tears streaking her cheeks, Belle tried to catch her attention. 'A sanctuary,' she said, half under her breath.

'Yes, a sanctuary,' Katarina repeated. 'A place for the cats to live with somebody to care for them. That is what is needed.'

The Signora had fallen silent. She seemed half-dazed.

'A place where they are fed and kept warm, treated for fleas, taken to the vet when necessary, by someone else, not me,' continued Katarina, her voice strengthening.

'Luciana loved the cats,' the Signora roused herself to say. 'The kittens especially. They brought joy to this house when there was so little to be joyful about. Now you want them gone?'

'Not all of them, Mamma,' Enrico reasoned. 'We can keep a few. But Luciana never imagined there would be so many. And Katarina shouldn't have to care for them if she doesn't want to.'

The Signora was as close to flustered as Belle had ever seen her. 'Who will organise this sanctuary?'

'I can do that,' said Enrico. 'I will start by finding a place, perhaps a *masseria* somewhere in the countryside, where there is space for them to roam. The Luciana Ginaro Sanctuary, that is what we will call it, she would have liked that.'

The Signora nodded, slowly. '*Va bene*. Is that all?'

'No,' said Katarina, finding her voice again. 'I would like to take over from Luciana in the archive. The new exhibition space in the foyer, I have ideas, I may not be creative but I am good at organising. And I want to be a part of Casa di Ginaro, like everyone else.'

She sank down onto her chair, as though saying so much had been a huge effort and she couldn't remain on her feet any longer. Gianni stared at her.

'Nothing has been decided yet about the exhibition,' he pointed out.

'I should be a part of any decision,' said Katarina, more quietly but still determined.

'Then you will be,' Gianni promised. 'If that is what you want.'

Katarina exhaled a breath, deep and heavy. 'Thank you.'

For once all of them gathered outside, seeking the cool of the evening, sipping bitter dark liqueur from crystal glasses. Perla sat curled around the shape of Pietro's body. Gianni lit lanterns that flickered candlelight in dark corners, even the Signora joined them for a little while.

'It was your suggestion, I think, this sanctuary?' asked Enrico, sitting beside Belle. 'If so then it was a very good one.'

'I may have planted the seed of an idea in Katarina's mind. And perhaps the timing was right.'

'It is the time for change,' agreed Enrico, nodding. 'I will have to look for a suitable place. Come sanctuary-hunting with me, Belle? We could make a start this week.'

'This week, Papa?' Gianni cast a worried look in his direction. 'Will there be time?'

'You are ready for this, yes?' Enrico turned to him, his voice calm and his gaze steady. 'Happy to take on more responsibility?'

'Of course I am ready.' Gianni sounded impatient.

'Then there will be time,' Enrico promised his son. 'And you should thank Belle; because it was her that helped me realise that I am ready too.'

Gianni stared away into the shadows. Belle couldn't see his expression or tell what he might be thinking. He was quiet as Enrico spoke about a *masseria* he knew of that was for sale and might meet their needs. And a restaurant in Monopoli where he and Belle could have lunch after they had been to view it. And all the places that property-hunting might lead them to that he would like to show her.

Only when Enrico went inside, to swap the empty Amaro bottle for a full one, did Gianni glance back at Belle. He didn't thank her, but managed a smile that didn't seem forced. And when he moved to sit beside his brother, cuffing him on the shoulder, saying something in Italian that made Pietro laugh, she thought that Gianni looked happier.

Glancing round at the circle of faces shining in the candle-light, she was pleased for them. But as Enrico returned, Amaro bottle held aloft, ready to fill glasses, it felt to Belle that the more things changed for other people, the more for her they seemed the same. She was an outsider here and always would be. She didn't fit in at all.

17

Summer Love

There was a pool at the first *masseria* they visited, and the day was so hot that Belle longed to plunge into it. Instead they were shown through buildings and rooms. A cellar that had once been a restaurant, suites where guests had stayed when the place was an *agriturismo*, sheds where rusted equipment was stored.

'It is more land than we need and it is run down,' said Enrico, staring out beyond the iron gates towards a wide grove of olive trees. 'But it is close to Ostuni so my mother could come and visit the cats if she wanted.'

The heat seemed to shimmer in the distance and the ground beneath the rows of trees was dry.

'I suppose you could sell the olive crop,' said Belle.

'That is an option.' Enrico agreed. 'But I don't know yet where this new freedom of mine is likely to take me. I may not be here to manage it all.'

Turning away from the view to follow a path down into a walled garden, Belle thought he might be wrong. It was easier to see what other people needed in their lives than understand your own, and what Belle could see was that Enrico needed his family. It seemed completely obvious to her.

The two of them could wander through Puglia, all the way down to the very tip of Salento where the landscape was bare and parched, west to Gallipoli, north to Bari but at the end of every day she was sure they would always return to the *palazzo* and its people. That was where Enrico belonged.

Sometimes his driver took them to look at properties in the Alfa Romeo, but mostly it was just the two of them in a small, dusty hatchback car. One *masseria* came with its own stray cats, another was more of a luxury resort. In one the farmer was burning trees afflicted by disease and the air was heavy with smoke as flames licked their twisted boughs. At another a very ancient nonna poured wine for them and insisted that they tasted her olive oil.

Enrico took the search seriously, but they weren't always searching. Some days they walked together through the narrow streets of old hill towns. They ate an entire afternoon away at a restaurant in Monopoli's historic heart, blackening their mouths with cuttlefish ink, sharing a platter of blue lobster and fried wild chicory, tasting the same flavours, watching other diners come and go but not feeling the need to move themselves.

Love seemed to build along with the summer heat. Belle sensed it shimmering between them as they stood in Locorotondo, beneath the blazing sun, looking out at the view. As they bought gelato in Polignano a Mare, sat in a piazza drinking Caffè Leccese, and followed the coast road trying to find a *masseria* that turned out to be little more than a ruin.

Their hunt went on as the days grew hotter. Belle almost hoped that each new farmhouse they visited would be unsuitable because she didn't want the search to end. What she wanted was more time with Enrico. And perhaps he felt the same, because at each place he would find something that was wrong. A *masseria* was too small or too large, too dilapidated or luxurious, too far away from home.

Despite him saying distance was a problem, they drove further and further from Ostuni each day. On those longer drives they talked at times about Ari and Luciana, but often they said very little at all. Increasingly it seemed to Belle that there was something they didn't know how to speak about.

One searingly hot day Enrico took her to the seafront town of Otranto. They explored, as they had everywhere, but were drawn back to the blue of the Adriatic, and the hint of a cooler breeze that it offered.

'It's beautiful.' Belle's gaze swept the wide expanse of water. 'Ari always needed a wild ocean, the waves made him feel alive, but I like this much more.'

'You are not so afraid now?' Enrico asked her.

'Not of this sea, it feels kinder and less dangerous.'

'It is very shallow and safe here. In the height of summer the beach and rocks will be covered in people.'

Belle felt the sun beating on her skin and wondered how much higher the temperatures might get here.

'This year the heat has come earlier than usual and so have the people,' Enrico told her, looking down on children splashing while parents or grandparents hovered beside them. 'I am glad my mother is spending more time in the office, where there is air conditioning. The *palazzo* is too old and large to cool properly. That is why in July and August we always go to the villa.'

Leaning back against the sea wall, Enrico talked about life at the beach. In the mornings he liked to wake early and walk down the pathway to the sea for a swim. Then he would drink a coffee in the gardens that surrounded the villa, and later go swimming again or take the kayaks out. Always there was good food and wine, and at night Pietro might play his guitar and sing them a song.

'At the villa I cook,' he told Belle. 'Probably you don't think I can but my nonna taught me and I like the chance to spend time in the kitchen.'

'What sorts of dishes do you make?' she wanted to know.

'Mostly very simple ones, because that is what summers at

the beach are for, a simpler life.' His gaze caught hers. 'I was thinking we might spend a few days there, you and I? Escape the heat? I will cook for us.'

Belle imagined being somewhere smaller and simpler, spending the days plunging into the cool sea whenever they wanted, eating feasts he had made. She imagined escaping the heat and also his family. The previous night had been especially tense. Belle had sat at the dining table in the *palazzo* listening to them clash, not understanding everything but aware the brief respite was over, as Gianni chafed at his grandmother's advice and what he seemed to see as his father's constant interference.

'What about work? Can you get away?' asked Belle.

'I think I have to.' Enrico's eyes fixed on the horizon and he sighed. 'Gianni, he is frustrated, he wants to take charge so I am trying to let him but ... after so many years it is difficult to put my faith in someone else, even my own son.'

'It must be harder when you are right there in the office every day,' guessed Belle.

'It is impossible,' Enrico told her. 'At the beach, perhaps I can relax, start to let go a little. I can try anyway.'

'What about finding a *masseria*? Will we keep looking?'

'I will make an offer on the first place we saw,' Enrico decided. 'If there is anything better out there then we haven't found it yet and it is too hot to carry on searching. Too hot for anything but the villa.'

Belle thought about being alone with him there. She stood thinking about it as the seconds and minutes ticked by. Was this what she wanted?

Driving back to the *palazzo*, he made up for her quietness with recollections of past holidays. Teaching his sons to swim, lighting bonfires on the sand, being alone with family or together with lots of guests.

'It would be good to spend time there with you,' Enrico said, parking the car in one of his cave-like garages. 'I hope you will come.'

Belle felt a rush of heat that had nothing to do with the weather. Turning to him, she saw that his eyes were lit with hope.

'Not too long, just a few days, to escape the heat, just you and me, if you would like it?'

Belle hesitated. 'Are you sure? It isn't too soon?'

He must have assumed that she meant too soon to leave the business, because Enrico only shrugged and said, 'Gianni will cope, I hope so anyway.'

Once Belle started packing she found herself filling her suitcase. Leaving the Casa di Ginaro clothes hanging in the wardrobe, she took her own belongings, aside from the dress she had chosen herself and the aquamarine scarf that felt like it belonged to her. Folding things carelessly and pushing them into her suitcase, she considered the prospect of days and nights alone with Enrico. Just a few days, just a few nights. Then he would come back here to his family. It was where he belonged.

She packed up everything that she had brought from home then glanced around the now barer room. Belle didn't belong here and never would. As she sent her suitcase down to the lower floor in a claustrophobically tiny lift normally only used by the old Signora, then wheeled it through the *palazzo* and along the garden path, it felt like she might be leaving for good.

Enrico was in the garage already, busy loading supplies into the hatchback – food, wine, clothes, books – piling it all into the boot. Setting eyes on the size of her suitcase, he seemed surprised.

'I should have given you a smaller suitcase,' he said, glancing back worriedly at the already full car. 'You only needed to bring a few things.'

'I'm never a light packer,' she told him, and it was only half a lie. The whole truth was that Belle hadn't wanted to leave any of herself behind. She didn't belong here and wasn't sorry to leave.

Somehow, Enrico managed to cram in her suitcase and arrange everything else around it. 'There, it is done. If something is forgotten then we will manage without it. We will only be gone for a short while.'

The night before, at the dinner table, his family had reacted in different ways to the news that they were heading away. Gianni had frowned momentarily and Perla raised her eyebrows, then they had gone back to clashing about something, an idea Perla liked that Gianni insisted wouldn't work, something to do with the business, that they felt equally passionate about. Their opposing views ended up involving everyone, the discussion growing louder, and they seemed set to argue all evening. These people cared mainly about themselves, realised Belle, sitting back and watching. Most likely they always had.

Now Enrico was reversing the car out of the garage and they were on their way, moving slowly through Ostuni's narrow streets away from the *palazzo*, then accelerating towards the open road. Belle wasn't sure if she was ready for wherever this journey was leading; all the same she was glad to be going.

She breathed out a sigh, and Enrico glanced sideways and back to the road.

'At the beach there are no rules,' he told her. 'We can relax, eat when we want, do what we like, be alone or spend time together.'

When had their friendship shifted and deepened? Casting back her mind, Belle wasn't sure. All she knew was it must have happened very slowly, as the rest of life rushed on around them.

'I would like us to be together,' Enrico said so softly that she only just caught the words. 'If you want it Belle. And if you don't then I understand. But I will hope.'

Their lives were different and their worlds far apart. 'Enrico, I don't know,' she said, eventually, although she was hoping too even if she knew it was impossible.

He gazed towards her again, but only for a moment since they were flying down the *autostrada* and the road demanded his attention.

'Let's go to the beach,' he said lightly. 'Take a break from everything else, relax. *Va bene?*'

'OK,' she agreed, glimpsing the sea and opening up the window to smell the salt in the air, still hoping because she couldn't help it.

The villa might have been where the Ginaro family headed for simpler times but to Belle's eyes it still looked impressive, a modern two-storeyed building with a flat roof, lots of blue mosaic tiles and two kitchens, one of them outdoors.

They spent some time dragging divans out onto the patio, opening shutters and windows. Then while Enrico went to check the pool, Belle explored a rambling garden overgrown with bright bougainvillea and prickly pears, then checked out the villa again.

Her room had a view of the dunes and sea, and a narrow balcony with just enough space to step out on. This must have been where one of the boys usually stayed because a few belongings were littered about: a pair of shorts folded on a chair, a bottle of cologne on the nightstand, a magazine that Perla might have left behind.

Downstairs the rooms were spacious and the furniture looked expensive. Everything matched, realised Belle. Other beach houses she had stayed at were shabbier places, furnished with odds and ends that people had brought from home, frayed cushions and lumpy sofas. Here it seemed like the Ginaro family had employed an interior designer.

'A swim first or lunch?' asked Enrico, coming across her in the living area.

'A swim,' Belle decided.

She changed quickly, gazing through her open window at the water shimmering against the sky. Then Belle walked in the harsh, dry heat through the garden and across a narrow lane, then down the pathway to the sea. Ahead of her, Enrico turned to check she was OK and nearing the bottom when they reached a set of uneven steps and a wobbly wooden handrail, he held out his hand and helped her down. As they touched, Belle felt something warm spark inside her, then her feet met the final step and he released her.

The beach was a river of sand flowing from a crevice in the rocks. Belle stood at the tideline as Enrico plunged in.

'Are you coming?' he called, and as he swam out further; she watched him, arms cutting through low ripples of waves, legs kicking.

The water lapped her legs, silky, salty, cool. Taking a breath, Belle ran in, swimming out until her feet no longer touched the bottom. Above her the sky seemed dizzyingly high and ahead was nothing but water. Only the sea and Enrico.

Then she let the shallow waves push her back toward the shore, and sat on a towel while the sun dried the drops of sea water on her body. She couldn't see Enrico now; he had carried on swimming past the point. Scanning the empty horizon, she felt a stab of anxiety, casting her mind back to another beach and a different time. The scars were there, they always would be. But Enrico had been marked by scars too, she was reminded, relieved to see him rounding the point and swimming back towards her. There was no hiding them from each other, no need to try.

She had expected a simple picnic for lunch, bread and cheese, perhaps a few tomatoes but it seemed that Enrico wanted to cook. Salty from the sea and still only wearing a bikini Belle sat with a jug of iced water at her elbow as he moved around the outdoor kitchen, bare-chested and lightly tanned.

'It is good to have the time to do this,' said Enrico. 'If it weren't for you, I would be at my desk right now, staring at a row of numbers or solving someone's problem. Often all I seemed to do was deal with problems.'

'Was it really me that made the difference?' asked Belle, watching him stirring a sauce bubbling in a pan and hearing something sizzling in oil.

'You have made such a difference to me.' Enrico looked down at what he was doing, then up at her again. 'There have been times in the past few years when I thought I would never be happy again.'

'Me too,' Belle told him.

He carried on cooking, testing a little of this and that, singing in Italian as he went about his work. They ate in the shade of a pergola, cooled by a light breeze. Little ears of *orecchiette* simply sauced with fresh tomatoes crushed and simmered with olive oil, slender stalks of chicory sautéed with anchovy and garlic, a dish of grilled mussels covered in toasted breadcrumbs and smoky shards of pancetta. Another of steamed razor clams with a fresh bite of lemon and parsley.

'You told me that you make simple dishes here,' said Belle, before teasing a clam from its shell with her tongue. 'Is this your idea of simple?'

'Perhaps I am trying to impress you.'

'It's worked, I'm impressed,' she told him, and as a smile spread slowly over his face Belle felt another warm spark rush through her.

Their lives were not the same, their worlds far apart, but perhaps she and Enrico could have this brief moment in time right on the edge of things, making a difference for each other. Belle wanted that more than anything.

Later in the sun-shimmered afternoon, they decided it was time for another swim, and Enrico offered his hand to help her off the low lounger. Belle felt looser-limbed in the heat, and as they stood close together, she lifted her gaze to his face. Tentatively her fingers touched his cheek and rested there. His arm circled her waist and tightened. They drew even closer. And their lips touched.

It seemed to happen naturally, like the steps of a dance they both knew. Her mouth dropped to the crease between his neck and shoulder, tasting the saltiness of his skin. He ran his fingertips down the length of her bare spine. She shivered with pleasure.

'Enrico,' she said, softly.

'Belle,' he replied.

Slowly, inch by inch, they travelled across each other's bodies, and Belle warmed and shivered as his touch moved. She had no idea at all how they went from the garden to the house. Who had taken the lead, were they still touching each other, how were the few clothes they had been wearing discarded on the floor? In the confusion of her mind only one thing was clear; she wanted him.

Later they watched the sunset from the tiny balcony of her room, their arms wrapped round each other. Time blurred and seemed to slow. Belle wished it could stop altogether.

Dinner was a picnic, leftovers from the midday meal that they grazed on sitting outside as the moon rose. They finished a bottle of red wine, then Enrico opened a second and they got drunk together.

'We have days of this, you and me, and nothing we need to do,' he said, and she heard the contentment in his voice and felt it in the way his body relaxed against hers.

That night they slept together. Belle kept half-waking, aware of his warmth beside her, his head on the pillow, the sound of his breathing. In the deep dark she couldn't quite believe it, but as dawn brought light and she made out Enrico's features, it felt more real.

They had no future together, she reminded herself. He was a part of something much bigger, a family, that she couldn't ever see herself becoming a part of. But they had the next few days at least, and Belle tried not to think about what might come after.

Time was unreliable. An hour drifted by but then a day seemed to speed away. Inevitably the outside world intruded now and then. Enrico needed to Zoom with his sons or call his mother, and Belle would be reminded of his other life. A boat might sail by when they were down at the beach, with the strangers aboard waving. A couple of kayakers go past. But mostly it was only the two of them, passing salt-soaked, sunlit days together, and sharing a bed at night.

Sometimes they talked about Ari and Luciana, mentioned them in conversation, nothing had changed about that. Belle didn't feel as disloyal as she had expected. This was only a few days after all, a short breather from normal life, a stretch of unreliable time.

It was Enrico who suggested staying for a little longer. 'I needed this break,' he told Belle.

And Belle had agreed, because she needed it too.

Some things about him were becoming familiar. The back of his neck, because she watched him sleeping in later than her every morning. His habit of singing while he was cooking, a little tunelessly at times. The way he powered out for his daily swim beyond the point. But other things stayed strange and new, his touch and the way it made her feel, his body against hers as they drifted off to sleep.

They made love every afternoon. Belle didn't open any of the books she had brought to read because they never seemed to run out of things to talk about. The one thing neither of them tried to discuss was the future. To Belle it felt as if there was an unspoken agreement not to. This was summer love, not meant to last.

One morning Enrico took the car to stock up on food supplies, and Belle stayed at the villa, afraid to leave and break the spell. Later he cooked a long lunch, red prawns wrapped in dry-cured ham, crisp strips of fried zucchini, aubergine baked with parmesan, meatballs in a puddle of sweet-sour tomato sauce.

'You should have been a chef,' she told him, because he seemed to understand the way that flavours worked together.

'It's a bit late now, but I am happy here, cooking for you.'

They took sea kayaks and explored the rocky bays and grottos. Walked the dusty beach roads and peered over walls at other people's villas, many of them shuttered and empty still. In the heat of a late afternoon, they basked in the pool, drinking Negronis. Sometimes Belle helped him cook, others she sat and watched.

Time might be unreliable but sooner or later it would run out and knowing that charged every moment.

In the strangest of ways, it was Ari that changed things. He was the one who had sent the young horse to Greg in the first place, with the best of intentions of course but knowing that half-wild horses could change in an instant and even good riders be surprised by the quickness of a movement. Not that Ari ever planned for his friend to get hurt, but unfortunately it was what happened.

'You've broken your ankle in two places?' said Belle in dismay, FaceTiming with Greg one evening while Enrico prepared a late supper.

'Yeah, I thought it was just swollen so I walked round on it for a couple of days but Matt made me have an X-ray.'

'What happened exactly?'

'Nothing dramatic,' Greg promised. 'We were in the arena, working well when he spooked. I popped off, landed on my feet, then overbalanced and went down. And somehow I must have crushed my ankle.'

'Ouch.'

'It's a bit sore but not as painful as you'd think. I managed to hobble up to the stables and sort out the horses. I'm not hobbling now though.' Greg showed her the plaster on his leg. 'I've had surgery and now I can't put any weight on it at all.'

While Belle had been here at the beach, he had been stuck in hospital. 'You should have called.'

'What was the point of worrying you? You're on the other side of the world, you couldn't have done anything.'

'How long will your leg be in plaster for?'

'Two weeks, then a moonboot for another four. It's so boring.'

'How are you managing?' asked Belle, aware how busy he always was.

'I'm fine on crutches, and Matt's been great. He's making sure I don't starve.'

'Is he any help with the horses?'

'Not really,' Greg admitted.

Enrico was setting the table, putting down plates and forks, a pepper grinder, a bowl of salad with its dressing in a jar; not eavesdropping on her conversation, but hardly able to avoid hearing.

'Please tell me you aren't feeding out hay on crutches,' Belle said to Greg.

'Don't worry, I'm fine.'

'But I am worried. You need to rest, give yourself a chance to heal, not do too much.'

'*Meh*,' he replied.

'Don't *meh* me,' she said, and saw Enrico smile.

'This is a very dull conversation,' Greg complained. 'Could we talk about something more interesting. How are things going there? How's Enrico.'

'He's right here.' Belle turned the screen to face Enrico, who was tossing a lemony dressing through a bowl of salad.

'I am sorry you are hurt,' he said, once she had introduced them properly.

'Not as sorry as me,' Greg told him. 'It's very inconvenient.'

Belle turned the phone back on herself. 'There must be someone you can ask to help? One of the neighbours or a local kid?'

'Yeah, yeah it'll be fine,' he said vaguely. 'It's only six weeks.'

'You'll have to rehab afterwards though.'

'I'm young and strong, I'll heal.'

Belle wasn't sure how old Greg was, but she presumed somewhere in his mid-forties. She did know he wasn't going to surrender easily to a quieter life. The property was hilly, and this time of year it would be slippery with mud. She hoped he wouldn't try to tackle paddocks on his crutches. Being near a horse at all seemed a bad idea. Greg risked getting hurt again.

Later she fretted as she ate the meal that Enrico had cooked, a dish of rice and shellfish in a rich saffron broth. Afterwards they navigated the coastal path by torchlight and he built a bonfire on the beach. It was dark aside from the firelight, still and starry, and sitting within its glow, watching the crackling flames, Belle still worried.

Searching her mind, she tried to come up with somebody that Greg could call on for help, but drew a blank. Ari had always been the one there for him, and after he had gone, she had stepped in. Greg worked hard from early to late, teaching lessons, schooling horses, mucking out loose boxes, harrowing paddocks. So many things needed to be done each day, things that a man on crutches shouldn't even attempt.

'You are very quiet,' observed Enrico. 'Are you worrying about your friend?'

'I am,' said Belle, resting her head on his shoulder.

'He has no farm-workers to help?'

It was unlikely that Greg ever made enough money to hire anyone except on the most casual basis. 'No.'

'What about his family?'

'None of them is horsey. If they don't know what they are doing they'll be worse than useless.'

They sat together, arms wound round one another. 'Do you need to go home?' asked Enrico.

'Yes, I think I do,' said Belle, reluctantly.

'You have been in Italy for such a short time. But I suppose you can come back here. Once your friend is on his feet again.'

Belle didn't say anything. She pressed her face into his shoulder and breathed him in.

'These past few days, Belle, this time together, it has been everything.'

'We always had to return to real life eventually though, didn't we?' she said, her voice muffled.

'This feels how I would like my real life to be.'

Belle booked a flight with a dull sense of inevitability. She and Enrico had a few more days and that would have to be enough. He would return to his family dynasty, she to her small, quiet life. Nothing would have changed really.

Those final days seemed hotter and brighter. They stayed mostly in the shade, moving very little, and Enrico told her constantly that he didn't want her to go, but never tried to persuade her to stay.

The very last night was spent on the beach, with a picnic they had prepared together. Enrico lit a fire as a beacon and they pulled off their clothes and swam naked in the dark sea. Later they made love and very much later climbed the path back to the villa and fell into bed.

In the morning his driver came to collect her. Enrico supervised the stowing of her suitcases in the car boot then they stood, a little way apart, arms hanging by their sides, and said goodbye.

'Thank you,' Belle said. 'For everything.'

'We will see each other again, before too long,' he promised.

Belle wasn't sure if they would. This seemed like it was meant to be an ending. And better to lose each other now than later on when it would hurt more, she told herself silently. Wiser to make a clean break. She should have said that to Enrico, but she didn't know how to so instead Belle kissed him one last time, and turned away with tears in her eyes.

On the journey home he stayed in her mind. Now he would be striding through the reception area of Casa di Ginaro, now returning to the palazzo and sitting with his family at dinner, now perhaps alone with a drink in his hand out on the terrace and thinking of her.

Her journey was long and provided plenty of time to think. By the time she had crossed all those thousands of miles and reached New Zealand, Belle had almost convinced herself. Summer love always ended, sooner or later.

18

Home

Home was as Belle had left it, colder and dustier, but still the same shabby place overfilled with things she loved. She put on a pot of coffee when she arrived, mainly to scent the kitchen and cover a slight musty smell. Then she sent Enrico a quick message to say she had arrived safely, took a long, hot shower and lay down for a rest in her own bed. Tomorrow she would go to see Greg, make herself useful around the stables, but for now she was exhausted.

Belle dreamed of a dazzling white Ostuni so vividly that when she opened her eyes to a familiar view of bush and sky outside her window, she felt displaced.

It was a crisp, cold morning and she wrapped up warm then went to see if the Land Rover would start. To her relief the engine fired at her first try, and she drove along the ribbon of road that wound between velvety green fields and led to Greg's place.

She spotted Tama as soon as she pulled into the driveway. The horse was standing on a rise, his breath puffing steam into the icy cold air. Stopping the car, she went to say hello and, although he snickered at the sight of her, he didn't make a move as she climbed the hill towards him.

'I'm home,' she said, slipping a hand beneath his rug to check he was warm enough. 'Home again.'

Belle thought he seemed happy to see her; but unfortunately, she couldn't say the same about Greg.

Matt had warned her what to expect. He was leaving the small farmhouse as she headed in, having dropped off a takeaway coffee and a blueberry muffin for breakfast.

'Good luck,' he said. 'The patient is being a complete arse.'

Belle recognised him as the youngish guy she remembered from the beach café. Friendly-faced rather than good-looking, tall, fair hair, nice eyes. She was pleased to find that he and Greg were still seeing one another.

'It's fair to say he's not dealing very well with being an invalid. Yesterday it was all I could do to keep him out of the paddocks,' Matt told her.

'Good thing I'm here, then,' said Belle.

'I think so, but he isn't going to.'

She found Greg lying on the sofa, his broken ankle stretched in front of him, television blaring, and the muffin that Matt had brought sitting untouched at his elbow.

'Didn't I tell you not to come?' he said, muting the television.

Belle helped herself to a piece of his muffin. 'Yep, you did.'

'What are you doing here then?'

'I think Ari brought me back,' she told him. 'That's how it feels.'

'Fuck's sake Belle, I fell off a horse, it happens.'

'You fell off Ari's horse.'

'Fuck's sake,' Greg said again.

'You're awfully sweary since you injured yourself,' she observed.

'You're awfully fucking annoying.'

He passed her the rest of his muffin and Belle sat on the far end of the sofa, listening to him complain about the many inconveniences of being stuck in a plaster cast.

'Matt's nice,' she said, when he finished. 'Seems like he's into you.'

'Maybe.'

'Does he bring you breakfast every day?'

'Like I need the carbs and sugar,' grumbled Greg.

'I needed them after that endless flight,' said Belle, finishing the last few crumbs. 'Long haul travel is brutal.'

'You shouldn't have come then,' said Greg.

'Ari would have wanted me to.'

Once she started hauling bales of hay through muddy paddocks and piling manure into the wheelbarrow, it was as if she had never been anywhere. It felt good to be outdoors and moving though. When the horses crowded her as she appeared with their hay supplies, she flicked a lead-rope in their direction, keeping them at a safe distance. She mixed feeds and picked mud out of hooves, brought some horses into stables, moved others onto fresh grass, swapped rugs and checked water troughs.

At lunchtime she wandered back to the house to catch up with Greg. His mood hadn't sweetened much.

'I don't like people looking after me,' he muttered, as she sliced bread for toast. 'I'm not used to it.'

'Ari looked after you,' Belle pointed out. 'All the time.'

'That's different.'

'There'll always be spaces in our lives where he used to be.' Belle put on a pan of eggs to boil. 'The least I can do is try to fill this one.'

'By making me eggs and soldiers for lunch?'

'Why not?' said Belle. 'Everyone loves eggs and soldiers, don't they?'

Greg's place was tidier than usual, but still she had to shift a cracked leather bridle and a pile of old *Horse & Pony* magazines off the kitchen table to make room for two plates filled with buttery strips of toast and soft-boiled eggs.

'What about the spaces in your life,' asked Greg, swinging over on his crutches and sitting down to eat.

'Nothing's changed,' she told him.

'I thought perhaps you and Enrico ...'

Belle treated him to the one-shouldered shrug that always seemed so cool when Mia did it.

'What's that supposed to mean?' he demanded, scooping the top off his egg and dipping a piece of toast into its runny yolk.

'Our lives are too different; it would never have worked out.'

'Something did happen with him then?' he pressed.

Belle didn't want to answer that question. 'Eat your eggs.'

'I'll get it out of you eventually.'

Belle laughed but didn't reply.

After lunch she took a solitary walk with his dogs to the top of the farm and stood looking out over the valley while they hunted rabbits in the paddocks. She would be coming here every day for as long as she was needed. Her tan would fade and Italy retreat into a distant memory. And Belle thought she was OK with that. It seemed how things were meant to be.

Mornings were for Greg and the horses, the afternoons Belle kept for herself. She tried to stay busy. Clearing out clothes she didn't wear anymore, sorting through the last of Ari's old canvases, rearranging things in the gallery ready in case she wanted to open it once winter was over. The days were fine, it was the evenings that were difficult. Once the view outside her windows faded into darkness, Belle felt more alone.

She avoided Zoom calls and FaceTime; life was too busy, she told herself and Enrico. But at night a stream of messages came from him. He always had plenty to say. He told her that the cat sanctuary was underway. That Pietro had crashed his car but was unhurt. That Mia had left for Rome to study. That he missed her and was looking forward to her return.

Going about her day, Belle composed replies in her mind. At night she sat with her laptop, still trying to put the words together. She wanted to tell Enrico what was really on her mind. The longer she waited, the harder it became.

By then Greg was out of the plaster-cast and wearing a moonboot; more impatient than ever to be moving around. To shorten the long evenings Belle had started going back over to his place for dinner. Sometimes she tried to cook things that Enrico used to make for her; pasta dishes and sea-food although none of it ever tasted exactly the same. They ate in front of the fire, sharing a bottle of wine, as bit by bit Greg coaxed out of her exactly what had happened in Puglia. It seemed dreamlike now, a salty-sandy haze of a dream.

'It couldn't last,' Belle told him. 'It shouldn't even have begun.'

'I don't understand,' said Greg. 'Why not?'

'We didn't have any future together.' Belle would never have asked Enrico to choose her over his family. But nor could she have blended in. 'It was impossible, and I think I always knew that but ...'

'Did Enrico think so too?'

'No,' Belle admitted. 'I'm pretty sure that he didn't.'

She had taken a risk, like plunging into the sea or galloping on a horse, been impulsive and daring. But this time the risk had been too big. People had got hurt.

'I have to find a way to tell him.'

It was a Zoom call, like so many they'd had before, and seeing him there, tanned skin, bright eyes, smiling from the screen, Belle's feelings surged. She almost couldn't say the words that she had practised for days. He had responsibilities, a family, a life. She needed to find her own life now. She was sorry.

When she told him, Enrico's face stilled and his voice sounded clipped.

'I thought you were coming back and then we would travel. Isn't that what we talked about?'

'I'm sorry,' she repeated.

'I thought you felt the same way I did. At the beach, when we were together, even before then. Was I wrong?'

'No, not wrong, not at all.'

'Well then why?'

'I can't lose any more of myself,' she tried to explain.

'And I don't want to lose you,' Enrico said, very softly and sadly.

Afterwards, she sat staring into the embers of the fire, remembering Enrico's voice as he said goodbye. Awake half the night, wrapped in a rug and curled in Ari's favourite chair, Belle told herself this was the only way, the best thing for both of them.

At least she was home. She looked at the old-fashioned plaid curtains drawn over the windows and the threadbare rug, the shelves crammed with books and pottery and the art covering up walls that needed painting.

Even once the moonboot came off, Greg needed time to regain his strength and balance. Belle was glad that he still needed her. She liked catching and tacking up ponies for children's lessons, then giving them a wash and feed afterwards before leading them back to the paddocks. There had been no flush of spring grass yet so hay had to be fed out daily. Horses needed to come in for the farrier, tack required cleaning, ripped rugs taken to be mended.

'I don't know how you do all this by yourself,' Belle told Greg, as she was working Ari's young horse on the lunge with his supervision. 'It's exhausting.'

'Toughen up,' he said, not unkindly.

Soon Greg wouldn't need her quite as much. He was conscientious about the rehab exercises to strengthen his ankle and desperate to get back to his normal life. Soon she would have to decide what her own normal was.

Sometimes Belle did question what she had done. It would hit her suddenly, most often when she was by herself, mopping the floor or weeding the garden. First an image of that dazzling white town against a cloudless sky then a memory of Enrico, walking through its streets with her. What if she had been wrong?

'You should sell that place,' her mother said without fail every time Belle spoke to her. 'It's too lonely out there, isolated.'

One person's loneliness might be another's idea of independence, argued Belle silently to herself, listening to her mother tell her how she ought to be leading her life. She couldn't imagine ever selling the place where she and Ari had been happy. Even so she tidied the garden and painted walls, keeping as busy as possible. She might want to rent the place out and move back to the city, get a job on a TV series, pick up her old life where she had left it. Or she might want to go travelling again, alone this time. Belle tidied and cleaned, half understanding now why her mother had done the same after her father had died. It did feel slightly better bringing order to the rooms she lived in when everything else seemed out of her control.

The photographs started coming in early spring, texted from a number that she didn't recognise. The first showed the Sagrada Familia in Barcelona and she assumed that someone must have sent it by mistake. Then a week later there was a picture that Belle recognised as Seville and a fortnight on another Spanish scene. Belle stared at the three images and wondered if they were meant for her.

'Who do you think they're from?' asked Greg. He was back in the saddle, astride Tama in the arena, with Belle watching to be sure the horse didn't move out of a walk.

'No idea,' she said, although by now she had a suspicion.

Belle liked receiving the pictures. There was no obvious progression to the journey. She could never guess where this person would go to next. One moment they were in a Nordic country, the next there was the Eiffel Tower. It seemed like they were sticking pins in a map.

They sent no clues, no words at all, only a scenic shot of a different location, often taken in the pale light of an early morning.

Belle hoped this was Enrico, following his dreams. She wondered who he was travelling with. She hoped he wasn't lonely.

Finally, there was a photograph with people in it. She recognised them straight away – Katarina and her new baby. They were both wearing white and seemed to be seated in the loggia and the infant was tiny, a creased little face peering out of its swaddle of Casa di Ginaro linen.

That week she sent off a card and small gift. No photographs came for a while after that. Belle assumed that Enrico must be back at home, easing into his new life there with more time for sailing, happy to be with his family.

One morning she was down at the beach café with Greg. He had taken her for breakfast, apparently as a thank you, although Belle suspected it was only an excuse to be near Matt.

A shot pinged onto her phone as she was biting into a cheesy egg roll. Belle half-choked as she glanced at it. The scene was a large marina with the spiky masts of hundreds of yachts and behind them in the distance a tower piercing the sky. The Sky Tower. Enrico was in Auckland.

Belle dropped her phone and the egg roll, staring up at Greg.

'What?' he asked.

She pushed the screen towards him. 'He's here,' she said.

'Your mystery photo bomber?' He glanced at the image. 'Hey, so he is.'

'It's not a mystery anymore. I know exactly who he is.'

'Enrico?' Greg guessed, studying her face.

'He may be right there looking at this view now.' Belle stared at the picture again. 'Or he might have taken the shot ages ago and only just decided to send it.'

'There's only one way to find out.'

'I know.'

'Come on, I'll drive you.'

Belle tried to argue but Greg was already putting on his jacket and fishing for the keys in his pocket. She followed him out to the car at a jog and he was revving the engine by the time she climbed inside.

Westhaven marina was forty minutes away, longer in heavy traffic. Greg put his foot down when he could but this was a blustery day, and she knew that Enrico might be out on the gulf already, sailing away.

She spoke her thoughts out loud. 'He may not be there.'

'If he is then we're going to find him.'

'Should you even be driving?' she worried, as Greg accelerated onto the motorway.

'Bit late to be thinking about that, isn't it,' he said, switching to the outside lane and speeding up.

Greg's car was the messiest of anyone's she knew. Belle sat surrounded by bits of old tack and discarded protein wrappers, still worrying. 'What if he doesn't want to see me?'

'Obviously he does, why else would he keep sending pictures?'

'What will I say?' she worried, as they sped towards the city.

'You'll think of something.'

The motorway ended and they pulled onto a main road, every traffic light turning red as they encountered it, slowing them down. Belle was a hot mess now. She glimpsed the harbour and saw there were boats out there. Enrico could be on one of them.

'You do know that Ari wasn't calling you back when I broke my ankle,' said Greg, as they neared the marina. 'He would never have held you back from anything. That wasn't his style at all.'

'I know,' said Belle, gripping the handle above the door as he took a roundabout too quickly.

Driving past the sailing clubs, he lurched to a stop in a car park. 'Let's check this side first and if you can't see him then we'll try the other, OK?'

'OK,' Belle agreed, already scanning the rows of yachts.

The gates onto the pontoons were locked so she could only look down on them from the wharf. There were so many boats moored there and people were moving round the decks of some but she saw no one who looked like Enrico.

'Nothing?' asked Greg.

'I don't think so.'

'Let's drive to the other side.'

They piled back into the car and Greg drove too fast over the speed humps, as Belle's heart hammered in her chest.

This part of the marina had a wooden walkway used by cyclists and people walking dogs. As Belle ran down it her footsteps sounded hollow. She wasn't sure Enrico was here. Suddenly it mattered more than anything that he was.

She heard a cry from Greg, coming up behind her slowed by his ankle, and turned to see where he was pointing. 'Over there?'

Belle looked but couldn't see anything. 'Where?'

There was a flash of pale lemon linen on a small yacht halfway down a pier. She saw Enrico sitting in the spring sunshine on the deck with a man she didn't recognise. Heart pounding still, Belle stopped. Had he hoped she would try to find him? Was that why he had sent the photo?

'That's him, yes?' asked Greg, although it must have been obvious from her face that it was.

Belle called his name but the wind was against her and the

sound didn't carry. Greg joined in, his stronger voice travelling further, then started jumping up and down, waving like an idiot, and Belle did the same.

Enrico must have caught a movement from the corner of his eye. He looked up and Belle saw a smile spreading over his face. Then he held up his hand in a wave and said something to the man he was with.

Belle stopped jumping. 'Oh God, he's coming.'

'I'll go and wait in the car,' Greg offered.

'No, stay there.' She didn't want to be alone with him, not yet.

Enrico was more deeply tanned than he had been before but his spare frame and long stride were familiar. He paused to unlock the gate, then was there beside her.

'I wasn't sure if you would come,' he said, still smiling.

They stood two metres apart, staring towards each other. Belle felt rooted to the spot, shy of him, uncertain.

'Your trip,' she said to fill the silence. 'It's looked amazing. So many places. Where to next?'

'Today I am sailing to Waiheke Island, for lunch at a winery. Would you like to come too?'

'Yes but ...' Belle was in the clothes she wore for farm chores, tattered jeans and an old shirt. There was no hint of make-up on her face and every chance she still had hay in her hair.

'Please come,' said Enrico. 'Just for the day.'

It didn't matter what she looked like. 'I'd love to.'

Greg was already leaving. As he headed back towards the car, Belle turned to follow Enrico onto the pontoon. The yacht belonged to a business contact, he was explaining, and although he didn't know him well, he seemed a nice guy.

He held out a steadying hand to help her on board and as their fingers touched, Belle felt a familiar rush of heat. She was aware how flushed she must look, as he introduced her to his friend Carlo.

Soon they were motoring out of the marina and sailing on towards the islands, Enrico at the helm and Belle sitting near him, watching the city retreating.

'This place,' said Enrico. 'This harbour, what a place to sail.'

'How long are you staying?' asked Belle. 'I could show you where I live. The west coast, that's beautiful too.'

'I would very much like to see it.'

They were still being carefully polite with one another as the yacht passed the distinctive volcanic cone of Rangitoto and sailed into choppier waters.

Reaching Waiheke, they followed its coastline filled with rich people's mansions, sandy bays and hillside vineyards, both of them staring at the view, not saying much at all. To Belle this felt like a necessary silence. They needed time to get used to being near each other again.

Man O' War Bay was on the eastern side of the island and the restaurant pavilion right beside the beach, with a stretch of grassy lawn for picnics and plenty of outdoor tables. It was still gusty, but they managed to find a spot sheltered from the worst of it.

Carlo, it seemed, kept forgetting that she didn't speak Italian, or perhaps he was just happy to be talking his own language, after years of living overseas. Either way Belle didn't mind not being able to understand. She was happy to sit with Enrico, tasting wine and eating creamy burrata cheese and tender fried calamari. Every now and then he caught her eye and smiled, or tried to bring her into the conversation, but Carlo was a loud, excitable man and Belle wasn't prepared to vie with him for Enrico's attention.

This was a place where you could easily while away an afternoon, but Carlo had an appointment and needed to head back and so before long they were on board the yacht again and sailing.

'I should text Greg to see if he can pick me up,' said Belle, as the city got closer and closer. 'It will take a while for him to get here.'

'I can drive you home,' Enrico offered. 'I have a rental car.'

At the marina, they berthed the yacht and said goodbye to Carlo with lots of hugging and promises to meet again. Finally, they were alone, heading along the pier, between the rows of boats. There were so many things Belle wanted to say, she didn't know where to start.

'How is your family?' she asked.

'They are all well. You received the photograph of Katarina with her baby boy Giorgio?'

'Your grandson, yes he is lovely.'

'I have many more photographs if you would like to see them,' he said. 'Video too.'

They were talking like acquaintances not two people who had been lovers, and in the car, which had the sterile feel of a rental, sitting close to him in the passenger seat, Belle still felt oddly distant.

'I look at Perla's Instagram page sometimes,' she remarked, to keep a conversation going.

Enrico started the engine and fiddled with his rear-view mirror although it didn't seem to need adjusting. 'Ah yes, and soon you will be able to watch her in the reality show.'

Belle's eyes rounded in surprise. 'I'm sorry, what reality show?'

'You hadn't heard?' Enrico fastened his seat belt. '*House of Ginaro*. It has almost everything – stylish fashion, beautiful women, two feuding brothers and a grand matriarch. What it doesn't have is me. I will be staying away for as long as they are filming.'

'A reality show, I don't believe it.' Although instantly Belle saw what a brilliant idea it could be.

'Another of Perla's schemes. It took a while for Gianni to agree, but now you might imagine it was his idea all along.'

'I don't even watch reality TV but I really want to see this.'

'I am dreading it.' Enrico laughed, a little helplessly. 'Can you imagine?'

'Oh yes, I can,' said Belle. 'I really can.'

'Everyone says it will be brilliant,' he said, ruefully.

'What about your mother?'

'Mamma tells me this is the modern way of doing things and we must embrace it. I expect her to be the star of the show.'

Belle thought so too. 'I literally can't wait.'

'They have only just begun filming so you will have to.'

His news had broken the ice. As she guided Enrico to the motorway, Belle felt easier in his company. They talked about his travels, the places he had seen and what he thought of them, as they edged through snarled-up traffic.

'I went back home when the baby was born,' he told her. 'But it seemed they are all doing very well without me and so I left again.'

Belle hadn't driven from the city through heavy traffic in a long time. She felt sorry for the people who needed to do it every day. But she wasn't in any hurry to arrive. If the trip took all night, she wouldn't have minded.

'Your friend Greg, he is all healed now?' asked Enrico as they proceeded at a slow crawl to the end of the motorway.

'He's back on his feet thankfully. I'm still helping out but I don't have as much of the hard physical work as I did over winter.'

Enrico glanced at her. 'This must be why you look so fit and healthy. You are glowing.'

As they took the turn-off to Muriwai and finally were in the proper countryside, she looked at Enrico's profile.

'Do you have to rush back to town?' she asked.

'I have no plans.'

'Stay for a while then,' she suggested. 'We'll go for a walk. I'll show you round my neighbourhood.'

They carried on past the driveway of her house and to the

forest below, where Belle took Enrico on her favourite walk along a riverbank and then out onto the wild black-sand beach, salt spray from the waves misting their faces.

'Is this where Ari surfed?' he asked.

'Usually, he went to a smaller bay to the south, but sometimes here.'

'I can't really imagine being out in a sea like that,' said Enrico, looking at the churning water. 'It looks so dangerous.'

'He'd surfed this coastline since he was a boy.'

Enrico watched the waves for a moment longer. 'Has it been any easier for you?'

'I've been too busy to have much time to think. So, in a way, yes.'

'Being busy; it helps for a while at least,' he agreed.

As they turned to walk back along the beach, pink streaked the sky and the evening light turned golden. Reaching a pathway through the dunes, they sat down on a hillock of deep sand to watch the rest of the sunset.

'Why did you leave me?' he asked, at last. 'What I mean is why did you decide never to come back?'

'I couldn't see how I could ever be a part of your life,' she said, honestly.

'But Belle, I wanted you to be my life ... not just a part of it.'

When they kissed, her body remembered then her mind caught up. Sitting in the dark dunes, shielded by fronds of grass, their hands found each other's bodies and they kissed as the sunset blazed orange and the wind chilled them.

'I still want you to be my life,' whispered Enrico.

It felt wrong to be together in Ari's house, so instead they went back the way they had come, Enrico driving the rental car to the hotel on the waterfront where he was staying. Belle barely registered the vastness of its foyer or the view over the Viaduct from his suite. They might have been anywhere.

'Come to Fiordland with me,' said Enrico, tugging her free of her old bush shirt. 'Come sailing in Dusky Sound. They say the birdsong at dawn is incredible.'

'Where after that?' asked Belle, stripping away his fine linen.

'Australia – the Great Ocean Road, the Barrier Reef; you choose.'

Once they were naked, tangled in bedsheets and each other, neither of them had words. Belle was only aware of her heart beating against his as their bodies held together.

'I could stay here forever,' she told him.

'Sooner or later, we will need to leave,' he replied. 'There are so many places to go.'

19

Home Again

As much as she loved roaming the world, there came a time when Belle wanted to stop and call a place home. The difficulty was deciding where home would be. She thought about it as they got to know modern cities and old towns, snowy mountains and tropical islands.

It was easier to say where home wasn't now. Their worlds were being reshaped without them. Ari's house was rented out, Matt was living with Greg and riding Tama; the palazzo had been taken over by a film crew, so even if Belle wanted to be there, which she very much didn't, Enrico wouldn't go near it.

'My family is living to be watched by other people,' he shuddered. 'That is no way to live in my opinion.'

Belle agreed with him. Wherever they went, she imagined how it would be to stay forever, but then they moved on to the next place. Often, they liked to surprise each other. There were times she didn't know where they were going until the destination was reached, others when she arranged the mystery. Enrico seemed restless and they might have gone on like that, shifting from country to country, living out of their suitcases, forever seeking the new. Except Belle missed the sense of being in a place where she belonged.

The *trullo* was tiny, the smallest she had seen, but it was all she could afford and it was important to Belle that she be the one to buy it. Katarina and Perla helped find it – Belle suspected house-hunting in the Valle d'Itria had provided scenes for a film crew to capture.

They sent photographs of houses they found. Some were in need of total renovation, others looked much too showy. The *trullo* that Belle bought sight unseen might have been small, but it had a blue rectangle of swimming pool and was hidden among olive and almond trees. Even from the photographs she could tell the kitchen was tiny and the living area cramped; still they would sleep beneath the *trullo* cone, behind thick whitewashed walls, and the moment Belle saw it she thought this funny pointy-roofed house might be the place to cure Enrico's need to keep moving.

'We'll still have adventures,' she promised. 'But this is where we'll come back to. Our first home together.'

'I always wanted to live in one,' he said, smiling like a boy, perhaps forgetting he had told her that before. 'It was my dream when I was a child but I never imagined it coming true.'

They were in Puglia for a few weeks over summer to stay at the villa. The family was to join them there, promising faithfully no film crew would follow.

'The first sign of a camera and I am gone,' Enrico had warned everyone. 'I will move so fast you won't notice me leaving.'

Now visiting the *trullo* for the first time, they imagined making a life together.

'We will have to buy new furniture,' Enrico told her, his gaze sweeping the rooms. 'Everything must be small and very simple.'

'Yes,' said Belle.

'And in the summer, we will live mostly outside so we will create more shade out in the garden.'

Belle nodded her agreement.

'And only one of us will fit into that kitchen so I think it had better be me.'

'You're very welcome.' Belle enjoyed nothing more than

sitting and watching, with a glass of red wine in her hand, while Enrico cooked for her.

He touched the whitewashed stone wall. 'I love this place already.'

They had a week together at the villa before his family started arriving, the driver making several journeys. First to come were Perla and Pietro's suitcases, followed by them.

'It is so wonderful to see you.' Perla enveloped Belle in a honeysuckle-scented embrace.

'No cameras,' Enrico warned, as she turned to greet him. 'Not even a photograph on Instagram.'

'Of course not Papa, I would never do that,' she promised. 'I understand that you want to keep your life private.'

She sounded convincing, but then Perla always did and Belle was sure she wouldn't be able to resist finding some way to show off her life at the beach.

Next to arrive were Katarina and Gianni, with little Giorgio and so many more suitcases that everyone had to help ferry them inside, Gianni directing the chaos.

The Signora was the last to make an entrance. She swept in issuing demands and finding fault with almost everything. With Belle she was restrained, making it impossible to tell whether or not she approved of her being there.

'We are in our fifties, we don't need my mother's approval,' Enrico made sure to remind her.

They gathered together to watch the first episode of *House of Ginaro*. A larger screen had been delivered to the villa for the occasion and they all sat in front of it in nervous anticipation.

It was strange watching them play out their lives on-screen, seeing the familiar backdrops and the family dynamics in sharp relief against them. Gianni and Pietro battling over some aspect of the business during lunch in the loggia, Perla bickering with Katarina beside the swimming pool, and the Signora with a cat on her knee, ruling over them all.

On-screen everyone was speaking in English, because this show would be viewed all over the world, but as they were watching the family exchanged quick comments in Italian, punctuated by laughter and shrieks. Belle didn't know what they were saying, but looking at their faces as much as the screen, thought they seemed pleased with themselves.

Enrico only managed to sit through ten minutes of it, then retreated to the outdoor kitchen to make a start on dinner.

'You hate the show,' said Belle, who had slipped out to find him busy scrubbing mussels.

'Is that what they are really like?' asked Enrico, looking up from his task. 'My family? The way they seem on-screen?'

'Everything is exaggerated, but yes, pretty much,' said Belle, moving beside him to crush garlic and reduce fronds of fresh parsley to fine confetti.

'I still can't believe they have done it,' said Enrico, putting a deep pan of water on to boil for the pasta. 'But I expect sales will jump and Gianni will open more shops and then he will be able to say he was right all along.'

Belle didn't bother going back to watch the rest of the show. The little she had seen was enough, and she would rather be with him. Besides there were plenty of chances to view it again. In the days that followed it was difficult to avoid. Perla seemed to be constantly examining scenes featuring herself. Gianni replayed the footage to mark down every outfit that appeared on a spreadsheet he was creating. Belle even caught the Signora tuning in a second time.

The villa wasn't so relaxing with them there. Despite the size of the place, it was remarkably hard to find a quiet corner. Belle was up in her bedroom, sitting beside the small balcony looking out over the garden and the dusty lane beyond it, when she saw two large vans making slow progress towards them. They stopped outside the villa's gates, because it was too narrow for them to turn in, and the drivers climbed out, beginning to argue. A few moments later, Gianni appeared on the scene, issuing instructions.

'Enrico, I think there is a film crew arriving,' Belle called to him.

He was in the bathroom and she heard a clatter as he dropped something. 'What?'

'Looks like it to me,' she said, gesturing to the trucks.

He stood beside her at the window. 'Perla promised this wouldn't be happening.'

'I think it's safer not to put any faith in what Perla tells you.'

'No, no, no.' Enrico repeated, looking so stricken that Belle couldn't help smiling. 'We have to leave, but where shall we go? The *palazzo*?'

'Let's go home,' said Belle. 'To our little *trullo*.'

'There is no furniture there yet.'

'I ordered a bed because I had a feeling this might happen. We'll need to take some linen though.'

Enrico stripped the sheets while she packed up their suitcases. By now they were so used to living out of them, it took no time at all. Loading everything into the car, Belle looked at the trucks blocking the gateway, and wondered how they were going to make their escape.

'There will be more cars arriving,' she told Enrico. 'If we're leaving then we need to do it now.'

'Oh, we're leaving,' he promised.

It took some shouting and hooting on the car's horn, entreaties from Gianni to stay, vows from Enrico that he would regret it if they did, then finally the vans reversed enough for them to squeeze out of the gate and past.

'At least we have the *trullo*,' said Enrico, as they bounced over the pot-holed lane. 'I don't think that you could even fit a film crew inside if you wanted to.'

Halfway down the lane they spotted a dented silver Smart car that Belle recognised. Mia must have been driving to the villa to do the Ginaro family's hair and make-up. She slowed as their cars met, winding down the window to exchange a few words.

'You are leaving? I thought I would be giving you another makeover.'

'No more makeovers,' said Belle, who was wearing an old cotton dress with Ari's greenstone lying against her chest, her hair in a tangle and tied with a scarf.

'Are you sure?' Mia sounded disappointed. 'You are not going to be appearing in the show?'

'Definitely not,' Belle told her.

'We wouldn't dream of it,' added Enrico.

As they drove on and away from the villa, he shook his head. 'I love my family but ... sometimes it doesn't seem like such a bad thing to have a little distance between us. Let us go to our *trullo*.'

They stopped to pick up a few supplies, then drove deep into the olive groves, raising dust from dirt roads, until they reached their new home.

'We wanted a simpler life, but not this simple,' said Belle, walking through the nearly bare *trullo* that looked shabbier than she remembered.

'We have peace and privacy here,' said Enrico, unpacking the food they had bought to picnic on. 'We have dinner, primitivo wine and cups to drink it from, we have somewhere to sleep. That is enough for now.'

They soaked in the pool till the heat had left the afternoon then sat side by side on a rough wooden bench eating bread, cheese and peaches as the sun was setting.

'Do you think we will be happy here?' asked Belle, winding her aquamarine scarf over her bare shoulders in case of a hint of chill in the air.

Enrico rested an arm around her, pulling her towards him. The sky darkened and the stars gleamed. A silver crescent of moon hung over the *trullo's* conical roof.

'I know we will.'

Acknowledgements

This novel is dedicated to my mother-in-law Margaret Bidwill although she won't be able to enjoy it. Dementia has stolen reading books from her, along with many other aspects of the life she once had. But while she may not remember what she ate for lunch, or where it is she lives now, or the last visitor who brought those lovely flowers, somehow Margaret has managed to hang on to a great deal of herself. Her sense of humour, stylishness, naughtiness, her ability to have a good time, her love of music, are all still largely intact. Oh and her favourite shade of lipstick remains MAC Morange (a vivid orange). Like so many things, the experience of dementia varies from person to person and we're grateful that for Margaret life has continued to have joy in it.

There are so many people who have supported me through the writing of fourteen novels (yes I know, fourteen, how did that happen?). For this one in particular I want to thank my editor, the talented Charlotte Mursell, for her patience, kindness and steady hand, and everyone at Orion who has helped my story reach readers.

Also thanks to my equally patient, kind and steady-handed agent Caroline Sheldon and the teams at Hachette Aotearoa NZ and Australia.

Last but definitely not least, a big thank you to all the booksellers and the readers who buy novels from them – it's

SO great to be able to meet some of you again at festivals and events.

This is a story about loneliness and connection, because that's been on my mind a lot over the past couple of years. I'm grateful for all the friendships that seem more important than ever. Particular thanks go to writers Stacy Gregg and Sarah-Kate Lynch for all the listening, and to Vicki Hoggard for coming to Puglia with me on a quick research trip, because I didn't want to travel alone.

Finally, thanks to all my whanau (family), distant and near, especially my husband Carne Bidwill who is highly unlikely to read this far, but just in case ...

Credits

Nicky Pellegrino and Orion Fiction would like to thank everyone at Orion who worked on the publication of *P.S. Come to Italy* in the UK.

Editorial
Charlotte Mursell
Sahil Javed

Copyeditor
Sally Partington

Proofreader
Laetitia Grant

Audio
Paul Stark
Jake Alderson

Contracts
Anne Goddard
Humayra Ahmed
Ellie Bowker

Design
Charlotte Abrams-Simpson
Joanna Ridley
Nick May

Editorial Management
Charlie Panayiotou
Jane Hughes
Bartley Shaw
Tamara Morriss

Finance
Jasdip Nandra
Sue Baker

Marketing
Javerya Iqbal

Production
Ruth Sharvell

Sales
Jen Wilson
Esther Waters
Victoria Laws
Rachael Hum

Anna Egelstaff
Frances Doyle
Georgina Cutler

Operations
Jo Jacobs
Sharon Willis

Also by Nicky Pellegrino

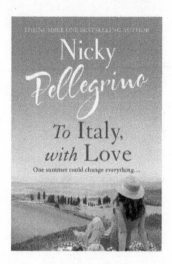

Love happens when you least expect it . . .

Assunta has given up on love. She might run her little *trattoria* in the most romantic mountain town in Italy, but love just seems to have passed her by.

Sarah-Jane is finished with love. She's buying an old convertible and driving around Italy this summer – it's the perfect way to forget all about her hot celebrity ex-boyfriend!

But when Sarah-Jane's car breaks down in Montenello, she has to stay longer than she intended! And the trouble is, love is *everywhere* . . .

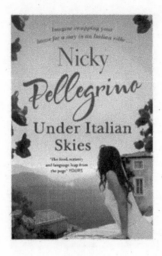

Can you change your life by swapping your home?

'It was a curious sort of feeling, being so cherished by a stranger . . .'

Imagine swapping your house for a stay in an Italian villa . . . and falling in love with the owner's life.

After Stella's boss dies suddenly, she's left with nothing to do apart from clear the studio. It seems as though the life she wanted has vanished. She is lost – until one day she finds a house swap website and sees a beautiful old villa in a southern Italian village. Could she really exchange her poky London flat for that?

But what was just intended as a break becomes much more, as Stella finds herself trying on a stranger's life.

Can Stella overcome her grief and find her way into a new future?

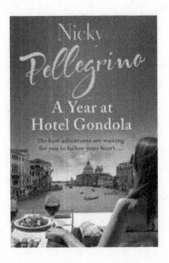

The best adventures are waiting for you to follow your heart . . .

Kat is an adventurer, a food writer who travels the world visiting far-flung places and eating unusual things. Now she is about to embark on her biggest adventure yet – a relationship.

She has fallen in love with an Italian man and is moving to live with him in Venice where she will help him run his small guesthouse, Hotel Gondola. Kat has lined up a book deal and will write about the first year of her new adventure, the food she eats, the recipes she collects, the people she meets, the man she doesn't really know all that well but is going to make a life with.

But as Kat ought to know by now, the thing about adventures is that they never go exactly the way you expect them to . . .

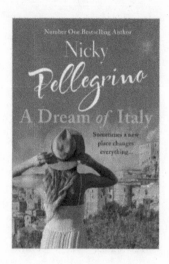

For sale: historic building in the picturesque town of Montenello, southern Italy. Asking price: 1 Euro

Cloudless skies, sun-soaked countryside, delicious food . . . In the drowsy heat of an Italian summer, four strangers arrive in a beautiful town nestled in the mountains of Basilicata, dreaming of a new adventure. An innovative scheme by the town's Mayor has given them the chance to buy a crumbling historic building for a single Euro – on the condition that they renovate their home within three years, and help to bring new life to the close-knit local community.

Elise is desperate to get on the property ladder. Edward wants to escape a life he feels suffocated by. Mimi is determined to start afresh after her divorce. And there's one new arrival whose true motives are yet to be revealed . . .

For each of them, Montenello offers a different promise of happiness. But can they turn their dream of Italy into reality?

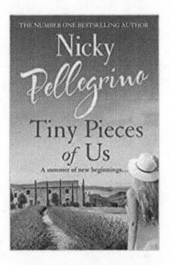

My heart is less than 1% of my body, it weighs hardly anything; it is only a tiny piece of me, yet it is the part everyone finds most interesting.

Vivi Palmer knows what it's like to live life carefully. Born with a heart defect, she was given a second chance after a transplant, but has never quite dared to make the most of it. Until she comes face-to-face with her donor's mother, Grace, who wants something in return for Vivi's second-hand heart: help to find all the other people who have tiny pieces of her son.

Reluctantly drawn into Grace's mission, Vivi's journalist training takes over as one by one she tracks down a small group of strangers. As their lives intertwine Vivi finds herself with a new kind of family, and by finding out more about all the pieces that make up the many parts of her, Vivi might just discover a whole new world waiting for her . . .

Join Vivi as she discovers second chances at life are anything but easy . . .